MELODY'S TEMPTATION

ERIN OSBORNE

Melody's Temptation

By: Erin Osborne

Photographer: Shauna Kruse

Cover Model: Matthew Hosea

Cover Model: Gina Sevina

Cover Design: Graphics by Shelly

Dedication

I've thought long and hard about who I was going to dedicate this book to. After changing it a few times, I have finally decided who I am going to dedicate it to.

Melody's Temptation is going to be dedicated to everyone that has ever taken a chance and followed their dream. It's not easy and you probably have a ton of obstacles to overcome along the way. The reward at the end of the day is worth it though. Without the encouragement of several people, I wouldn't have had the courage to follow my dream. So, this book is also dedicated to everyone that has helped me and given me encouragement along this amazing journey. Whether it was fellow authors or readers, without all of you, I wouldn't be living my dream right now. So, thank you from the bottom of my heart!

Character List

Clifton Falls Chapter

Grim
Bailey
Cage
Joker
Skylar
Irish
Caydence
Tank
Maddie
Ma
Pops
Glock
Melody
Blade
Rage
Summer
Storm

Dander Falls Chapter

Gage
Steel
Crash
Trojan
Darcy
Shadow

Phantom Bastards

Slim
Playboy
Killer
Wood
Boy Scout

Table of Contents

Part One
The Past

Prologue
Glock

Eighteen Years Old

I WAS A SENIOR in high school the day that Melody Michaels walked into my life. She was a new girl in school and I knew as soon as I saw her that things were going to change for me. Melody had long chestnut hair that she wore curled and flowing down her back. When she looked at me, her sky-blue eyes were shining with the innocence of her age and bright with the laughter you could see waiting to escape her lush lips. The first time she turned those eyes on me, I felt like she could see right through my soul and see all the secrets I tried so hard to hide from everyone.

There were about three months of school left when Melody transferred here. Over the course of this time, we were paired together for a few different assignments. It led to us spending time together in and out of school. Melody is easy to talk to and would make me laugh over the silliest things or get me to talk about things I didn't talk about with anyone, not even my closest friends and brothers by choice. One day we were studying at the library when it started raining out. Immediately, she got excited and grabbed my hand before dragging me out to dance in the rain. I've never done anything like that before and that is the only time I think I'll ever do it.

Another time, I opened up about my brother, Anthony. He was older than me and when things hit the fan with him, he turned to drugs to escape reality. On several occasions, I tried to get him clean and keep him that way. Unfortunately, it didn't stick, and he ended up paying for it with his life. Anthony's death tore my world apart and made me want to keep everyone else in my life at arm's length, so it wouldn't happen again.

Other than when we were studying, Melody and I didn't spend as much time together outside of school as I would have liked. Our time was our time, and I didn't want it any other way. My closest friends were man-whores already and tried to nail anyone they could. Personally, I had been too busy with my life to worry about it. While they were out fucking every girl in our class and some of the club girls, I was spending my time getting the grades I needed to get out of school and start prospecting for the Wild Kings MC. I've known my entire life that's where I would end up. Just like my dad and my uncle, Dec's dad.

One day, about three weeks before school was done, Melody came up to me between classes. "Mason, I have a question to ask you," she said before looking at the floor.

"What's up?" I asked, tilting her chin back up to look at me. I had never seen her unsure of herself or nervous.

"I was wondering if you wanted to hang out later."

"Did you have anythin' specific in mind babe?"

"I just want to drive until we find a spot to park. I want to lay in the bed of your truck and watch the stars. Is that okay?" She asked, letting her eyes look everywhere but at me.

"Yeah, we can do that. I have somethin' to do for a while, but I should be free by seven or so. Am I pickin' you up where I usually drop you off?"

"Yeah. Are you sure I'm not taking you away from your friends?" She asked, looking over my shoulder.

Turning my head, I see the guys walking down the hall towards us. "I'm sure. I'll pick you up no later than eight."

"Okay. I'll see you then." Melody says before leaving me standing there.

As I watch Melody's retreat down the hallway, Dec slaps me on the back. "When you gonna introduce us to your girl?"

"She's not my girl!" I tell him, making sure that I look him in the eyes. None of them need to know how much Melody has gotten under my skin.

"Then why are you always with her?" Levi asks me.

"We've been paired up on some projects. When I've been with her, we've been studyin' and that's it. Her dad's a preacher, you think I need that shit?"

"Preacher's daughters are always down for some dirty and nasty fun," Brock pipes in.

"I wouldn't know." I answer, trying to shut them down before they really get started. "I'm goin' to class."

After school, we went and helped my dad and uncles pack some stuff up. Apparently, the club is going to do some renovations on the garage and we were needed to help the prospects do the grunt work. They let it slip that sooner or later, we'll be moving to a new location. I guess a prime spot was located a few hours from one of the other chapters of the Wild Kings and they want to be closer. So, we'll be moving half-way across the country when they get everything worked out.

As soon as we're done with moving and packing things up, I let everyone know I'm heading out. The guys have to give me a hard time. They're staying at the clubhouse for a while to see what trouble they can get in to and I'm not staying with them this time. Usually we all sit around, play pool, and sneak a few beers. Our dads know, and I don't know why we try to hide it, but it's not where my head's at right now. I've been thinking about Melody since she asked me to hang out. I'll be honest, there's been some dirty thoughts running through my head. I want to know how soft her skin is under my hands, what she tastes like, and a million other things. She would run as far as she can if she knew the thoughts running through my head. But, I can't push her away no matter how much I want to. Melody has already sunk her claws in deep!

It's about ten minutes to eight when I finally pull up down the road from her house at our meeting spot. When I look out my window, I don't see anyone there and I begin to wonder if she went home instead of waiting for me. It's not long though before I see movement from behind one of the trees lining the road. Melody approaches the truck and I lean across to open the door for her.

"I didn't think you were here," I tell her when she pulls herself up on the seat.

"My parents went out and I didn't want them to see me waiting for you."

"Which direction?"

"Wherever you want Mason. I want to find a field or something where we can pull over and just lay back and relax."

"I know the perfect spot. You want to tell me what's goin' on babe?" I ask her, resisting the urge to pull her in the middle next to me.

"I just wanted to see you. I mean, we've studied and spent time talking, now I want to just relax with you. Without the pretense of having a project to finish."

"Why is that?" I ask her, somewhat confused at her answer. She's never shown an interest in me before now.

"Mason, I'm not good with letting people in. With you, it's easy. We laugh, you indulge my crazy ideas, you let me in, and I like spending time with you. School's over soon and I'm sure I won't see you after that."

"Sure you will. We have all the time in the world to spend together. Well, when I'm not busy with the club."

"You don't understand. My parents are sending me away after graduation. They don't like the way I talk about you at home, that we've had to work together, and that I like you and want to be more than friends."

Melody's response floors me. I never thought she would tell me that she wanted more from me. "You sure about that angel? About wantin' more than friendship from me?"

"Mason, I've wanted you since the first day I came to this school. You stand out to me and you make me believe that I can be anything that I want to. I don't have to listen to my parents about what my future should be. I can make my own path and find happiness."

"Angel, I have wanted you so bad. The thoughts I have about you would make you run as fast as you can."

"No, they wouldn't. Mason, I want you. Tonight. Now." She responds, moving over next to me, and placing her hand on my thigh.

My foot presses down a little harder on the accelerator so I can get to the field behind the clubhouse. I place my hand over hers and link my fingers with hers. I can't believe the way tonight is going to turn out. When Melody asked me to hang out, I figured we'd hang out and talk. I never once thought she'd offer to give herself to me.

It takes me less than five minutes to get where we're going and the closer we get, the more nervous I'm becoming. I doubt that Melody has ever been with anyone, and I know I haven't so it will be the first time for both of us. What if I fuck up and she ends up hating me for it?

"Are you sure this is what you want, angel?" I ask her, pulling over and shutting the truck and lights off.

"I've never been more sure of anything in my life. I want it to be you, Mason. No one else but you."

I lift her chin up again and look into her eyes. I'm not sure who moves first, but before a few seconds pass, our lips are meeting. Melody's lips are the softest lips I've ever felt beneath mine. Yeah, I might be a virgin, but I've made out with my fair share of girls. Okay, club girls. I gently bite down on her bottom lip and swipe my tongue over it, taking the sting out. Knowing that I want access, she doesn't make me wait for it and opens her mouth to me. There are little moans coming from her mouth and I can feel her breath picking up speed the more she gets into our kiss.

Suddenly she breaks free of me and gives me a devilish little smirk. Turning the radio on, she flips stations until she finds a song that I've never heard before. It's country. I don't listen to country music. At all.

"Don't look at me like that Mason," she says, showing her sassy side. "I love *Die A Happy Man*. It's going to stay here."

Without looking back, she climbs out of the passenger door, grabs the blankets stuffed behind the seat, and heads to the bed of the truck. I sit here stunned at the sass she just showed me. It's not very often that she lets it come out. Scrambling to help her set the blankets and pillows up, I climb in the bed of the truck after toeing off my boots and smooth everything out. Once I'm done, I hold my hand out to her so I can help her climb in.

"I have to know, are you sure about this Melody? We don't have to do anythin'." I ask her, laying down and pulling her down with me.

"I am Mason. I want it to be with you and only you. I even got condoms from the health room."

"I have a confession to make then," I tell her, making sure she's looking in my eyes. "I've never done this before, so I can't reassure you about what will happen next. We'll both be flyin' blind here angel."

"That just makes me want you more. I know it's going to hurt and I'm ready for it."

I lean in and take her mouth with mine again. This time, I let my hands explore. Running my hand down to the bottom of her shirt, I bring my hand under it and run it back up her silky skin until I reach her tits. Pulling her bra down, I pinch and pull on first one nipple before moving on to the other one. Since I'm not sure what to do here, I take my cues from her responses. Melody's back arches up into my hand, trying to get as close to my teasing fingers as she can. Moving away from her mouth, I make my way down to her neck. The only time I stop is when I lift her shirt from her body and toss it behind us in the truck.

Melody's hands are doing their own exploring of my body. After I remove her shirt and bra, she helps me take my shirt off. I'm fumbling and I have no clue where to go from here, but I'm determined to make this good for her. So, I take a nipple in my mouth and suck it until I hear a moan escape her mouth. Moving down her body, I kiss and lick everywhere I can reach on her until she starts squirming under me. At the same time, I undo her jeans and push them and her panties down her smooth legs. I sit up enough to get her pants the rest of the way off and take her in for the first time, completely bare to me. Her pussy is bare and I can see how wet she is already. There's no way that I'm not getting my first taste of her.

I scoot between her legs and lock my gaze on hers as I lower my head to her body. I take my first tentative lick of her. She arches up and meets my mouth as I move from her slit to her clit. Taking it in my mouth, I suck on it gently. Melody moans out and I feel her hand in my hair. Grabbing a handful, she pushes my head where she wants me to go. In this moment, I can feel that we're both just going on what we feel is the right thing to do. But I can't get enough of her.

When I sense that Melody is getting close, I insert a finger into her and feel how tight she is. I don't know how the hell I'm going to fit there, but I've listened when the club girls and the guys have talked about that kind of stuff. I slowly slide my finger in and out of Melody's wet slit a few times until I feel her clenching around my finger, trying to keep me there. Carefully I insert a second finger and scissor them a little bit, trying to stretch her out a little bit for me. I can feel every ripple and spasm of her as she gets closer to her release.

"Mason!" Melody screams out as I feel her shatter under my tongue and finger.

Stopping what I'm doing, I use my forearm to wipe my mouth and move back up her body. On my way up, I undo my jeans and pull them down one handed. Melody senses what I'm doing and reaches down to wrap her hand around my length. Fuck, that feels good.

"Angel, you gotta stop," I tell her after she works her hand up and down for a few minutes. "I'm gettin' close and I want to make this good for you."

Melody pulls her hand away from my dick and licks the pre-cum from her fingers. That's fucking hot. She reaches behind her head and grabs the condom that she must have put there after we laid down. I take it and rip it open, sliding it down my length before I move between her creamy thighs once more. Looking up at me, I can see the trust and desire shining from Melody's eyes and I hope I don't hurt her too bad.

Taking a hand away from her face, I make sure that she's still wet so it will be easier to fit inside her. I remember overhearing one of the guys saying that you have to make sure the girl was ready every time. She lifts her hips up to meet me and I lean down to kiss her. Finally, I place myself at her entrance and start to push inside. My gaze doesn't move from hers so I can see what she's feeling and I can read the discomfort on her face. There's no way I'm going to be able to hurt her like this, so I start to ease back out.

"Don't stop Mason!" She cries out. "I'm fine, it will get better. I promise."

Pushing back in a little bit, I pull back out and ease my way back in further than before. As I go to push back in a little bit further, Melody reaches down and pulls me to her while pushing her hips up to meet me. There's no stopping me from going balls deep. She lets out a small shriek of pain and I immediately still my body. I can feel myself trembling from holding still and I know she feels it too. A tear escapes her eye and I feel horrible that I hurt her.

"I'm so sorry, angel," I tell her, leaning down to wipe her tears away and kiss her.

"It was going to hurt either way," she tells me, running her hand down my face as I lean into her touch. "Start moving Mason. Please, start moving."

Slowly I pull out and push back into her. Within a few minutes, my angel is meeting my thrusts. She's so tight, I can feel every ripple of her. Needing more, I wrap her legs around my hips and start moving faster within in her. I can feel her getting close to exploding if the way she's gripping me is anything to go by. I know that I'm getting close to finding my release. Melody doesn't wait for me to help her get her release, she reaches between our sweat slicked bodies and I feel her rubbing her clit.

"So…close…Mason." She pants out.

I start moving faster and it's not long before Melody is pulling me over the edge with her. She shudders beneath me and clenches my dick like a vice trying to keep me within her body. There's no holding back from me as I thrust my hips into her three more times and fall over the edge with her.

"Melody!" I roar out through my release.

Rolling us to our sides, I pull my sweet angel into me and wrap the blanket up around us. Even though it's hot out, the breeze has a slight chill to it and I don't want her to get cold. It takes a few minutes for our breathing to even out as I rub my hands up and down her back. Before I can move to get us more comfortable, I feel something leaking down our entwined legs. What the fuck?

Slowly sliding out of her, I look down to see that the condom broke. Fuck! How the hell do I tell her this after she just gave me one hell of a gift? But, I can't lie to her about it.

"Um, angel, we have a problem." I tell her, pulling the broken condom off my dick. "The condom broke and I'm guessin' you aren't on anythin'."

"No, I'm not." She says sitting up and looking me in the eye. "I'm sorry, Mason. So sorry!" She finishes, starting to cry.

"It's not your fault baby. This happens sometimes." I say, trying to reassure her and pulling her into my arms.

Honestly, I'm not mad this happened. I'm scared that we just might have created a life together because we're young and I don't want to stop my angel from reaching her goals, but not mad. Whatever happens, we'll deal with it together and figure out what our next steps are. I tell her all this as I hold her close to me. After a while, Melody calms down enough to fall asleep in my arms and soon, I'm following her into a peaceful slumber. Something I don't ever get.

Melody

It's been a few weeks since my night with Mason. After he calmed me down, we both fell asleep in the bed of his truck and didn't wake up until one of his friends stumbled upon us. He was drunk as hell and thought Mason was alone. Unfortunately, he saw more of me than I was prepared to show anyone else. Since then, things have been absolutely crazy with finals, getting ready for graduation, and my parents basically forbidding me to see Mason ever again.

I haven't told anyone, but I haven't been feeling the best right now and most days I'm sick throughout the day. The craziest things turn my stomach and I have to rush to the bathroom. Knowing that I can't put it off any longer, I buy a pregnancy test from a pharmacy out of town. I had to ride the bus there and back while my parents thought I was studying at the library. Now, I'm actually at the library, locked in the bathroom waiting for the results of the test to show up. The directions said that I have to wait a few minutes, but the results show up almost immediately. It's positive.

Silently freaking out, I know that I have to tell Mason what's going on, but I have no clue how to do that. I know I should tell him face to face, but I've been avoiding him. It's nothing that he did wrong, I just didn't know how to deal with the possibility that I was pregnant. Now, I think that I'll write him a letter or something and tell him. That way he can process it and talk to me when he's calmed down. I know that he said we would deal with whatever happened, but now that it's a reality I don't know that his answer will be the same.

Now that my decision's been made, I decide to sit down and write him a letter. Thankfully it's the weekend and no one is in the library.

Mason,

I'm sorry that I've been avoiding you these last few weeks. It honestly has nothing to do with you or what happened between us. I just didn't know how to deal with the fact that I might be pregnant. Now, it's not a possibility that I'm pregnant. I have taken a test since I haven't been feeling good and I'm late. The test came back positive.

I know that you said we would deal with the result of whatever happened, but I don't want you to give up your dream of becoming a Wild King. That's not going to be easy, add in a kid, and it's going to be even harder. I'm prepared to raise the baby alone and you can visit whenever you want to. No matter what happens between us, I would never keep you away from your child.

The only reason I'm even writing you this letter is so that you can process the information and calm down. Then we can talk about it and make a decision about where to go from here. I'll let you come to me when you're ready. You know how to get a hold of me.

Melody

Folding the letter up, I stick it in my book and make my way out to wait for my mom to pick me up and take me home. Until I can get the letter to Mason, I'm going to have to hide it. It's Sunday so I'll put it in my dresser until I go to school tomorrow. That way, if my parents search my stuff, they won't find it. To my knowledge, they never go through my dresser.

As soon as I get in the car with my mom, she starts in on how I missed the dinner after church so I could come to the library. So, I still got to hear about all of the gossip and stuff when I had no interest in it and I was dealing with my own world crashing down around me right now. I want to tell her to shut her damn mouth, but I know that it will only be harder for me. She loves it when I talk back and stuff so that she can punish me. There's just too much on my mind right now to be worrying about getting punished. Like normal, I sit back, don't say what I really want to, and make the appropriate comments when necessary.

"When we get home, I want you to get your room cleaned up and then we'll have a talk." My mom says as we pull in the driveway. Her voice has that fake, sugar-like quality to it when I know shit is about to hit the fan.

"Okay mom. Is someone coming over or something?" I ask.

"You'll find out when I'm ready for you to find out." She says, finally showing the attitude that I know she usually has.

I've been searching and searching for the letter to Mason since I had the conversation with my parents last night. It's not here anywhere though. I'm guessing that when my mom disappeared for a little bit she went through my stuff and found it. Now they'll know my biggest secret and I don't know what they're going to do to me about it. I wish now that I knew so I could do something before anything happened.

Mason has been trying to seek me out in school since it's the last day before graduation. I've managed to avoid him so far today and his friends have passed me in the halls giving me knowing looks. I'm not sure if it's because he's been bragging that we had sex or if the one that found us opened his mouth. Or, maybe it's because they all know I'm avoiding him for whatever reason. Just as I go to turn the corner, I run right into someone.

"I'm so sorry!" I mutter, looking up into Mason's eyes.

"Angel, we need to talk. Why are you avoidin' me?"

"I'm no…" I start to respond before he cuts me off.

"You are. Now, I know somethin' is up, and we need to talk." He says, leading me to a quiet corner.

"We do need to talk. My parents found a letter I wrote you and I don't know what's going to happen to me now."

"Why would you write me a letter instead of just talkin' to me about whatever was in it? What do you mean that you don't know what they're goin' to do to you now?" He asks, getting more confused the longer we stand here.

"I can't explain everything right now. My mom will be here any minute to get me. I wish things were different and we could just be together Mason. If that's what you want, that is."

"I want that more than anythin', angel. Why can't you just come with me? I'm goin' to start prospectin' for the Wild Kings today or tomorrow. But, I've got enough money saved to get an apartment now. We can move in together and just be happy. Hell, my dads got an apartment out behind the house we can stay in for now."

"That sounds wonderful! I wish we could really do that." I say, feeling the tears starting to gather in my eyes.

"I'll send you a message in a little bit after I talk to him. I know he won't have a problem with it since we're both graduatin'. Meet me in our spot with whatever you want to move in with. We'll figure everythin' else out tomorrow, angel. I promise, everythin' will be okay."

"There's something that you don't know Mason. Something that might change the way you feel about everything."

"What is it?" He asks me, moving his body that much closer to me.

Before I can answer him, I hear the horn honk outside the door we're standing at and I know without looking it's my parents. So, I don't tell Mason the news he needs to hear. He can find out when he picks me up tonight. It's honestly the only way that we're going to be able to be together without my parents ruining everything. I leave Mason standing there looking after me and go running out to the car before whoever is here decides to come in looking for me.

"I don't know what you were thinking young lady, but you are *not* going to embarrass your mother and I with this sin you have committed!" My dad shouts before I have the door closed. I know that Mason is hearing him since he's standing just outside the door.

"I'm sorry Daddy!" I say, trying to calm him down while shutting the door behind me.

Before he pulls away from the curb, my dad backhands me so hard that my head hits the window and tears instantly fall from my eyes. I can see Mason running towards the car after witnessing my dad's abuse. He's running with everything in him, but he's just no match for the speed my dad is starting to pick up.

"You're packing a bag when we get home and you're going to stay with family down south until that sin you're carrying is born. It will be adopted out, you *will* sign the papers, and then you'll come home as if nothing ever happened. Once you get home, you will do everything your mother and I say with no back talk and no letting go of your routine. Do you understand me you dirty whore?" My dad shouts, the spit flying from his mouth more and more as he yells. His face is turning bright red and the veins are starting to stick out.

"Yes sir," I mumble.

If there's any way that I can escape without having to go wherever my parents are thinking of sending me, I'm going to do it. Mason deserves to know he fathered a child and he deserves to be in that child's life. I'm not going to be the one to take that away from him. Even if it means that I have to give my child to him and walk away. I will do it if I have to because some stranger is not going to call our child their own. They didn't create this child, Mason and I did.

As soon as we pull in the driveway, I don't bother waiting for the car to stop. Climbing out, I run into the house and make my way up to my room to throw some stuff into a few bags. I know I'll need more than I'm packing since I'll be gone for the next eight months or so. At least that's what my parents are going to think. The entire time I'm packing, my mother is watching me like a hawk to make sure that I don't take anything they don't want me to. She's already pulled books, hair products, magazines, and a few other things out of my growing pile and thrown them to the floor. That's okay though, I'll buy more when I get to wherever I'm going. I've become a master at buying things I'm not supposed to have and hiding them so they don't get discovered. Unfortunately, my entire room has already been gone through, and I know that they've probably found all that stuff.

Finally, I'm finished packing what I'm allowed to take. I try to send a message off to Mason since I've been feeling the phone that I bought vibrating like crazy in my back pocket.

The only reason my parents haven't found it is because I keep it in my bag when I go to school and wear loose clothing when I get dressed. So, walking into the bathroom I close the door and pull the cell phone out only for my mother to whip the door open and pull it from my hands. She looks me in the face as she throws it to the floor and stomps her heel down on it multiple times. Now I'll never be able to get ahold of Mason since that was the only place I had his number.

They lead me out to a car that's waiting and put my bags in the trunk. I'm basically shoved into the backseat and they make sure that the child safety locks are engaged so that I can't open the door from the inside. Some man I've never seen before gets in the front seat and pulls away without a word to me or my parents. I look back and they aren't even standing there. I guess I'll have to figure out a way to get back here so that I can tell Mason what's going on and that he's going to be a dad. No matter what, I will get back to him some day!

Chapter One
Melody

A week later

FOR THE PAST WEEK, I've been holed up in a hotel room with my transporter. He's a man from my parent's church and he's been tasked with driving me to my aunt's house. The only reason we stopped is because I've been so sick and he was worried about me. My parents wanted him to just continue driving, but he put his foot down.

Every day that I've been gone from Mason, I think about him from the time I wake up until I close my eyes to go to sleep. He's in my dreams and there's no escaping him or the memories of things we did. The best times we spent together were when we would just drive somewhere and park. He didn't care if I just wanted to lay in the grass and look at the stars or sky depending on what time it was. If I wanted to do something, he had no problem making sure it happened. The best day was when it started raining when we were at the library. Mason went out with me and we danced in the rain like fools. We laughed and just had fun. It was amazing.

I wouldn't trade my time with him for anything in the world and I want him to be happy about the life we created. Even if we're not together, I want him to be happy no matter who he's with. It will break my heart to know that he's with someone else, but I will never deny him his happiness.

I cry myself to sleep every night missing him, and my heart hurts so bad with every passing day. It might be different if he knew about the baby and chose not to have anything to do with him or her. At this point, I don't know what he would say about the baby. I just know that I'm going to go through the pregnancy and raising this baby alone. Unless I can find him.

The only thing I can do at this point is document every stage of my pregnancy and delivery in the hopes that Mason will be able to see everything someday. Once the baby is born, I'll take so many pictures everyone in his or her life will be sick of seeing me with a camera in my hands. Not that I plan on anyone being around. I'll never open myself up again to lose everything I hold dear. Mason is the only one that will get that from me again.

A day or two ago, we stopped in a gas station and there were a few girls there that were talking about the guys Mason hangs out with. Apparently, they're moving somewhere near a town called Dander Falls. I'm not sure why they're moving or anything like that, just that these girls are mad as hell that they won't be able to party with them anymore. I'm sure the girls get more than partying out of this though. They are in a gas station in clothes that look like they belong on a child. Nothing is being left to the imagination and it's the exact type of thing I'm sure that Mason is going to figure out that he wants. Ones that aren't afraid to try new things and learn new things sexually.

So, even if I could get away from this guy, we'll call him asshole, I wouldn't be able to find Mason. I don't have any clue where Dander Falls is. How the hell am I going to tell him about the baby now? It was never a plan to not tell him about the life we created together. Now, I don't know what to do and I don't have anyone to talk to about it. Fuck my life!

"Melody, we're gonna be moving on in the morning. Are you feeling good enough to travel?" Asshole asks me.

"I guess so. The morning is the worst so far for me today. So, as long as we can wait a little bit, I should be fine."

"Okay. We'll get you some dry toast and ginger ale and then wait a bit before we leave."

Seriously this guy isn't truly that bad. He's been doing everything in his power to make sure that I'm comfortable. It's just the point that he won't help me escape and get to Mason. Asshole is going to make sure that I get to my aunt's house and that I'm delivered there safely.

Asshole was true to his word and let me have a reprieve this morning before getting back in the car. Now, I'm laying down in the backseat thinking of ways that I can find Mason to talk to him. I need to see him. It's been a week and he's all I think about. Every night I cry myself to sleep and I just want to hear his voice one more time. Even if it's him telling me that he hates me for trapping him with this baby. Honestly, I don't care if he has nothing to do with our baby, I just want him to know so he can't hold it against me.

As I daydream about the things I thought we'd be doing after graduating, I hear a rumble start. With every passing second, the sound gets louder and louder. Sitting up, I look out the back window and see a large group of motorcycles. They're heading up to the back of the car faster than Asshole is driving. The only thing I can think of is Mason.

Before they get too close, the bikers move over into the next lane along with trucks and vans. My heart rate accelerates and I can feel myself staring out the window to try to get a glimpse of who's going by us. Too bad their faces are concealed by helmets and stuff. Not that I would know who I'm looking at anyway. Unless it's one of the trucks. I know Mason's truck. Unfortunately, the windows in this car are tinted so no one can see in. Guess my parents don't want anyone to know that they are basically kidnapping me and hiding me away because I'm pregnant and didn't follow their plan.

The bikers are now almost completely past us and I can see the trucks and vans coming up. Spying the second truck in the line, I see Mason. He looks pissed off and there's another guy that I've seen around school riding with him. They could be twins. Seeing Mason makes me the happiest I've been since I had to leave. I see him look at the car and for a moment our eyes meet, he just doesn't know it. The scowl on his gorgeous face deepens and I can almost see the wheels turning in his mind. As they get side by side with us, I can see him almost slowing down to keep pace with us.

"Mason!" I scream, trying to roll down the window. Asshole has them locked though and it doesn't move an inch. "Mason, I'm here!"

"Calm down Melody! Don't make me do something we'll both regret." Asshole says.

"Please, just let me go and no one will have to know." I beg and plead with tears streaming down my face. "We can make it look like we got into an accident and neither one of us survived. Please, I'll do anything!"

Asshole doesn't say anything. He just speeds up and blocks out my voice. As he speeds up, Mason speeds up too. He has to know something is wrong since we're randomly speeding up with their caravan traveling beside us. Maybe he'll follow us and see that it's me. My hope rises as I see him pull out a phone and put it to his ear. The entire time he's continuing to stare the car down while the guy riding with him cranes his neck to try to see the license plate.

"Please babe, please follow us so you can help me get away." I beg quietly.

Too soon though, Mason pulls ahead of us. The caravan continues moving steadily down the highway and I know that all hope is lost now. Mason is never going to know that it's me in this car. He's never going to know that he's the only man that I'll ever love. Someday, though, I will get back to him and tell him everything that happened. Including my parents threatening to kill our baby.

Someday, Mason will know about the baby and make a decision as to whether or not he wants to be a dad. That's the only thing I can hope for now. By the time I find him again, I'm sure that he'll be happy with someone and they can be a part of raising our child. The way I feel about that is that if he's happy and the woman treats my child the way they deserve to be treated, then I won't have a problem with them at all. I'd rather be on the same page as them when it comes to raising my child and them on the same page as me. There's nothing more I can really ask for than that.

Chapter Two
Glock

Three weeks later

IT'S BEEN ALMOST A month since I've seen my angel. In such a short amount of time she became my entire world and I'll never love another. Melody is the only one that I want in my life. I want to marry her, put my babies in her stomach and watch her grow round, raise our babies and grandbabies, and grow old together. It doesn't take a genius to know when you've found something good, someone that makes breathing easier.

"Mason, you ready to go to the clubhouse?" Dec asks me.

"Guess so." I reply.

Dec, Levi, Logan, Brock, Connor, and I are all prospects for the Wild Kings MC now. This is what I've been waiting for my entire life and now that it's here, I could care less about it. Honestly, the only thing I want in my life is my angel, Melody.

The day that we moved to Clifton Falls, I saw a car on the highway that drew my attention for some unknown reason. Dec was riding with me and I made him get the license plate number while I called Pops to get someone to run it for me. Nothing came back, and it was the worst trip in the history of the Wild Kings MC. We got all the way to Clifton Falls to have to turn around because the building the club thought was a done deal fell through. So, we had nowhere to set up home. Thankfully the sale of the old clubhouse hadn't gone through so we could go back.

All of my friends, my brothers, know something is wrong. They just don't know what to do to get me out of my funk. I've had women thrown at me, enough alcohol to drown a horse, and every drug under the sun. The only thing that has taken away the pain is the drugs. None of the guys know how truly bad I've gotten though, and for that I'm thankful.

The only time I'm at the clubhouse these days is when I absolutely have to be there. Other than that, I'm out looking for my girl every place that I can think of and taking away the pain with whatever I can get my hands on. Alcohol doesn't even numb the pain I feel anymore. Pills and other drugs are the only thing that numb me enough I can get through the day.

I know the last day I saw Melody that she was trying to tell me something important. Unfortunately, her dad got there to pick her up too soon and she couldn't tell me. Now, I wonder every day what it was and wonder if the main thought running through my mind is really true. The night we were together, I know the condom broke. It was only a matter of a time before her parents forced her away from home. Melody carrying my baby is the only thing I can think of to cause her parents to react like that.

I'm going to miss her growing round with my baby and everything that she's going to be going through. I can just imagine the thoughts running through her mind right now. Having no one there to support her or help her when she needs it. No one there to take care of her when she's sick and needs someone to be there for her. I should be by her side through every stage of her pregnancy, and I'm going to miss it.

The day her dad picked her up and backhanded her so hard her head hit the window, I followed her home and waited in our spot for her to come to me. My parents already agreed to let us stay out back in the apartment, I was just waiting for her to show up. For over a week, I stood in our spot waiting hours and hours for her to come out. Until, finally one day, a girl appeared and told me that she was taken away to her aunt's house. When I questioned her, she didn't know more than Melody was being sent to live with an aunt for a while.

"Mason, you with us here, or are you dreamin' 'bout that bitch again?" Logan asks me, breaking me out of my thoughts.

"Don't ever call her a bitch again!" I scream, jumping up ready to come to blows over Melody with one of my best friends.

"Mase, I didn't mean anythin' by it. You just haven't been yourself in a while and we know that chick from school has to do with it." Levi pipes in. "You need to talk, talk."

"Listen, she came into my life and blew me away. Now she's gone. End of story." I gloss over everything that Melody means to me. I'm not going to tarnish her memory by talking to these guys about her.

"There's more to it than that." Connor says, heading out the door. "Let's get a move on. Pops wants to see you Mason."

Fuck! I know he's been watching me like a hawk and is going to know something is wrong. Hopefully I can give him a little more than I just gave them, and he'll be happy with it. The only way that's going to work is if Ma isn't with him though. Levi's mom is like a vulture. She'll keep digging and digging until you tell her what she wants to know. Ma will not leave you alone until she's satisfied that you've told her the whole story and haven't left anything out. They know I'm using and I don't want to think of what the repercussions will be. Not only from them but from the club.

Pulling into the lot of the clubhouse, Pops is the first person I see. Just looking at him, you can tell that he's a man on a mission and isn't happy about having to wait. Knowing I have to get this done, I park my bike and make my way over to the picnic table I see him heading towards. Smoking is another new habit I have these days, so I pull a smoke up and light it before I take a seat across from him.

After saying nothing, just looking at me for a full minute, Pops finally begins. "I don't know what's goin' on with you Mason, but somethin' is and it needs to end. Now!"

"I'm good Pops."

"No, you're not and we all know it. Somethin' happened to you right around the time of graduation and it's killin' you inside."

"I'm fine, I promise Pops. Guess I didn't really think of everythin' that we'd have to do when we started prospectin'. It's a bit overwhelmin' at times." I try to play it off like I'm stressed out about prospecting and nothing more.

"Then why you leavin' the second that you can and not returnin' sometimes for days? Why are there times we have to hunt you down and finally find you in some questionable places and situations? And, why is it that you're barely spendin' time with the guys anymore?"

There's no way I can answer him honestly without giving too much away. So, I'm going to have to pull something out of my ass and hope that it's enough to get him off my back. Unfortunately, I don't have any clue about what to say to make that happen. And, I've never once lied to anyone involved in this club. My family. They have always known me and everything going on with me.

"Listen, I'm just goin' through some shit right now. I need to get it handled and then I'll be back to normal. I don't need help, don't need a babysitter, and I don't need anythin' else. I show up when I need to, do everythin' you guys ask of me, and I don't need to spend every waking second with the other guys. I can do my own thing. We done here?"

"I guess. Just know that when you hit rock bottom and the pills, the lines, the alcohol, and the loose ass pussy isn't enough, I'll be here to pull you up. Got me son?" He asks.

There's nothing I can say to that. I'm in shock that he's nailed everything that I've been doing since Melody left me. I don't have a problem, I just need to get her off my mind for a little bit each day so that I can try to live my life. Man, I wish she were here with me right now. None of this would be happening if she were still here and we were getting ready to welcome our little one into the world. Instead, it's a sea of nameless, faceless pussy with drugs and alcohol thrown into the mix.

"Mason, you comin' with us tonight?" Dec asks me, pulling out the chair and flipping it backwards.

"Nope."

"You don't even know where we're goin'." Levi says.

"Don't care. I'm busy and already got plans."

"Which loose pussy is it today? Never seen anyone go through it like you do these days." Dec says.

"None of your business what I do. It doesn't affect you and so you need to stay the fuck out of my shit. Got it?" I say, getting pissed off and standing up from the table. My chair crashes to the floor and everyone stops moving around to stare at me. "I'm out. Need me, call."

Hopping on my bike, I think about where I'm going to go and what I want to do today. I know a trip to Crystal is in order. She's got the ability to get me high enough to take my mind off shit and then make sure I get my release. Too bad the only face I see is Melody's and the only name I call out is Angel. Crystal would be a good woman to be with, but to me, she's just a temporary distraction. One that has what I need when I need it.

Pointing my bike in the direction of her house, I make it there in record time. I need to let go of some of the anger from being questioned by everyone, so I rode hard and fast. Crystal is opening the door as I park my bike along the curb and a wide smile breaks out on her face.

"Hey handsome. Looking for me?" She asks, going into flirt mode. It's kind of disgusting how much she thinks I truly want her.

"I am. Got what I need?" I ask, setting my helmet on my bike and taking the first step towards her.

"I sure do. Let's go inside and I'll make everything disappear baby."

Glaring at her, I continue making my feet move in her direction. She knows not to call me baby or any other stupid ass shit. My name is Mason and that's what she's to call me. The glare I send in her direction is enough to make her realize what she did, and I can see her skin pale just a little bit. Yeah, she doesn't want to lose my cock to ride.

"Keep that shit up and I'll be cuttin' you loose Crystal. You know better than that." I growl out at her.

"I know. I'm sorry Mason. It won't happen again." Crystal whines.

"Let's just get this shit done with. I need to get shit out of my head."

I'm pounding into Crystal like my life depends on it. She's moaning and panting, but I don't hear any of it. I hear Melody's sweet moans and her whispered words in my head. Nearing my release, I call out 'Angel' and roll off the warm body. Quickly I pull on my clothes and get up. I grab the baggie off the stand by the bed and drop some money.

"See ya around." I grumble before leaving the house, and Crystal, behind.

Every single time I make a trip here, I feel like shit and guilty as fuck. It's like I'm tarnishing Melody's memory by sticking my cock in someone other than her. And every time I say it's going to be the last time, but it never is. I always have to go back and get my next fix. Sure, I could get it without fucking Crystal or the other faceless women. Most times Melody's face pops up and memories creep in and I need to forget about her for a little while. Too bad that doesn't happen though.

Pulling back into the apartment I share with Dec and Levi, I make sure my stuff is hidden. All I want to do is take a shower and hit my bed. Hopefully the guys aren't coming over tonight to party and shit. Again.

"Nice to see you made it back in one piece." Levi comments as I walk in the door.

Flipping him off, I make my way to the bathroom to take a shower. They better have already taken theirs because I'll use all of it. Not only to just get my head back in the game but to finish taking care of myself. I might have found release with Crystal, but I'm nowhere near satisfied. Melody is the only one I'll ever find satisfaction with.

"Don't use all the hot water Mase. We need to take a shower for tonight." Dec says.

"Sorry. If I use it, I use it." I tell him, walking in to the bathroom and slamming the door in their faces.

Once I'm in the shower, I hang my head down and just let the water run over me. I need to get my shit under control and quick. I'm starting to snap at the people closest to me and that's not like me. Usually I'm so easy going that nothing bothers me.

Before too long, thoughts of Melody take over and I'm instantly hard again. It's to the point that I have to think of her just to get hard when I'm with someone else. Just one little thought and I'm ready to go. Including as soon as I'm done with whatever warm hole I'm sinking in.

Taking my hard cock in my hand, I stroke myself thinking of everything I want to do to my angel. There's so much that I want to do to her and teach her to do to me. One day, I will find her, and she will be mine again. I just hope it's not too soon and I don't miss out on everything important.

I find my release quicker than anything when thoughts of Melody enter my head. I know it's not her and that must be the reason. Because as soon as I can finally sink balls deep in her again, I know I'm going to take my time and treasure every second with her. She'll know that I worship everything about her and I'll teach her how to worship my body the way I want it to be worshipped. Plus, she'll know that I'll treasure everything about her. Not just sexually. But in everything she ever wants to do. Melody is the only one for me and one day, she'll know it without a doubt.

Chapter Three
Melody

Seven Months later

THE LAST SEVEN MONTHS have been a rollercoaster ride for sure. I did make it to my aunt's house and it was a miserable place to be. Seriously, I would rather have stayed with my parent's. I had to be up at three in the morning every day and I was basically her servant. Well, hers and my cousin Kim's. Kim is a twenty-year-old that acts more like a five-year-old because her mom doesn't make her do a damn thing.

It took me a month before I got their routine down to the point I could pinpoint a time to leave and then another six months before I had the courage to actually leave the house. Every Wednesday they would go to get their hair done. It would take them about two hours plus the time to get there and back. They always left me home and gave me a list a mile long to get done in the amount of time they were gone.

About a month ago, I finally made my escape. It was scary as hell, I'm not going to lie about that. I was heavily pregnant and had no money to my name to truly go anywhere. The only thing I was thankful for was the fact that I was so close to Dander Falls. My aunt lived just outside of there.

I started walking along the road, hoping my aunt didn't come home sooner. About two miles into my walk, a truck pulled over and a guy gave me a ride into town. Honestly, I wasn't going to get in the truck with him but there was a girl about my age with him and they both looked like they were truly trying to help me.

As soon as we got into town, he dropped me off at a diner and told me to tell the owner that Hank had dropped me off. Said she would help me with a job and finding some place to stay. Little did I know, that day would change my life for the better.

Walking in, I could feel myself getting shaky and knew I had to get something to eat soon. A girl about my age saw me and rushed to my side. She led me to a booth and made sure that I had something to eat and drink before sending a woman in her early forties over to help me.

"Honey, I'm Karla and Kiera told me you need some help. Is she right?" The woman asks, sitting down across from me.

"Yes ma'am. I need a job and somewhere to stay. I'm supposed to tell you that Hank dropped me off." I tell her, looking down at my hands.

"There's no reason to be looking down at your hands honey. Everyone needs some help sooner or later in their life. I'm just here to make sure that we get you and that baby the help that you need." Karla tells me, lifting my face up to look her in the eyes.

"Thank you so much ma'am." I tell her honestly.

"Stop with that ma'am stuff honey. My name is Karla and you can call me that. Now, I'm going to give you a job here working a few hours a day. I don't want you on your feet for full shifts with you looking like you're about to pop. I will also talk to Kiera and see if she still has that extra room in her apartment that you can use for a bit."

"Oh, I couldn't impose like that. I'm sure that she likes her space and in a few months, I'm going to have my little boy here. She won't want to be around a crying baby."

"Nonsense. Kiera is good people. Having a baby around won't mean anything to her. If anything, she'll spend all the time she can helping you out with that precious angel."

At Karla's use of the word angel, I feel my eyes start to fill with tears. Mason always called me his angel and it's just making me miss him more. Karla wraps her arms around me and pulls me in the back room. Once in her office I spill the entire story of Mason, my parents, and escaping the hell of my aunt's house.

Karla asks if I know which club Mason's family belonged to and I can't tell her. I know he told me, but I can't remember which club he's a part of. She tells me that there's a local club and that if I ever want to talk to them and see if they know Mason to let her know. That's not something I can do though. It's hard enough for me to talk to people, but make it guys in a motorcycle club that I truly don't know, and I'll never be able to open my mouth.

Once I have myself back under control, Karla calls Kiera in and asks her about the spare room she has in her apartment. Kiera gets excited and tells me that she's more than happy to let me stay with her.

"Are you sure?" I ask. "I don't want to disrupt your life and I'm sure that my son will do nothing but that once he's born. I don't want you to think that you have to tiptoe around us or anything in your own home."

"Hush now. I seriously have no life and would love the company. Just think that when you can come back to work, we can take opposite shifts so that you don't have to worry about finding a sitter for your little guy." Kiera tells me.

"Okay. Well, thank you both so much. Karla, when do you want me to start?"

"You can start tomorrow morning at open. Kiera, take her to your place and get her all settled in. Take this and get her what she needs." Karla tells Kiera, handing her a bunch of money.

"Oh, no, I couldn't take your money."

"You can pay it back when you're able to. Now, go get some clothes, some toiletries, and some more food for the apartment. I'll see you both back here at five tomorrow morning."

Kiera takes me out of the diner and around back to her car. I'm constantly looking over my shoulder making sure that my aunt is nowhere to be found. The last thing I need is her finding me here and trying to drag me back to her fucked-up little world.

"You okay honey?" Kiera asks me.

"I'm looking to make sure that my aunt doesn't see me. I'm sorry to be bringing this drama to you."

"You tell me what's going on and I'll help you make sure that your aunt never finds you. Deal?"

So, for the second time in less than an hour, I find myself telling my story to someone I just met. Kiera doesn't interrupt me the entire time I'm telling my story. She just sits back, driving us to a store, and listens to me ramble on and on about everything that has happened to me over the last seven months.

"Damn girl! I thought I had a fucked-up past, but I got nothing on you honey." Kiera says. "We'll make sure that no one ever finds you and your little one. I don't care what we have to do. If that means we move and run every fucking week, then that's what we do. You're not alone in this anymore."

"You don't have to do that Kiera. I would never ask you to do that."

"You're not asking me to do it. I'm telling you I'm going to do it. I got your back from here on out and you're not getting rid of me any time soon." Kiera says, looking at me so I see that she's serious.

Finally pulling into the store, Kiera makes sure that the car is locked, and no one has followed us before I get out. She leads me inside and directly to the women's clothes. There, a cart is loaded with all different types of maternity clothes from dresses to capris and tee shirts. Our next stop is for bras and panties, which I get to choose myself. It only takes us a half hour to get everything we need and head back out to the car.

"Kiera, I think that's my aunt's car over there." I tell her pointing out a blue sedan.

After looking in the direction I'm pointing in, Kiera starts walking faster towards her car. While I get inside, she loads all the bags in the trunk since my aunt doesn't know her. From there, it takes us about a half hour to get to a cute little house that Kiera tells me she has to herself.

It's a two-story house that looks like a cottage with a wraparound porch. Inside there's an open floor plan and the biggest room is the kitchen. It's almost a gourmet kitchen with all the appliances I can see from just inside the doorway. There's no way in hell I'd ever ask Kiera to give this little place up to help me.

"Welcome home!" Kiera says, coming in behind me and shutting the door.

"You know I'm never going to let you give this place up if I have to leave here. Right?"

"It's just a building babe. You need to leave, we leave and find a new one."

It's been the calmest month I've ever had, and Kiera has been a tremendous help. If I get sick, she's there to help me, when I want to take a picture or video of something new happening to my body, she takes it, and if I want to take a nap then she lets me. Karla has been amazing too. When she sees me getting tired on my feet, she tells me to sit down and relax. Guys from the motorcycle club she talked to me about before have come in and she's let me take their order and wait on them so that I can get to know them. She's hoping that I'll get the courage to talk to them one day about Mason and find out if they know where he is.

Every time the club comes in and I take care of them, I always get a large tip. I'm pretty sure it's just because of the fact that I'm pregnant, but I'm not going to complain about it. The guys are really nice and joke around with me and laugh the entire time they're in. A few times one or two have even come back for lunch and made sure that I was their waitress then too. I really want to talk to them about Mason, but it's been almost a year and I'm sure that he's moved on by now. Yes, he needs to know about the baby, but I'm not ready to face him. Maybe I can just let one of the younger guys know that Mason is having a baby and he has the right to know.

"That couple is back again." Kiera tells me, pointing my line of vision to the back-corner booth.

"I hate it when they come in. You can just tell that he's a prick that's controlling the shit out of that poor girl."

"I know. Cassidy has their table this morning. So, we don't have to worry about him staring at our chest while his girl is sitting right there."

"Yeah. I hope she wises up before she gets hurt." I say, turning to go back to check on a table of bikers.

I've been at the diner about a month and my aunt has yet to be in while I'm working. Karla told me that she's been in once or twice to inquire about a missing niece that she's so scared for, but that's it. About the only thing I can say is that I have seen her car drive by and I've seen my cousin walking down the street.

"Is everything okay?" I ask the table full of bikers.

"Yeah, honey, we're good." The older one at the end of the table tells me.

"Melody, it's about time I find you!" I hear being shrieked from the doorway. "I've been looking all over for you!"

Turning around, I see my aunt standing there with her hands on her hips, glaring at me. Before I can say anything or make any moves, I feel a wall of heat at my back. Looking over my shoulder, I see that every single one of the bikers has stood and is now surrounding my back. Why they feel the need to take this on, I'm not sure, but I am thankful.

"We got a problem here?" The older gentleman asks.

"No, you do not. If my niece doesn't get her ass out to my car in the next minute, she'll be having a whole lot of problems." My aunt sneers.

"Do you want to go with your aunt honey?" One of the other bikers asks me.

"No." I whisper.

"Looks like she's not goin' anywhere. She's good where she is, and you can't make her do anythin' she doesn't want to. I suggest you back out the way you came in and forget this place even exists."

"Nope. I'm not leaving until she comes with me. Or do I need to tell your father that you're nothing more than a whore for a bunch of bikers now?"

"She isn't a whore for anyone!" Kiera screams out.

"Ma'am with all due respect, your niece isn't going anywhere with you." Another younger guy says stepping in front of me.

Before anyone can utter another word, the worst pain I've ever felt shoots through my stomach and doubles me over. Arms shoot out from all around me to make sure that I don't hit the floor with the force of the pain. This can't be happening, I can't be in labor. I still have just under a month left to go.

"Sweetheart, what's wrong?" The older biker asks.

"I think I'm in labor." I whisper. "It's not time yet."

"Okay. Just do me a favor and try to calm down a little bit. We'll make sure everythin' is okay." He responds.

As I go to stand up once the pain starts to subside, I feel a warm gush from down below. Fuck! My water just broke. The guys all pull in closer to me despite the liquid all over the floor and lead me to the back door. Kiera already has our stuff and is holding the door while another biker goes to open the car doors for us. Karla is telling me she'll be at the hospital as soon as she can and for us not to worry about anything.

One of the bikers helps me lay down in the backseat while Kiera gets in the passenger seat and a second biker drives us to the hospital. Kiera is spending her time facing me in the backseat trying to keep me calm while the two bikers are concentrating on making sure we get where we're going with no problems.

"Th-thank yo-you." I stammer out to the biker in the back with me.

"Darlin' it's nothin'. We're just helpin' someone out that needs it." He tells me.

"I don't ev-even know your names. I'm s-s-sorry."

"I'm Digger and the one in front is Gage. He's new to our chapter from back East."

"Y-y-you know Mason?" I ask.

"You mean Glock?" Gage asks me.

"Don't know. I just know him by Mason."

"If he now goes by Glock, then yeah, I know him."

"Oh."

"How you know him?" Gage asks me, just as another contraction hits.

"He's her baby daddy. They went to school together." Kiera answers for me.

"You the girl he's been pinin' over for months now?"

I don't even have time to answer as the contractions start coming one after the other. Digger tells Gage to speed up and get us to the hospital. Thankfully, I don't think it takes us another five minutes to get there because I can't handle this pain any longer.

The guys and Kiera rush me inside by carrying me while the bikers that followed us make sure no one gets in our way. Kiera is screaming her head off for a nurse, doctor, someone to help us while the bikers lay me on a gurney that's in the hallway. Before I can take a breath, I'm surrounded by nurses and other hospital staff. They're bombarding me with questions and giving me weird looks since I'm surrounded by a ton of bikers.

"Gage, I need you!" I call out as they begin to wheel me to delivery.

"What's up babe?" He asks, coming to my side and pushing a nurse out of his way.

"You can't say anything to Mason. Please, I'm begging you!"

"I don't know Melody." Gage starts. "He's my brother and I really should tell him that he's got a kid."

"Listen to me," I pant. "My parents were going to kill our baby if I didn't leave and go to my aunt's house. As soon as he's born, I'm supposed to be giving him up for adoption, but I'm not going to do that. That's why I ran away from my aunt's. Well, part of the reason. No one is going to take my baby away from me. But, if he knows and comes here, I can't guarantee that he's not going to be followed here."

"I still don't know Mel. What do you think is goin' to happen to me when he finds out I didn't tell him?"

"I'm sure it's nothing pleasant. But, you don't know who my parents are and what they do to me. The things I've been put through growing up have only gotten worse since I hit puberty and my body started developing. There have been beatings, whippings, nails almost through my feet, kneeling on cement floors for hours on end. There's been a ton of shit like that I've been through and that's just the nice stuff."

"What do you mean that's the nice stuff?" Gage asks me, and I can see the rage on his face.

"I don't want to go into more detail, but I will if I have to. Please, I need you to do this for me. I'm going to tell him when I find him again. I just can't do it right this second. Please, Gage, I'm begging you as much as I can right now."

"I'll keep it for a little bit, Melody. That's the best I can do. What are you goin' to do now that your aunt knows you're in Dander Falls?"

"We're going into hiding again." Kiera answers him, walking through the door.

"What does that mean?" Gage asks.

"It means that you won't know where we are. We'll be underground and no one will know where we're at. Don't worry, Glock's baby will be more than taken care of."

"It's not just the baby that I'm worried about. I'm worried about you guys too." Gage says, standing guard by the door so that we can apparently have this conversation while I'm in labor. "If I think that you're runnin' away, you know I'm makin' that call now, right?"

"You can't make that call now. Please!" I beg. "Besides, by the time he gets here from wherever he is, we won't be here."

"You have to stay in the hospital for as long as they need you and the baby here. We can protect you, especially since you're Glock's woman. You're one of us." Gage says, coming closer to us.

"I don't need you guys. I'm not involving you in my shit. I got myself into this and I can get myself out of it. We'll be fine. We always are. Aren't we, Kiera?" I ask, looking at her.

"I'm sure you are. But, you're club now, and club looks after its own."

"I'll think about it, Gage. I promise. Now, I need to have this baby, so can we please do this some other time?"

Gage nods his head once and leaves my room. As soon as he's gone, the nurse and doctor come in. Thankfully, it's time to push. I don't have anything for the pain, but that's okay. I'm used to pain. I've lived with it every day of my life. Now, it's pain that will bring our child into this world. I'll handle that all day long.

"Okay, Melody, on your next contraction, I want you to start pushing. Okay?" The doctor asks, looking at me.

Nodding my head, I can feel another contraction coming on. Kiera is on one side of me and she helps me pull my leg up on her side while a nurse helps me on the other side. I'm already so tired that I don't think I could hold them up by myself.

After almost ten hours, our son finally made his appearance into the world. He was screaming so loud and it was the best sound in the world to me. He weighed in at just over eight pounds and was about twenty-two inches long.

"What's this handsome little guy's name?" One of the nurses asks me.

"Anthony Mason Greene." I tell them.

Kiera doesn't really know what that name is going to mean to Mason, but I do. Anthony is the name of his brother that died from an overdose. Mason tried his hardest to get his brother clean, and keep him that way, but it didn't work out. He took it hard as fuck and it's going to haunt him the rest of his life. By naming our son Anthony, I am hoping that he knows that I've listened to everything that he's ever told me and I'm trying to honor his late brother's memory.

"That's a good, strong name." The doctor tells me.

"How long am I going to have to be in here?" I ask, suddenly remembering that I need to go in hiding.

"Well, we'll have to check you and the baby out, but I can probably release you tomorrow." She tells me.

"That long?" I basically plead with her.

"If I can release you any sooner, I will try, but I'm not going to guarantee anything. That's the best I can do honey."

After making sure that I'm cleaned up and I don't need anything else, the doctor tells me that she'll be back to check on us later. Kiera is holding Anthony while the doctor finishes up with me. She's looking down at him like he's the most precious thing on Earth. To me, he is.

Suddenly, I can't stop the tears from flowing down my face. Mason should be here with us for this. He should be the one holding our son right now, and he's not. He's missed everything. How am I ever going to make this right for him? There's nothing I can do to make it possible for him to be there during the pregnancy, delivery, and watching our son grow into an amazing man.

"Babe, why are you crying?" Kiera asks, handing Anthony over to me.

"He's missed it all. Kiera, is he ever going to meet his son and know that I wanted him with me through this?"

"Mason will know his son. He will know that you tried to find him while hiding from your bitch of an aunt. And, he will never hold this against you."

"You don't know that. But, I'm going to have to cross that bridge when I come to it. For now, I need to concentrate on making sure our son has the best life I can give him. I also need to figure out how I'm going to make sure my parents don't find us."

"*We* are going to make sure your parents don't find you. As soon as you get out of here, we're moving, and no one will find us babe. I promise you."

Chapter Four
Glock

Two years later

MY DAYS ARE A constant routine. I get up, go out looking for my angel, get pissed I can't find her, get high, and find some random pussy to try to take her memory away. It's a shit way to live and I know I'm slowly killing myself.

I've done every drug under the sun except for one. I will never touch heroin. It's what killed my brother Anthony and in my mind, I'm okay as long as I don't do that. Honestly, I don't even care if I live these days though. The only person that ever made my life bright after Anthony is Melody and she's gone. She's out there with my child somewhere.

I'm still just taking a guess that she was pregnant with my baby, but the thought won't go away. Those two are my reason for getting out of bed every day and I have no clue where to even go looking for them. I've been all over this shitty little town and three towns over all the way around. Using the club's contacts, I've put the word out all over that I'm looking for her. Still, there's been no word on her. I refuse to believe that she just disappeared. Melody wouldn't do that to me without a good reason.

"Glock, get the fuck up!" Cage yells through my door at the clubhouse. "It's time to head out."

"Fuck off! Not goin'." I holler back, pushing the club girl off of me and telling her to get the fuck out.

"Not sayin' it again Glock. Get the fuck out here and let's roll."

Strolling to the door naked as the day I was born, I fling it open. "And I said I'm. Not. Going."

"The fuck is your problem these days? It's been two fuckin' years of you fuckin' up and not holdin' up your end of the deal. We're goin' to the lake and everyone is supposed to be there."

"Don't give a fuck. Got plans today that don't involve that shit."

Cage is my cousin and one of the closest people to me here. Even though I grew up in the club, Cage is still the one I'm closest to. He knows that something's been off, I've just gotten good at hiding what I'm really doing. So far, no one has questioned me or gotten me in too much trouble with the Pres.

"Glock, we're done fuckin' around with your ass. Get the fuck out here now!" Joker tells me, standing his ground next to Cage.

"You both need to fuck off before I do somethin' I'll regret later."

"Like what?" Cage asks.

"Kickin' both your asses." I mutter before turning around to get back in bed.

"Bring it Glock. You can't beat shit up these days." Joker says, stepping just inside the doorway of my room. "I'm surprised you even come back here. Too busy lookin' for some bitch that don't want to be found."

"I warned all you motherfuckers!" Is all I say before spinning around and going on the attack.

My fist finds purchase in the side of Joker's head. Catching him off guard was the plan and now it's on. The adrenaline is flowing and I'm ready to take out some of this pent-up aggression on someone. Too bad one of my oldest friends happens to be on the other end. Now, I can't kill him, I can just hurt him.

"Glock!" Cage yells, bringing attention to my room and the fight.

Joker catches me in the gut with a right hook, knocking me to the floor. He climbs on top of me and continues to land punch after punch. Just as he starts slowing down, I see my opening and flip him over so that I'm now on top. My fists don't stop and they land everywhere. I'm landing blows to his head, chest, stomach, and anywhere else I can reach.

"Enough!" Pops bellows from just outside my door. "Cage and Joker, get the fuck out of here. Go with the rest of the club to the lake. Glock and I are gonna sort some shit out."

"You gonna meet us there, dad?" Joker asks him.

"I don't know yet. Just get everyone the fuck out. Now!"

Pops doesn't say another word until no one is near my door. Then he tells me to take a shower and wash the stench away and to meet him in the kitchen. Ma is cooking us breakfast and I better be there for it in less than five minutes.

Picking my broken ass up, I make my way into the bathroom. While I wait for the water to heat up, I stare at my reflection in the mirror and realize how low I've sunk. I'm honestly no better than Anthony was right now. He didn't care who was hurt while he was high or trying to find his next fix. I've been doing that for just over two years now. Not only to my blood family but to my club and my brothers. Fuck! What have I done?

Knowing that Pops isn't playing around, I take a quick shower and throw some clothes on. Making my way into the kitchen, I see Pops and Ma sitting at a table, waiting for me with three plates of food on the table. My stomach rumbles and I realize I don't even know when the last time I ate was.

"You're goin' to eat and then you're goin' to tell us what the fuck is goin' on with you. You will not leave anythin' out and I want the fuckin' truth from you Glock. You got me?"

"Yeah Pops, I got you."

I stuff my face with the hot breakfast Ma made and gulp down the piping hot coffee without taking a breath. Ma and Pops sit back and watch me eat instead of eating their own breakfast. Normally, we'd be talking, joking, and laughing. Instead the seriousness of what is about to happen is weighing down the good mood. If only they knew what I was about to unleash on them.

Honestly, I've wanted to get off the shit I've been doing for a while now, but it was just easier to stay numb to everything. I'm not proud of the man I've become and I'm happy as fuck that Melody isn't here to witness it. Living without the other half of my heart though isn't something I was strong enough to endure without numbing a little bit of the pain.

Yeah, everyone can say that we were too young and we didn't know what we were talking about. But, I know what I feel for Melody is real and I've damaged her memory beyond repair with my fucking random pussy and all of the drugs I've put in my body. Fuck! Let's hope that she still takes me back when she learns of everything I've done.

"You about done son?" Pops asks me.

"Yeah. Pops, I'm gonna start off by sayin' that I need help and I don't want anyone else to know what's goin' on right now. I'm goin' to explain everythin' to you and Ma and hope that it stays between the three of us. No one, and I mean no one, else knows everythin' that I'm about to tell you two."

"We'll take it to our grave." Ma says, leaning forward and grabbing my hand. "Pops and I will do whatever we can to help you, but you need to be completely honest with us. That's the only way it's going to work."

I nod my head and take a minute to gather my thoughts and courage. This is going to be the hardest thing that I've ever done so far in my life. Not because I'm admitting that I have a drug problem, that's the easy part. I know I have one and have for a long time now. No, the hard part is going to be facing two of the most sacred people to me, besides my own parents, and see the disappointment in their eyes every time they look at me.

"It all starts back in high school. I met the love of my life, the lightness to my dark. Melody was so smart, funny, never afraid of anythin' I thought I represented, and wanted to be with me for me. Not for what I could give her, what the club meant, what being a biker meant. She got me to talk about things I've never opened up about, like Anthony. She's just that easy to talk to, get along with, and she makes me want to do things I've never thought about doin' before. Fuck, I'm content just to lay in a field with her somewhere and talk." I pause, trying to gather my thoughts once again. I could talk about Melody all day long and not get tired of it.

"Anyway, we ended up havin' sex together, losin' our virginity to one another, in the field at the back of the clubhouse. The condom broke and I told my angel that we'd take care of anythin' that resulted from the condom breakin'. No, Ma, I don't mean her getting' an abortion. I mean, I was ready to settle down with her and raise our child together. Mel started avoidin' me at school until just before graduation. She said we had to talk but her dad got there to pick her up before we could. She took off like she was afraid to make him wait for her. When she got in the car, a few words were exchanged and before I knew it, he was backhandin' her. He hit her so hard,

Pops, that her head bounced off the window of her door. I tried to run after them, I tried to get her out of that car and away from him, but I couldn't keep up. That's the last time I saw her. I have a feelin' that she was goin' to tell me that she was pregnant, but I can't know for sure. Now, I've missed everythin' with the pregnancy. Hell, I don't even know if the baby was born or if somethin' happened to it or her."

Stopping again, I have to put my head down. I can feel the tears starting to come at the unknown about my angel and our child. I hope that Melody is okay first and foremost. Any child that we could possibly have made is also important to me. But at this point in time, that's an uncertainty and Melody is not.

"I spent days and days waitin' for her to show up at our spot so that I could tell her dad said we could move in to that little house at the back of his property. I'd sit there for hours and hours just waitin' for her. Finally, I realized that she was never goin' to come out to me. So, I've been searchin' for her ever since. I have feelers out with every contact we have to look for her and let me know if they see her. That's not what I need help with though. Give me a minute please." I say, needing to brace myself for the disappointment that I'm about to see cross their faces.

"To numb the pain from the loss of my girl, and possibly our child, I've been doin' almost every drug out there. For obvious reasons, I haven't touched heroin, but I've come close a few times. When the pills, lines, and alcohol don't work at numbing the pain enough for me to forget my girl for just a few minutes, I turn to the random pussy. Fuck, I can't even get hard these days without thinkin' of my girl though. No matter what I do, I can't forget her. I need to stop this shit if I ever hope to find her though. There's no way I'm showin' her this version of myself. I need to detox, and get clean of this so that I can start my life again. I need to be clean for her and our baby. If there even is a baby." I tell them, finally looking up at their faces.

In Ma's face, I see nothing but pure love shining through. There's no disappointment or anger. Instead, it's love, understanding, and a little bit of pride. On Pop's face, I see anger, pride, and love. I don't know if I'm happy that I don't see disappointment, but Pop's anger is almost as bad.

"Son, I've been waitin' for two years for you to come to me with what was goin' on with you. Why would you ever think it was okay to turn to fuckin' drugs? There's more than enough of us here to help you with whatever you need." Pops asks. "Wait, this is the call you made to me when we were movin' to Clifton Falls, wasn't it? You thought your girl was in that car?"

"I know she was. I can't explain it, but I know she was in that car. The only reason I didn't follow them was because I didn't want to lose you guys. Otherwise, I would've made sure that she was in the car and brought my girl home a fuck of a lot sooner. I would've been there for her if she was pregnant and made sure that I didn't miss a thing."

"We're gonna help you get this shit out of your system Glock. And, we'll keep it quiet from everyone else. You ever start this shit again, I'll never help you again. When you get clean, that's it. Is that a deal?" Pops asks me.

"That's more than a deal. I promise you both that I won't ever go back to this shit. I'm better than that. I know I'm better than that and I need to get back to who I am. Instead of snappin' at my brothers and losin' my life over some stupid ass shit."

"Ma, I want you to go in and search his room. Get everythin' you find and destroy it. Then go to the apartment and search that place. I'll make sure that the guys don't go back there some way."

I thought someone going through and taking my stash was going to drive me insane, but it's really not. I'm relieved that someone is taking it away from me so I don't have to. I let them know the main areas I keep things in so that Ma won't have such a hard time locating it all. But, I know she's going to tear my shit apart to make sure she's gotten it all.

The last week and a half has been pure torture. I knew detoxing wasn't going to be easy, but this is pure hell. Ma and Pops have been by my side through every single thing. They've taken all the abuse I've dished out and let me say whatever comes out of my mouth. Pops has had to restrain me more than once when I was determined to take the pain away by getting another fix. Most times Ma only comes in when I'm in the shower or asleep. I don't want her around me when I start losing it. If I did anything to hurt her, I'd never forgive myself.

I told Pops that I don't want her in here until I get through the rage part of this detox, but he says she's going to do what she wants to do anyway. We all know this is true. So, I've told Ma myself that I don't want her around me right now. I was almost in tears when I talked to her about it and, so she's limited the time she's in with me.

Pops has had to force me to eat more days than not. And I usually just get sick after I do get done eating. Ma is just wasting her time and talents on me right now, but she's getting to mother someone so she's fine with it I guess.

"Son, the boys are pretty much demandin' to see you. They want to know what's goin' on but we haven't said anythin' to them. It's your call." Pops tells me one day.

"I don't want them to know. Please, tell them I'm sick or somethin' and I can't see them right now. Let me get through the rest of this and start feeling normal before I see them. But, all this stays between us and only us."

"Okay son. Like I said, your call. I'll put them off again."

Pops leaves the room and I can feel the sweat starting to pour off me. Just talking to Pops took what little energy I had and now I'm ready to go back to bed. That seems to be the main thing I do these days. Ma has to change the sheets and wash them daily, some days it's more than once a day. They just don't want me any more uncomfortable than I already am. And I really want a fix, but that would be breaking a promise I made to them and myself. I can beat this, and I will. I'm not going to be like Anthony and let it destroy me. I have too much to live for.

It's been about six months since Ma and Pops took me into their home to put me through detox. Life is definitely looking better again. I still miss Melody like crazy and think about her every second of every day. Just like I still wonder whether or not we have a child together, and what I'm missing right now.

I've built myself back up and I'm proud of the man I'm becoming. The club is the main thing I focus on right now and my job for it. I manage one of the strip clubs and handle all the books for it. I'm the first one to volunteer when a run comes up, and I've quit all the loose pussy. I can't even tell you the last girl that I was with or when it happened. Melody deserves to know that I'm clean when I find her again.

"Glock, you ready to head out?" Cage asks me.

"Yeah. Give me one second to make sure I got what I need." I tell him, checking my bag again.

"We'll be outside waitin' on you then."

Making sure I got enough clothes and smokes to get to Clifton Falls, I close my bag up and make my way out of the clubhouse. Crystal became one of the club girls and is still trying to get my cock back. Too bad for her that Melody is the one that it belongs too. Hell, if anyone paid attention to my bike they'd see that shit.

I had my bike repainted about three months ago, saying I needed a change. Really, I had it painted to match my girl's eyes. If you look close enough in the paint job, you'll see other reminders of my girl, but that's for you to find out. I don't tell anyone about it and so far, no one has commented on anything other than the color.

Right now, Cage, Joker, Grim, and I are heading to Clifton Falls to see if we can finalize the sale of a new clubhouse once and for all. It's still going to be a bit before we can move in, but at least we'll know we have it. The pictures we've looked through showed an old factory. We're going to have to start work on it a little bit before we can move everything down there. Or we'll just take our chances and see what happens when we get there.

It's going to take us about a week to get there and then who knows how long we'll have to stay there. I think that Gage might come down for a while if we have to stay there. This is going to be the first big test for me since going through detox. I haven't been away from Ma and Pops for more than a few days. Now, we're talking weeks of being just with the guys. I'll just have to stick to my routine as much as I can, and make sure that I find something else to do if the temptation gets too bad.

"Roll out!" Grim calls before taking off.

Chapter Five
Melody

Eight years later

TO SAY MY LIFE has changed over the past eight years is an understatement. Anthony has changed me in ways that I never dreamed possible. He's my whole world and I wish that I were doing better by him than what we are. But, he's one hell of a kid and never complains or whines when we have to randomly pick up and move somewhere new. I wish we could just settle down in one place, but that can't happen as long as my parents are still out there looking for me.

Kiera has also been a major part of our world. Without any questions, concerns, or angry outbursts, she packs up and moves right along with us every single time. We both still work as waitresses, but Kiera has taken her job in a different direction than what I could. She's now a waitress for one of the local strip clubs. Actually, I think the guys from the MC own the club, but she doesn't say one way or another if they do or not.

We have moved a total of fifteen times between the day that I was released from the hospital with Anthony and now. I hate making him change schools, but it's better than my parents getting their hands on him. Now, I'm a waitress at another diner that Karla recommended me to and I'm so happy. I work the day shift still so I can be home at night with my son.

Every day he looks more and more like his father. I have a total of one picture from high school of him and Anthony has taken it in his room where he can talk to his dad when he wants to. I've heard him telling Mason how sad I am, how he wishes that his dad could be there with us, how he's going to be the man of the house in no time at all so that we can stop running from my parents. Our son is years beyond his age in some ways and younger in other ways. I blame myself for keeping him so sheltered and having to hide out more times than I can count.

The school that Anthony is currently in is trying to help me get him into counselling and get him some extra help so that we can get him where he's supposed to be. He just turned eight about three months ago and there's days that he acts so much younger than that. Until he gets in his comfort zone and feels he can be himself. At this point, even when he's in his comfort zone, there's time he still acts young. We will get this fixed though and help him in any way we can. Kiera is on board with whatever we have to do to make that happen.

It's been a long day at the restaurant and I'm just getting ready to clock out when I hear my boss calling my name. She's a young girl that thinks her shit doesn't stink and takes her bad mood out on all of the waitresses. I guess today is my turn to have her wrath turned on me. It's been a while, so I really can't complain too much I guess.

"Melody, I need you to stay late tonight. There's been two call offs and no one else can cover them." Rachel tells me.

"No. I'm going home to my son so my roommate can get to work herself. You know that I can't stay late and you're just going to have to find someone else to do it."

"Then you can start looking for a new job." Rachel says, throwing her hands on her hips and staring me down. It's funny when she tries to intimidate me.

"No, I won't. You can threaten me all you want, but all I have to do is call Mike and he'll make sure you're the one that doesn't have a job. You've already been warned once Rachel and I'm tired of your shit. Now, I'm going home and I'll be back in the morning. Try to get me fired and you'll find yourself in the unemployment line instead. Do I make myself clear?"

"W-w-well, we'll see what Mike has to say when I tell him I caught you stealing from the tip jar." Rachel tries to blackmail me. Everyone knows it's her including Mike.

"Honey, don't threaten me. We all know you're the one taking our tips when you don't do shit to earn any yourself. Mike knows this too and you're really on thin ice with everyone here. Now, like I said, go ahead and try to get me fired. You'll see that I'm not lying and I don't have to resort to games to try to get my way." I say, turning my back on her. "By the way, you might find that people would be more willing to help you out if you tried being nice to them instead of acting like a bitch every day."

With that I make my way through the restaurant and out the front door. We still don't have a car, so Kiera and I make sure our jobs are close enough to our apartment that we can walk wherever we have to go. Once a month we get friends to take us to the store for food and anything else we might need at the apartment. It's not a good life, but it's our life and we're doing the best we can with what we have to work with right now.

I'm about three blocks from home when I hear footsteps coming up behind me. It's not unusual to have other people walking this neighborhood during the day, but for some reason I'm getting a horrible feeling about this. The only thing I can think of is that my parents have found me. Too bad that's not the case though.

Before I can turn around, a hand covers my mouth and I smell something horrible. It's the worst body odor I have ever smelt in my life. I can feel an overweight body pressing up against mine before feeling the pinch in my neck and everything starting to turn fuzzy. I'm not sure what the fuck they just injected in me, but I can barely move my arms and legs and my vision is leaving quicker than I like. Hell, I can't even yell for help between him covering my mouth and the fact that nothing on my body seems to want to work the way it's supposed to right now.

"That's a good little girl." The man whispers in my ear. "You're going to fetch a pretty penny when I turn you into the boss. We'll get you where we want you in no time at all."

'No' is the only thing running through my head as I'm pulled backwards. I'm guessing that he's putting me into some sort of vehicle to take me to whoever he's talking about. Now, the only thing I can do is accept my fate I guess.

Anthony and Mason's faces keep running through my head on a loop and I can't stop the tears from leaking out of my eyes. As long as these assholes have me, they'll leave the men I love alone. At least that's my hope if my parents are behind this shit right now.

The only thing I can do when I get thrown in the back of a van, is see. My eyes are still open, but the rest of my body is not moving at all. I can see a few other girls laying in similar positions to what I'm guessing I'm lying in. They all have a wild look in their eyes and tears streaking down their faces. What the fuck is happening to us?

"Alright ladies, I suggest you behave if you know what's good for you." The man leers at us. "Your new, temporary, owner expects obedience from his girls until they get sold to their new owners. You lot will be no exception."

After slamming the door, I can hear him whistling a show tune as he makes his way to the front of the van as if nothing unusual is happening right now. This guy is crazy, if he thinks that no one is going to report seeing a bunch of girls being taken in broad daylight, starts running on a loop. If only I knew the hell that we were all about to endure would, in fact, not be reported to any cops at all.

Honestly, I can't even tell you how long I've been with the assholes that took me so long ago. I know it's been more than a few months if the way the new girls are talking is correct. According to the dates they're saying, it's been almost six months since I've seen my son and Kiera. Six months that I've been beaten, tortured, raped, and drugged. This happens on a daily basis and I'm almost numb to it now. In the beginning, I put myself in the forefront so the men would leave the younger girls alone. Some of these girls are very young.

In the beginning, I would cry out with pain, but soon realized that they like hearing our screams and pleas. So, now, I remain as silent as I can and don't give them anything. I don't even cry now until after they leave me alone in my cage. There I curl up in a fetal position and let my tears flow freely. No sound even comes out when I cry anymore.

We've been moved several times now and I'm not sure why that is. I know a little while ago one random girl was brought in but she's kept separate from the rest of us. None of us know why she's so special, but we don't take the time to find out either. The only ones we truly worry about is ourselves. Wondering if today is going to be the last day that we have alive or if we get to survive the torture another day.

The pain in my body gets worse and worse every day. In the few moments of clear thinking when I first wake up, I can tell that I have a fever and that something is very wrong with me. Before I can think about it too much though, they inject me with more drugs. Some days, I almost wish that they'd just overdose me and put me out of my misery. But then Anthony's little face flashes in my mind and I want to live more than I want to die.

The only face that I'm truly losing sight of is Mason's. It's been so long since I've seen him and the changes that he's gone through that I can't even pull up images of us when we were in school. Maybe I don't want to right now because I know he deserves someone better than what I am. I'm just a dirty, used-up whore if the men holding us are right. That's what they tell all of us on a daily basis anyway.

"Get up bitch!" A man screams at us. "Time for your daily medicine. Then you'll go two by two for showers."

That's what they tell us the drug of the day is. Apparently, it's because we won't feel any pain or anything else once it gets coursing through our system. Then the night guards will give us just a little bit more to get us through the night without crying. It's kind of hard not to when your wounds have wounds and they continue piling up every day.

Now we all sit in our cages as close to the door as we can so when they open the little hole we can stick our arms out. They've gotten everything down to a science so that they're in and out. We all know the days that the big boss is coming because they let us get cleaned up. Looks like today is one of those days.

"You all know the routine. Wash, rinse, dress in what's laid out for you, and make sure your hair is brushed." A second guard barks out.

Just before the men get to me, I hear shouting and gunfire starting to explode all around us. I'm not sure if it's my imagination or if someone is actually coming in to save at least one of us. The guards forget what they're doing and run to grab any weapon that they can get their hands on. I've overheard the owner telling them that they are to protect us with their lives if necessary and make sure that no one rescues us. Maybe today someone will actually be rescued from this nightmare and make it out alive.

The gunfire and screams get closer and closer. I can hear doors slamming open and closed down the hallways until someone shouts that someone has been found. I'm betting it's the girl that has never been put in a cage with the rest of us. Now that they have the one they came for, I'm guessing they'll be on their way to make sure she's okay. So, I put myself close to the front door of the cage so that I can stick my arm out when it's my turn to get my 'medicine'. It's going to happen whether I want it to or not, so I might as well be prepared for it.

Closing my eyes, I wait for the needle to hit my arm and the pain to melt away. Whatever they inject into us daily, melts whatever pain we're feeling completely away for a little while. When we start coming down off our high, the pain is ten times worse than before. Instead of the pain being taken away, I hear the main doors crash open and shouting growing louder and louder until finally three or four men come bursting in the room.

Turning my attention towards the sounds, I see a man that closely resembles Mason. But, it can't be him, he's nowhere near where I am right now. Still, there's just something about him that makes me unable to take my eyes away from him. Is this too good to be true? Is it really the man that can tempt me to do almost anything?

"Mason!" I yell out, not knowing if he can even hear me.

Chapter Six
Glock

WE'VE FINALLY FOUND out where Maddie is and we're at the warehouse. Tank has found his girl and now we're clearing the rest of the warehouse to make sure that there's no one else here. After making our way into the main room, I see cages and cages of girls ranging from very young to a little bit older. Just as I go to look down in the first cage, I hear someone yelling.

"Mason!" is yelled out. I haven't heard that name in so long.

Turning my head, I see a girl that looks like my angel. She's the only one that would be using the name Mason. The girl is extremely skinny, and I can tell that they've been feeding her drugs, the same as the rest of the girls here, but the face still kind of looks like my angel's face.

"Angel, is that really you?" I ask, not giving a shit about anything else right now.

"Mason, please tell me I'm not dreaming." She says.

There's no doubt about it, this is my angel and I'm going to take her home. As soon as the guys that are playing guard are taken care, we start letting the girls out of their cages. Fuck, I can't believe they've been caged like dogs or some shit. My angel has been caged like a fucking dog and fed who knows what through a fucking needle in her arm.

One of the other guys goes to help Melody out of her cage and I lose my shit. No one is touching my angel except for me. Cage and Joker can see how close to losing my shit I am so they pull everyone back and let me get her out. As soon as I'm close enough to her, I can feel the heat from a fever radiating off of her. Fuck! Who knows how long she's been sick and no one has helped her at all.

Right now, I'm only touching under her arm pits because I can see all of the wounds on her body. There's no way I'm putting her in more pain than I absolutely have to. But, that's not going to be a problem considering the fact that as soon as she was mostly clear of the cage, the strength left her and she passed out. So, I lift her up in my arms and Cage covers her as gently as he can with his tee. Not that I want anyone else's clothes near my girl, but right now she needs to be covered from their eyes.

Melody is covered in dirt and grime from head to toe. Her hair is matted and a complete mess and the injuries all over her once flawless skin are red and angry looking. She's only wearing a filthy bra and skimpy pair of panties that are torn on one side. These motherfuckers put their hands on my girl and made her suffer more than anyone should ever have to. I will be sending them to a special place in hell.

"Someone get doc here now!" I yell out as I take my girl outside to get some air to her overheated body. "My girl needs help. Cage, please get me some help for her!"

Cage must see the desperation and tears on my face at seeing the most innocent and beautiful person I have ever known suffering. He runs inside and suddenly I'm surrounded by doc, Cage, Joker, and everyone else that has come with us besides Tank. I'm sure he's with his girl right now making sure that she's okay.

"Doc, you gotta help her. Please! I can't lose her when I've just found her again!" I scream, pulling him in closer to look at my girl.

"Son, I'll do what I can, but she might need a hospital more than the help I can give her."

"No!" I shout, knowing that there's a reason my girl has basically been in hiding if my resources couldn't find her. "She's got someone after her I'm sure and they'd be able to find her in a hospital. Please, just help me. I'll take her somewhere safe and do everythin' you tell me to do. I *need* you to help me with this."

Doc takes a second to look around and gets the nod from Grim to do as I've asked. I know that Gage has a cabin they use as a safe house. If I have to spend all the time in the world there to make sure my girl is okay, that's what I'll do. Melody means more to me than the club and I'll leave if the guys don't understand that I need her in my life. She's not getting away from me. Not this time.

After making sure that Melody was stable and could travel, Doc loaded me up with medicine and ointments for her. Not only am I to give her antibiotics, I have to continue to put the ointment on her wounds and then bandage them. Since she already has an infection, he's worried about her getting a worse one from something getting into one of the open wounds. That's one of my main concerns too.

Gage let me borrow his truck so that I could transport her up to the cabin they use as a safe house. There I'll monitor her, make sure that her wounds are clean, and that she gets over this infection running rampant through her body. If I have to go without sleep for weeks on end, I will. That's how much Melody's health means to me.

"You sure you wanna do this Glock?" Cage asks me.

"There's no one else that's gonna take care of my girl. She's my responsibility and I'm goin' to make sure that she gets better. Grim, you need me to turn my patch in, that's fine. Don't know how long I'll be gone."

"You ain't turnin' in your patch. Take all the time you need. We ain't goin' anywhere." Grim tells me, turning to head back towards the warehouse.

"We'll miss you." Pops says, giving me a man hug. "You need anythin' at all, you call us. Even if it's just to talk if things get to rough."

I know what Pops is talking about and he's not going to have to worry about it. There's no way in hell that I'm going to relapse knowing that my angel is back in my life. She's all I need in my life and I am not going to give her any reason to leave me. Drugs are not as important to me as she is.

"I'll be fine Pops. My angel is back and I'm not fuckin' it up for anythin' in the world." I tell him. Making sure that I look him directly in the eyes so that he can see the truth in them.

Pops nods to me and leaves. One by one all of the guys head back towards the warehouse. They let me know to call them if I need them for anything. I won't though. It's going to be hard enough on Melody with just me around after so many years and I'm not bombarding her with the rest of the guys from the club, not from any of the chapters of the club. She's never met any of them and I don't want her to be scared as hell when she meets them all for the first time.

I load Melody up in the back seat of the truck and take off. The bag doc gave me is in the passenger seat and I only have to stop to grab some groceries real quick. Joker is actually going to be meeting me at a store to run in for me. That way I don't have to worry about what I'm going to do about Melody while I'm in there.

Since the cabin isn't too far outside of Dander Falls, we decide to stop at a store about ten minutes from where the warehouse is. I text Joker my list and see him run in grabbing a cart from outside as he goes. I hope he doesn't take forever while he's in there. Getting Melody laying down in bed is the only thing I want to do right now.

While he's in there, I keep checking on my angel to make sure she's still breathing and that her fever isn't spiking more than it already was. That's the last thing I need right now. Although, I'm pretty sure that there's meds in there for that too.

"I think I got everythin' you wanted man. There's a few things in there for her too. I'm pretty sure that for the first few days after she wakes up fully you're not goin' to want her eatin' more than basically clear liquids." Joker tells me, helping me load everything in the back of the truck.

"Thanks. I didn't even think of that."

"You might want to put a call in to Karen too man. I'm just sayin' she's been a tremendous help to Sky and I can't recommend her enough. We don't know what all she's been through so she might need to talk to someone."

"Yeah, that's true. Text me her number and I'll call her when we get there."

"Done." Joker tells me before giving me a man hug and getting back on his bike.

It's taken me about an hour to get to the cabin. Usually it wouldn't be that long, but I've tried to go slow with Melody in the back seat. I don't want her jostling around back there and cause more damage.

I've unloaded everything and now I'm going back to get my sweet angel out of the truck. She's still passed out and hasn't stirred at all, which has me worried. But, doc told me to expect her to be out of sorts for a while. At least until the infection starts to leave her body. It's just scary as fuck to see this shit happening to someone that you've given your heart to.

It doesn't take me long to get her settled in the bed downstairs. I grab a cool washcloth and lay it across her forehead before grabbing a basin and soap to wash her up a bit. There wasn't much we could do while outside the warehouse, but now is a different story. I can get the dirt and grime off her body and worry about her hair in the morning. I don't want to do too much to her right now.

Now, it's time to make the call to Karen. Thankfully I don't have to leave a message for her, she answers almost immediately. I briefly go over what little I know she's been through with her parents and that I just rescued her from being kidnapped and held hostage for who knows how long. Karen tells me to let her know once Melody is out of the woods and that she'll clear her schedule to come out and spend some time here at the cabin with her. I can't believe how amazing this woman is. She doesn't have to do this, but she's willing to just because Skylar has gotten so much help from her and that's her passion.

I pull a chair in next to the bed and make myself as comfortable as I can while keeping an eye on my girl. It's been a few hours now and I have barely moved a muscle. My eyes are trained on her to catch any little movement she makes. There's been a few times I've caught my name and someone named Anthony cross her lips. I'm not sure who Anthony is, but if he's another man in her life, he won't be for long.

Chapter Seven
Melody

I WAKE UP IN a strange looking place, in a bed I know isn't mine. At first, I'm confused and scared because the last thing I remember is being trapped in a cage and having drugs forced into my system. Then I realize that I'm not being held prisoner anymore and that I'm not handcuffed to the bed I'm lying in.

My body is absolutely killing me no matter what I do. I can feel my skin stretched tight in some areas on my back and I know that the cuts I have are healing. That means that I haven't been beaten in a little bit of time. However, I'm still just about naked, other than a tee shirt that covers my upper body. I look down to see some sort of symbol and something about Wild Kings. Who the hell are the Wild Kings?

"You're awake." I hear a male voice say from off to the side of me.

Turning my head, the sight before me makes my breath catch and my heart feels like it's stopped beating. Tears pool in my eyes, and I want to reach out to touch him to make sure that it's really Mason standing in front of me. He moves slowly over towards the bed and I hope he doesn't think that I'd ever be afraid of him.

"Is it really you?" I ask, my voice in an almost whisper.

"It is angel. I've been by your side for weeks now. You were really sick and I made sure that you didn't get worse."

"You've nursed me back to health?" I ask, astonished.

"I did. I finally got you back in my life and there's no way you're goin' anywhere. I wasn't goin' to lose you for any reason."

There's no words I can say to that. I always dreamed that I would find Mason again, not that he would have to nurse me back to health. But, I'll take him any way I can get him right this second. I need to get stronger so that I can tell him the secret I've carried for years. My only concern is that he'll hate me because of it.

"I thought I was dreaming that I saw you in that warehouse."

"No angel you weren't dreamin'. I wouldn't let anyone else there touch you because I needed to have my hands on you. I've missed you so much angel."

"I've missed you too. There's so much that we need to talk about. Right now, I need to sleep though."

"You sleep and I'll be right here when you wake up. I'm not goin' anywhere."

I'm not sure how long I've slept again, but I do feel just a tiny bit better. I don't feel quite so achy or hot. In fact, I'm actually really thirsty. Just as I go to get out of bed though, Mason is handing me a cup.

"Thank you, Mason." I tell him.

"Haven't heard that name in a long time angel." He tells me, sitting on the edge of the bed.

"What do you mean?" I ask, the confusion written on my face.

"My road name is Glock. That's all I answer to now."

"Oh. I'm sorry. I'll try to remember to call you that, Glock."

It just sounds weird coming out of my mouth when he's always been Mason to me. I'll just have to get used to it though when we interact for the sake of our son. Fuck! I hope there's a reason to interact because of Anthony and that Glock doesn't turn his back on his son. All you have to do is look at him and know that he's our son's father. Anthony is a mini version of Glock. Even though I haven't seen him in many years, they still look identical. Especially the eyes.

"Angel, we need to talk. And I hope you don't get mad at me."

"Why would I be mad at you?"

"I made a call when we got here a few weeks ago. There's a lady here that is goin' to talk to you and try to help you fight whatever demons you have from your parents and bein' kidnapped. Is that okay?"

I take a minute to digest what I've just been told. No, I normally wouldn't take my problems to a perfect stranger, but in this case I think I might need to. "Yeah, that sounds good. Is she here now?"

"Yeah. She's out in the other room. Do you want to talk to her now?"

"Yeah, I think I do. At least until I can't keep my eyes open anymore."

Glock goes out and brings a lady to the doorway. After introducing her as Karen, he leaves the room and shuts the door behind him. I'm actually thankful that he's not trying to stay for this. I don't want him to know the extent of things that my parents have done to me. Let alone what those animals did to me.

"Hi Melody. I want you to know that we can talk about anything that you want to talk about. We'll make goals and track your progress of completing them. Whatever you're comfortable with." She tells me, holding her hand out for me to shake.

"Hi. Well, I just really don't know where to start. There's been so many things." I begin, trailing off.

"Glock filled me in on a little bit about you having some problems with your parents and then that you were kidnapped and tortured."

I take a minute to breathe and begin by telling her about growing up with my parents. Nothing is left out, from the torture of a small child for the most innocent mistakes, to the torture of a teenager for daring to hit puberty. Karen hears about having to stand on a board with nails poking through for hours on end just because I forgot to put the dishes away, getting beaten with my dad's belt in front of his church because I smiled at one of the members, kneeling on cinder blocks at the end of my bed while reciting certain passages that my dad had marked out based on my perceived crime. I tell her about the time that I was out five minutes late at the library studying for a paper and my mom backhanded me so hard that I hit my head and needed to have stitches. My dad has broken my bones more times than I can count and my mom just sat there and watched it happen. There's absolutely no judgement coming from Karen, she's just sitting there, taking notes and listening to me.

"I'm sorry, I feel like I'm rambling on here." I tell her.

"No, you're not honey. This is what I'm here for. Now, what are some goals you want to make based on the past you had with your parents?" Karen asks me.

"Well, I want to learn to stand up for myself without worrying about what's going to happen to me. I don't want to constantly hide and keep moving from one place to the next because I'm afraid my parents have found me."

"What do you mean?"

"This is strictly between you and me?" I ask nervously.

"It is."

So, I tell Karen about finding out I was pregnant with Glock's baby after the one and only time we ever had sex. How my parents forced me away to go hide out at my aunt's house and I ended up running away from there. Now, I have to run every time I think that my parents have found me and my son is the one suffering because of it.

"So, he doesn't know?"

"No, he doesn't. I had no clue where to even begin looking for him. When I had Anthony, Gage was one of the men that helped me to the hospital and I made him promise that he wouldn't say a word. I told him how my parents threatened the life of my baby and that of Glock's. Gage didn't want to keep the secret from him, but he eventually caved in. As far as I know, he kept his word and never did say anything to Glock about the baby."

"Okay. Do you plan on telling Glock now?" Karen asks me.

"I do. I just haven't been strong enough to do it yet. I know he's said that we've been here for a few weeks, but I honestly don't know how long in total I've been gone."

"Well, we're in the middle of the year right now. And I know that Glock called me about four weeks ago, if that helps you out any."

"So, that means that I've been missing a total of almost seven months. Including the last four weeks that I've been here with Glock. I think I'm ready to tell him though. If you could give us just a few minutes."

"I can do that. Why don't we stop here for today, and I'll come back in tomorrow morning? We'll have your sessions first thing in the morning that way we can worry about the rest of your recovery throughout the remainder of the day. Does that sound like a plan?"

"It does. Thank you so much Karen."

Karen leaves the room and within a few minutes, I hear Glock entering the room again. He's standing at the end of the bed and I can tell that he wants to say something. But, he's waiting for me to say the first word.

"First of all, I want to say thank you for everything that you've done to help me since finding me. Including calling Karen. I think she's really going to help me. But, there is something that I need to tell you about. Please just know that if things were different, you would already know."

"Go on angel. Tell me anythin' you want to tell me and I promise that I won't be mad."

"You can't promise me that when you don't know what it is."

"I think I have a good idea and I've been dyin' to know." He tells me, sitting on the bed and taking my hand in his.

"The thing that I was trying to tell you the last day I saw you was that I was pregnant. My parents shipped me off to my aunt's house until I had the baby and could give it up for adoption."

"You what?" Glock yells, interrupting me.

"I didn't give him up. I promise you Glock. I escaped from there shortly before I gave birth and had the help of some amazing people. My aunt did find me the day I went into labor but some nice men made sure that she didn't get anywhere near me. So, you have a son named Anthony." I finish, looking away from him for a minute so he can gather his thoughts.

"And where is our son right now?" He asks, tipping my head towards him.

"The day I was kidnapped, my friend Kiera was with him. As far as I know, he's still with her and she's taken him on like he is her own son. That's the plan we had in place in case something happened. I'm just hoping that they're still in the same place since we moved so much before I was taken."

"How old is he now?" Glock asks, trying to absorb the information.

"He'll be nine soon. He looks just like you."

"As soon as you're strong enough, we're goin' to get our boy." Glock tells me, leaning his forehead against mine. "What do you mean you moved so much?"

"Every time we thought my aunt or parents were closing in on us, we would move. There was no way that I was going to let them try to take our son away from me. They threatened him and told me that they would kill him if I didn't give him up for adoption. Then they threatened you too. So, I've not done right by our son by continuously moving him from place to place." I tell him, trying unsuccessfully to hold the sobs in.

"You did the best you could with what you knew. If I were around, you wouldn't have had to do that, but things are goin' to change now angel. You're both comin' home with me when the time is right." Glock tells me, folding me in his strong arms to protect me from the demons I carry about our son.

It's been a few weeks and I've healed in more ways than one. My body is completely healed with just a little scarring in a few spots. Karen has been amazing, listening to me continue on about my parents and being tortured. We've worked out goals for me to work on and things that I want to accomplish while introducing Glock to Anthony and letting them become a family. I'm still not sure where Glock and I stand and I don't know that we'll ever be together again, but that's okay. He's always been a temptation for me and he always will be.

Karen has told me that there are a few people that Glock knows that would be great to talk to about my experiences because they've been through similar things. I'm not sure that I'll ever be ready for that, but we'll see what happens down the road. I'm content with the goals that we've set and the strategies we've put to use a few times when I feel that I'm getting overwhelmed by things.

Glock has been amazing and has stayed by my side the entire time we've been here. If I need space, he gives it to me. When I want to go out and get some fresh air, he takes me on walks around the property. One or two times, Glock has even taken us into town and gotten us dinner and dessert. Just because it's something that I wanted to do.

I know that he's been getting restless and he has a life he needs to get back to. So, I've been trying to get myself better. I've taken all the medicine Doc has given me, yeah, he made the trip here once to check me over and make sure that I was healing properly. Then Glock spent some time with him outside. Now, I just want Glock to get back to his life.

The day we leave is going to be bittersweet. He hasn't really said much, but I can't help but think that he's got a girl back home and he's just been trying to help me because of our past. I don't ever want to keep him from anything that he loves or makes him happy. As long as he plays a role in our son's life, I'll be happy. So, I'm ready to let him go if I need to and ready to go see our son. Hopefully he's ready to leave too.

Part Two
The Present

Chapter Eight
Glock

IT'S TIME TO TAKE my girl to go get our son. We need to get back to the clubhouse and I need to see what's going on with everything. Melody has had weeks to heal and fight the infection she had raging through her system. Almost every single cut and open wound on her body was infected and it ended up running through her entire body. I just have to convince her that it's time to leave this town and head back to my own club.

"Angel, we need to talk babe." I tell her, sitting next to her on the bed.

"What's going on Glock? It's going to take me forever to learn to call you that name." She says, giving me a weak smile.

"We need to go get our boy and then go to Clifton Falls, angel. I need to get back to my club and brothers. I'm talkin' we need to leave now and head out. It's goin' to take us a few hours as it is to get there."

Melody just gives me a blank look as I'm telling her that we need to head back to Clifton Falls. I know it's probably the last place that she wants to go, and that's partially my fault. She doesn't know any of the guys since I never brought her around when we were in school. Now, she probably doesn't want to be around a lot of men that she doesn't know. I mean there's Skylar, Bailey, Summer, Maddie, and Ma. They'll be all up in her face though. Finally, I know my angel is going to answer me.

"The only reason that I'm going back with you, Glock, is because of our son. You both deserve the right to get to know one another. As far as anything between us goes, we don't know each other like that anymore. We've both grown and changed in the last nine years. There's something that you need to know about Anthony though."

"What is it?"

"There's times that he doesn't act like a normal nine-year-old boy. We've spent all of our time sheltered and running from my parents. So, at some points he acts younger than what he is."

"You think that matters to me angel?" He asks, sitting down beside me. "The only thing I want is to meet my boy. Everythin' else, we'll take care of and handle when we get into a routine and he gets to know me better. You guys are done runnin'."

"I just wanted you to know before you thought I did something wrong. Well, I mean I did do something wrong by not finding you sooner and by continuing to let them run my life."

"I'm not lettin' you go again, angel. I didn't fight for you before but I'm gonna fight like hell for you this time. I've already got Rage workin' on buildin' a house for us and we're gonna work on gettin' to know one another again," I say, getting real close to her. "You are worth fightin' for. No matter what you've been through and what's been done to you. Melody, you've given me the greatest gift of all with Anthony and I don't even know him yet. So, let's go get our boy."

We pack up our meager belongings and head out to the truck that I'm borrowing from Gage. He doesn't know it yet, but it's gonna have to get us back to Clifton Falls now that I have to get three of us back. The trip to Melody's friend's house only takes about twenty minutes and my angel stares out the window the entire ride. I'm sure her head is spinning with everything I've just told her, so I'll give her the space I know she needs right now. It won't last long though, and I'm sure that she knows that.

Giving me directions, Melody jumps out as soon as we pull in the driveway. Hell, I don't even have the truck stopped all the way before she's running up the stairs and banging on the door. Not wanting to be left out, I park and turn the truck off before rushing up the stairs after her. Just as I hit the landing, the door flies open to reveal a girl that seems to be in her late twenties. She's got red hair that goes almost down to her waist and the brightest green eyes that I've ever seen in my life. As soon as she sees Melody, she drops to her knees and tears stream down her face. Mel drops down with her and wraps her up in her arms, like she wasn't the one that's been to hell and back again.

"Melody, I can't believe you're back!" She says, standing up and looking up and down the road. "Get inside. Now!"

This girl is pulling my girl inside and I'm standing there wondering what the fuck is going on. I follow them knowing that's going to be the only way I'll get answers. Her friend rushes past me and locks a million different locks on the front door. Don't get me wrong, I'm all for security and taking preventative measures, but this seems crazy.

"This him, Mel?" She asks, looking at me.

"It is." Melody states when she can get a word in. "Where is he? Where's our son Kiera?"

"He's upstairs. I don't let him go outside these days unless I can be sure that no one else is going to come sneaking in the backyard."

"I'm Glock. Why don't you let my boy go outside?" I ask, curiosity getting the better of me.

"Does he know them Mel? Has he met your parents?" She asks, sitting down in the living room. We follow her in and sit down so that we can talk before I meet my son.

"He's seen them. Have they been here? What did they want?" My girl asks, clearly shaken at the thought that her parents have been here.

"They've been here a few times. You know I can handle myself, Mel. Hell, I'd beat your mom's ass and not even think twice about it for everything she's put you through. When it comes to Anthony though, I wasn't gonna take any chances. I knew you'd be back and I wasn't gonna let you hear that he wasn't with me anymore."

"What. Did. They. Do?" I grit out between clenched teeth. I remember the day that I saw Melody's dad back hand her so hard her head hit the window. That's all I can see as I wait for Kiera to answer me.

"They came here looking for the two of you. I don't even know how they found us Mel. I've been really careful. Anyway, I made Anthony stay upstairs and said that I didn't know where you two had gone. I was only bringing him to you since you were finishing up something. Neither one of them bought my story. So, instead of leaving, they started threatening to take Anthony away from me. If I didn't give him up, your dad said he would burn the building down and hope that we were in it when it went up in flames. Nothing would ever be traced back to him, he said. According to them, they were going to bring you both home and beat the sin out of you. You for having sex when you weren't married and Anthony for being born." Kiera says, tears filling her eyes. She's looking back and forth between us and I know that she would give her life for my boy, and for my girl.

"Motherfucker!" I yell, not caring who hears at this point. "I'm makin' a call, then I want to meet my boy, angel."

Leaving the room, I go into the kitchen and pull Blade's name up on my phone. He's always been a loyal brother, doing whatever we threw at him and not complaining once about the bitch work. If he's not busy with anything else right now, I want his help with what I know has to be done now.

"'Lo." He answers.

"Need your help brother. You and a prospect actually." I tell him, hearing rustling in the background. There's muffled talking before he's back on the line.

"Whatcha need Glock? You know I'll be there as quick as I can."

"I know. Listen, didn't mean to run your pussy away, but this trumps that. I'm in Dander Falls still and I need you here like yesterday. I have to move a few people back with me because of a situation. Take the phone to wherever Grim is so you can both hear me at the same time."

"Give me one second. He's in the office."

I wait for Blade to get wherever Grim is and put the phone on speaker. Suddenly, I hear Grim on the line. "What's goin' on Glock? When you comin' home?"

"That's why I'm callin'. I found out some information from my girl. I've got a son. He's eight and I'm bringin' them home with me. We just stopped to get him from her friend and she let us know that Melody's parents have been by here. They've threatened them, said they would take my boy, and if she didn't cooperate, they'd burn the buildin' down. I'm not leavin' her friend here to die because she was protectin' my kid, Grim. I need Blade and a prospect to come help me pack them up and move them to the clubhouse."

"You sure you can get it done with just Blade and a prospect? I can send more brothers if you want me to."

"No. Melody's still real scared around a lot of people. Blade and Slim Jim only. Please Pres?"

"Yeah, if you need anythin' else, you let me know and we'll get it to you. I'll have the girls start gettin' rooms ready. And, congrats on the boy. What's his name?"

"Anthony." Is all I say. Grim will know how important that is to me. Hell, anyone that I grew up with will know. Especially Cage.

Hanging up, I make my way back inside to finally lay eyes on my boy. As soon as I enter the living room, I see that he's joined the girls and is hugging his mom with everything in him. So, I stand back and watch for a few minutes to let them have the reunion that they need to have. I'm sure my boy was suffering without his mom around and not knowing what was going on. Melody is facing me, but her face is buried in our son's neck. They're both crying and not letting go. Finally, my girl looks at me and I can see her pain written all over her beautiful face. She whispers something to our son and he slowly wipes the tears off of his face.

Anthony turns around and my own grey eyes are looking up at me. I see the wonder, amazement, and shyness burning through my own miniature features. He looks exactly like me from his dark hair and grey eyes that are filled with the look of someone that is going to be up for causing trouble. For a little guy of only eight, he's already tall for his age and he's stocky as hell. The same way that Cage and I looked when we were his age.

"You're really here, Dad?" He asks, starting to edge closer to me.

"I am. I'm so happy to meet you little man." I say, kneeling down so that I can be on his level. "I can't wait to get to know you Anthony."

Without any warning, he runs and jumps up in my arms, his little arms going around my neck as if he's hanging on so that I don't disappear from his life. Yeah, there's no way in hell that I'm going anywhere. I look up at Melody and see her reaction to us meeting for the first time. I mouth 'thank you' to her and stand up with my boy in my arms. I won't be letting him go anytime soon, that's for fucking sure.

Lifting Anthony up a little bit, I sit down on the chair so I can face Melody and Kiera. They need to know what's going to be happening and start moving their asses to get everything that they want to pack up and take with us. Maybe taking Kiera with us will help Melody get used to the fact that I'm not letting them go. She and Anthony are my world now and that's how it's going to remain.

"We have to talk guys. I know this isn't goin' to be a popular decision, but all of you are comin' with me. The fact that her parents have been here puts you in danger Kiera. I'm not goin' to leave you here to suffer whatever consequences they decide to make you suffer. On the plus side, angel, this might help you relax a little about goin' to the clubhouse with me."

"You're saying that you're taking me with you guys when you leave?" Kiera asks.

"Yep. We'll get everythin' figured out when we get there as far as livin' arrangements and workin' go. You okay with that?" I ask, silently begging her to be on board with this plan.

"Hell yes! I'm ready to move away from here. I don't want to deal with her crazy ass parents anymore. If you can stop that, I'll go wherever you want." She exclaims.

"Angel, you okay with this? I want you to be comfortable and make this move with me so that we can be a family and give little man here what he really needs."

"Yeah, I'm good with it Glock. I know that you guys have to get to know one another and I would never keep your son away from you. Not intentionally."

"I know you wouldn't angel. Now, I've got two guys comin' from the clubhouse to help us get you there. So, we have to get everythin' packed up that you want to take with us in the next few hours. I don't even wanna leave you to get boxes knowin' they're in the area. So, I'll have a few boys drop them to us."

Kiera gets up and runs up the stairs to start packing I'm guessing. Melody sits still for a minute before she takes Anthony up to his room to start packing his stuff up. Meanwhile, I text Gage to have a few of the brothers here bring us some boxes and lunch while we wait for Blade and Slim Jim to get here. I'll help out where I can, but other than that, I'll stay out of the way so everything that needs to get done can. All of a sudden, I hear my son yell 'daddy' down the stairs.

Melody

I watch Anthony pack up everything that he holds dear in his little world. He's going on and on about how his daddy is here and he's taking us away to make everything better. For his sake, I hope that Glock can do that for him. Anthony is going to place him above everyone else that he has in his life and Glock needs to realize that before our son gets his heart broken and realizes that his dad isn't who he thinks he is.

"Daddy! Daddy, come up here! Please!" Anthony yells down to his dad.

Glock comes upstairs, meeting our son at the top, and enters the room Anthony has here. Kiera has done the best that she can with our son while I was held captive and Glock didn't know he existed. His room is a testament to everything that he loves at his tender age of eight, almost nine. Man, he's growing so big and I've missed so much the past six months. That's nothing compared to the almost nine years that Glock's missed with Anthony. Time that he'll never get back again. So, I'll let them spend as much time as they can together and see where their relationship goes.

"What's up little man? Are you gettin' all your things together?" He asks, sitting on the small bed that Kiera got him.

"I got all my toys and teddy bears packed up. Momma said she'd help with my clothes. Daddy?" Anthony asks, talking a million miles an hour in his excitement.

"Yeah buddy?"

"Are there other kids there to play with? I really don't play with anyone here."

"There are other kids, but they're younger than you. So, you'll be the big man at the clubhouse."

"We're going to a clubhouse?" Anthony asks, astonishment lining his features.

"Not the kind of clubhouse you're thinkin' of buddy," Glock says through his laughter.

"Then what kind? Is it for big people like you and momma?" Anthony asks, sitting down in front of his dad on the floor.

"It is. You'll meet them all as soon as we can get back there, buddy. For now, you'll get to meet Blade and Slim Jim. They'll be here soon, so we need to get this packed up. Want me to help?"

"Would you?" He asks, looking up.

"Yeah. That way your momma can do what she has to do and get it done."

Since I've been dismissed by Glock and our son, I make my way into my room and stare at everything that I used to know so well. The pictures of Anthony on the wall representing each month of his life, pictures of Glock and I from high school, little decorations that I fell in love with throughout the years, and albums of all the other pictures I've taken to show Glock. My clothes are where I left them that fateful day and I can't wait to wear my own stuff again.

Looking at the bed, I know I despise the lumpy mattress and how I could never get comfortable. Right now, it's looking really comfortable though. It won't hurt anything to lay down for just a minute or two and shut my eyes. Anthony is with his dad and Kiera is running around packing everything up like a madwoman. So, I climb up and lay my head on the pillows without removing my shoes or covering up. Within minutes, I'm out like a light.

I'm jolted awake by someone sitting on the end of my bed. I bolt upright and see Glock sitting there looking through one of the photo albums. It's the very first one that starts with my pregnancy photos. For a few minutes, I just watch him. He's so engrossed in the pictures that he doesn't realize I'm awake yet. Now is the time I can study the changes to him since I last saw him so many years ago.

He's always had dark hair and kept it short, almost a buzz cut. Now, it's grown out a little bit, but it's still short as hell. Glock's grey eyes are more perceptive and see through a person, finding what they want to hide away. I don't want him to know all my dark secrets from when I was held captive though. On top of all those changes, there's more noticeable changes. What parts of his body I can see are covered in tattoos. Tribal work goes up his arms, disappearing under the sleeves of his tee. One or two peek up from the neckline of his shirt and I'm sure that there's more that I haven't seen yet while I was out of it during my recovery. I've also caught a glimpse of a tongue piercing along with the one in his lip.

"Why do you have so many pictures of your pregnancy?" Glock asks, breaking me out of my own head.

"I wanted to document everything so you wouldn't miss seeing anything," I answer. "Eventually, I knew I would find you and wanted to be able to show you what I was going through. The changes that my body went through."

"Thank you." Is the only response I get as he continues to flip through the pages. Every so often he stops and a smile graces his handsome face.

"I'll get up and get packing. You continue to look all you want." I tell him, standing and stretching my body.

"It's mostly done in here." Glock says, finally looking at me.

Looking around the room, I see that almost everything is, in fact, packed away. Whoever he called earlier must have brought a ton of boxes. Before I can comment, Anthony rushes in the room and jumps on my bed, crawling over next to his daddy. He tucks himself under Glock's arm and starts looking at the photos with his dad.

"That's me in momma's belly." He points out.

"I know buddy."

"Look how big I made momma's belly get Daddy. She tells me it's because I'm a big, strong boy and needed a lot of room."

"Your momma's right buddy. Which means, I'm gonna need your help in carryin' things out when my brothers get here."

"I gots uncles?" Anthony asks.

"You have a lot of uncles, buddy. When we get back, you'll meet them all. I'm sure that Cage will be one of the first you meet. He's my cousin."

I watch the exchange between father and son. Anthony is Glock's mini me in every way. His looks mirror his dad's, the mannerisms he has are identical to Glock, and he's already becoming so perceptive. Even when I don't want him to know things are messed up and not going the way they should, he knows that I need him a little bit more. Anthony won't leave my side in those times and he really hasn't gone far since I walked back in the door and he laid eyes on me for the first time in months.

When I go to say something to our son about making sure everything in his room is packed up, there's a pounding on the door. Glock goes into full protective mode and ushers me farther into the bedroom with Anthony. Kiera is just about to go into the bathroom until she is pushed in the room with us. It's not long before we hear multiple sets of boots pounding up the stairs and towards us. I sure as hell hope that it's Glock returning with whoever he's been waiting on all day.

Peeking his head around the corner, I let out the breath I've been holding seeing his dark hair and grey eyes staring at me. Anthony goes running up to him and wraps his little arms around his neck. At least until he sees the two men standing behind his dad. Then his face goes into Glock's neck and he takes a few small peeks at the two men.

"Buddy, remember I told you you'd be meetin' Blade and Slim Jim?" He asks, kneeling down and standing Anthony on his feet. Once our son nods his head, Glock continues. "Well, this is them. Blade and Slim Jim this is my son Anthony, his mom Melody, and her friend Kiera. Guys, this is Blade and Slim Jim."

I look at Kiera and see her staring at the guy that's standing directly behind Glock. Her eyes are trying to take in every inch of him she can see, and he's returning the same interested look right back at her. Interesting. I've never really seen Kiera take such an interest in a guy. I'm glad to finally see it and I'll do what I can to help her along. Although, I'm not sure that she'll need much help.

"Well, hello there sexy." She says, starting to move closer to him. "Why don't you help me out with my stuff while this little family has the other guy help them."

The guy doesn't say anything in response. He just follows along behind Kiera and I can see his head tilted down a little. Yeah, he's checking her ass out as she puts just that much more swing into her step. Damn, the girl works it when she sees something she's interested in. This whole moving thing just got a lot more interesting for sure. I can see something happening between these two and I just hope that one of them don't get their hearts broken. Especially Kiera. She deserves nothing but happiness and what she wants out of life.

"Slim Jim, I guess you're helpin' me since Blade is apparently goin' to be busy for a while. Most of the stuff is already downstairs. How many vans did you bring?"

"We brought two and the enclosed trailer. Weren't sure how much stuff we needed to move. And I see you got a truck if we need it."

"Yeah. It's Gage's. I'm not sure if they're takin' any of the furniture, but all the personal stuff they want is already packed up and waitin' downstairs. While you go start loadin' that up, I'll find out what's goin' on with everythin' else."

I watch as Glock's friend walks back downstairs and I wonder what the hell is going to happen when we get to wherever we're going. Hell, I'm wondering what's going to happen in the next little bit with everything. I have to get used to everything again now that I don't have to worry about men coming in whenever they want to violate me, however they want to. And since I can walk about when I want to instead of being stuck in a cage, I'll have to get used to being free again.

"So, what furniture do you want to take, angel? All of it, none of it. It doesn't matter what you want to take, we'll get it there one way or another."

"Personally, I don't want to take anythin'. I mean as long as Anthony has a bed, I'll be fine sleeping on the floor next to him."

"You aren't sleepin' on a fuckin' floor angel. You're in my bed, and only my bed. Our son has a bed waitin' for him. I'm sure the girls are gettin' everythin' ready as we speak. He'll be in a room connectin' to ours so we can leave the door open when we aren't busy." Glock says, wrapping his arms around me and nuzzling my neck. I used to love when he did that to me. Now, I'm not sure about it.

"Glock, we need to slow down here. Please, give me time and space. I need to figure things out here before we decide what's going on with us."

"I already know I'm not givin' you up again, angel. You're mine and I'll spend my life makin' sure you know that. Now, let's get this show on the road and get things loaded up in the vans." He tells me, turning and walking down the stairs to help move things out to our transportation to his world.

Since I'm sure Blade and Kiera are busy, I usher Anthony down to help load things up in the van. We'll be ready when they're done doing their thing. Then, Kiera can decide what furniture she wants to take with us. I'm not sure that she'll want any of it since most of it was second hand stuff we found for a great price at yard sales and things like that. Nothing was brought as a family heirloom or anything so there's no attachment to anything here.

With the men loading up most of the boxes, we're almost ready to head out when they make their appearance. Glock doesn't give us a chance to talk or anything though since he wants to head out. It's going to be a long drive with me wondering what the hell is going to be expected of me and our son. I don't know anyone there, but I know that Glock won't let anything happen to our boy, so the best decision is to go with him. I'll figure everything else out when we get there.

Chapter Nine
Melody

WE FINALLY ARRIVE at the clubhouse about five hours after leaving Dander Falls. The guys made multiple stops for bathroom breaks and food along the way. I'm sure it was just for the three of us, but I appreciate them answering the millions of questions Anthony had and helping win a few things out of one of the games at one stop. Our son is so excited to be going somewhere that has a bunch of other people around and, of course, motorcycles. He's been grilling his dad almost non-stop about whether or not he has a bike, if he can get one, will he be taught how to ride one, and so on and so on.

I've just been sitting here, dozing on and off for most of the ride. Other than resting his hand on my thigh, Glock has let me be and concentrated on Anthony. I'm grateful that he's letting me have this space right now since there's a ton of thoughts running through my head. Since I wasn't around when he became a prospect, and finally patched in, I'm not sure what Glock's role in the club is, whether or not anyone will want us staying there with him, or if anyone even knows about us. I'm sure he mentioned something since his friends came to get us, but now I don't know what to think.

"What's goin' on in that pretty little head of yours, angel?" He asks, breaking me free of my thoughts.

"I'm just trying to figure out how all of this is supposed to work. I mean, we're not together and I'm sure you've got someone there waiting for you to get back after being gone so long. I don't know what's going to be expected of me and Anthony or how I'm going to get to know anyone. You always kept me away from your friends when we were in school."

"That wasn't anythin' against you angel. It was because they're all a bunch of perverts and I knew they would make you uncomfortable. I didn't want you scared away from me before I got the chance to know you, and you to know me. I was fully intendin' to bring you around them."

"Now it may be too late Glock. I mean, we're walking into a world that's yours. You know everyone, know what's expected and acceptable, and you have an entire life there. Anthony and I are walking into a completely different and strange world. What happens if we mess up and do something wrong?"

"You won't do anythin' wrong, angel. And it's not like you'll be the only girl there. Grim, Cage, Joker, Pops, Tank, and Irish all have old ladies. They'll show you the ropes and let you know what you have to know. The only thing I'll say right now is that there are goin' to be things that I can't tell you. If I say it's club business, then it's club business."

"I have a lot to think about and a lot to decide. Then I guess we'll have to talk and see what's going on with us. I know where you stand on it, but I need to decide where I stand on it too. It's not just what you want Glock. I get a say in whether or not I want to be with this new version of you."

"You got nothin' to worry about. I told you that you're mine, you just need to realize it and we'll go from there. Now, there's one other thing you should know about before I walk you in there." I watch Glock take a deep breath and try to figure out what he wants to say before he begins again. "There's club girls that you'll see. Yes, I've been with a few of them a time or two. But, it was just a way to get a release and not worry about tryin' to be in a relationship with anyone. You are honestly the only one that I've ever wanted and I won't be with them anymore. I can promise you that."

"What's a club girl?" I ask, completely confused as to what that means.

"It's a girl that is with whatever brother there that wants her at any given time. She has a roof over her head, our protection, and money in her pocket. In return, we get what we want without the strings attached of a regular girl."

"So, you're saying that you've been fucking whores for the past nine years?" I ask, almost disgusted by the thought that I was in the same position up until recently. The fact that I wasn't given a choice in the matter doesn't really hit home with me though. "I mean, if that's what you want, then have at it. I won't stop you unless Anthony sees something that he shouldn't be seeing."

"I don't fuckin' want that angel! *You* are the one I want. Tomorrow, I'm gettin' tested so you know for sure that I don't have shit. Melody, *you* will be the one in my bed, the one by my side, and the one helpin' raise my babies. We've already got Anthony and he will have brothers and sisters at some point in the near future." He tells me. "I will never force you to do anythin' you don't want to do, but it's always been you for me."

"There's so much that I want to do still though. I want to go to school and get a degree since I never got the chance. I want to have a steady job and a good home for Anthony before I bring any more babies into the picture. I *need* to be able to stand on my own two feet without the help of someone else to know that if something happens to you, I won't have to depend on Kiera or anyone else. I want to experience different things and grow more. Can you understand that? All I've been for the last nine years is a mother to Anthony. Then I was kidnapped and held captive for months. Now, I want to be free and live a little bit." I try to explain to Glock so he knows where I'm coming from.

"I get where you're comin' from. All I'm sayin' is that I'm not goin' anywhere. And, you *are* mine. So, where you go, I'll go."

"Even if it means leaving your club?" I ask, knowing what his answer will be.

"I won't leave the club angel. With them, we have someone always at our backs. Without them, anyone comes after us, we've got no one. I stay in the club and you do what you gotta do angel."

"Okay. I get where you're coming from. But, you can't expect the three of us to live at the clubhouse forever. Can you?"

"No. We won't be livin' at the clubhouse forever. Once I know what's goin' on, I'll show you what's already been started. I just don't want you to see until I know the progress on it."

"We'll see what happens. I'm not going to stay there long. And I can guarantee that Kiera won't either. Plus, we need jobs and stuff too." I tell him. "How much longer until we're there?"

"We should be there in a little bit. Probably about another fifteen minutes or so.

Glock

One way or another, my angel will understand that she is mine. I'm not letting her and our son go anywhere. The past nine years has been hell and torture knowing that she was out there somewhere, but not having the first clue as to where to start looking for her. Now, I wish I had tried harder to find her. Then, I wouldn't have missed so much time with my angel and son. Melody never would have been through the hell she's been through since being kidnapped either. No one would have gotten to her!

Finally pulling up to the clubhouse gates, I breathe a sigh of relief. It's been a long day with meeting my son, packing up a house, knowing that angel's parents are out there searching for my family, and the long drive back here. But, we're back now and I'm sure that Grim and the guys are going to want to talk.

After Melody didn't meet me, I changed and became someone I didn't like. For a long time, every drug out there was going in my body, alcohol was the only thing I would drink, and I can't tell how long I went without eating anything solid. It took Pops talking to me and getting the whole story out of me before I got my head out of my ass. He might actually be the only one that knows most of the story concerning Melody and me. The guys know there was a girl from school and that's about it. I guess talking about her felt like I was tarnishing her memory or something.

"Angel, we're here. When we get inside, the guys will probably need to talk to me, so I'll show you and Anthony to our rooms and then meet you back there. Or, you can stay in the common room and get to know some of the girls here. It's up to you."

"I guess it depends on what Anthony wants. If he's hungry, then we'll probably get something to eat. Can you show me to our rooms though? That way if we want to go to bed or get away from everyone, we can. I don't mean to sound rude, but neither one of us are going to know anyone other than Kiera and I'm not sure what she's going to do since she's with your friend." Melody asks me, looking away so I can't see whatever emotion is flitting across her face.

"I can do that, angel. As soon as we walk through the door, I'll take you there. Do you want me just to grab big man back there or do you want to wake him up?" I ask, not sure how she usually handles this type of situation. I'm just going to follow her lead for now.

"If you want to grab him, I'd rather not wake him up. Unless he wakes up on his own. He can be in a bad mood when he gets woken up. It's not a problem for me to sit in the room with him until he wakes up and is hungry or something. We'll be fine Glock."

Parking the truck as close to the door as I can get it, I tell Melody to get of the clothes they'll need now and Anthony's toys that he can't live without out of the backseat. Opening the driver's side back door, I see my boy half laying down and half sitting up, fast asleep. There's no way in hell that he's comfortable like that. Oh well, he can lay stretched out in a bed now. Hopefully someone changed the sheets on his bed so I don't have to worry about who, or what, has been there.

Blade, Kiera, and Slim Jim meet us at the clubhouse door and Kiera is whispering with Melody. I'm not sure what it's all about, but I'm not sure that my girl is happy about whatever she's being told. I'm guessing that Blade has convinced Kiera to stay in his room with him and Melody is thinking she's never going to see Kiera. That couldn't be farther from the truth though. I'll make sure that they get to spend plenty of time together. They really haven't had a chance to spend time alone since we walked up to the house in Dander Falls. Blade will not be monopolizing Kiera's time until I know that the two women have had enough one on one time.

Slim Jim opens the door for us and I can hear the music playing, not blaring though, and a few people talking. Cage, Joker, Pops, and Grim are the first people I see. Immediately they stop talking and laughing to look at us. Cage stands up to come over to us, but I shake my head at him so no one wakes my son up. He nods in understanding and sits back down. Pops is grinning like a damn fool knowing that my family is home where they belong. I'm sure he wasn't surprised to hear about me having a kid at all. And I know that's exactly why they're all sitting at a table close to the front door.

The two of us make our way down the hallway towards the rooms. Mine is at the far end of the hall since there's another room attached to it. I'm not sure how I ended up with this room, but I'm glad I did now. A bathroom is the only thing we'll share with our son though. So, we'll have to watch what we're doing if he goes to the bathroom in the middle of the night. And, I guess there's no sleeping naked for now. Not until I learn his nighttime habits.

After making sure my son and girl were set in our room, I make my way back out to talk to the guys. They're all sitting in the same position. Except they've moved another chair over for me to sit in.

"It's good to have you back Glock. We've missed you!" Grim says, slapping me on the back and motioning for Summer to bring me a beer.

"I've missed bein' here too. But, I had things to take care of and Melody needed me more than I needed to be here."

"We know. As soon as we saw you flip out when someone else tried to take her instead of you, we knew it was her." Cage says, taking a sip of his drink.

"Her who?"

"The girl from school. We all knew it was her when you wouldn't let anyone else near her. I mean we never got to know her in school, but that wasn't because we didn't want to. You were the one that always kept us away from her. It's not happenin' this time Glock." Joker tells me.

"It's not that I didn't want you guys to get to know her. I just didn't want her scared away by the brutal honesty and perverted ways you guys have. Hell, I thought I would do the job myself. I've already tried to talk her into comin' out here tonight. Our boy is sleepin' right now though and she doesn't want to leave him alone with it bein' a new place."

Pops looks at me from across the table. He knows exactly who just walked in behind me and what her disappearance meant to me. Hell, the other guys don't truly know the extent of the damage I was doing to myself. Ma and Pops are the only ones that saw me at my lowest. Not because I was trying to hide it, but because they knew I wouldn't want the other guys to see me like that.

"I know who that is, son. Know what her bein' here means to you. My only concern is whether or not she'll make it here after everythin' she's been through. That boy in there has to come before everythin' else you think you want to happen." Pops says, making sure I know that Anthony has to come before whatever else happens with Melody and me.

"I know Pops. He'll always come first, no matter what happens with us. Anthony is my son and he'll always know how loved he is by the both of us. Nothin' will ever get in the way of that!"

"You sure he's yours?" Cage asks me.

"Fuck you! He's mine. Anthony has our eyes and he's a mini version of me mother fucker!"

"Just wanted to make sure you would back that statement up against any one of us. You know there's gonna be talk with her bein' gone for so long and now sayin' you got a kid." Cage answers. "I love you, you are blood, and that little boy in there is too. Melody isn't hidin' away this time and you aren't keepin' her from us."

With that, Cage gets up and leaves the table. I knew he was hurt when I wouldn't bring her around before. I just never knew it was as bad as it apparently is. My intention was never to hurt anyone by keeping my angel to myself. She was timid and not someone that was used to hanging around guys like us. It was a matter of getting to know her enough for her to know that they wouldn't hurt her or that they meant anything they said to her.

The rest of us just sit around the table, talking about nonsense when I hear my name called softly. If there were more people here, I would have never heard Melody calling for me. Thankfully it's basically just us and a prospect behind the bar.

"Come here, angel. Everythin' okay?" I ask pushing back from the table so she can sit on my lap. Instead she pulls out Cage's empty chair and sits between Joker and me.

"Everything is fine. Anthony is awake and I wasn't sure if you wanted us to stay in the room or not."

"No. You guys can come out. Let me go get him." I say, standing up and heading to the hallway.

Walking into our room, I see my son sitting on the floor by the bed. He's not really doing anything, just sitting there with his head laying on his knees. He looks so lost and scared right now. So, I go to him, sit next to him and pull him in my lap. Anthony curls up into my lap and wraps his little arms around me. After only a day I'm addicted to him wrapping his little arms around me.

"What's wrong buddy?" I ask, leaning back a little so I can see his face.

"I'm scared Daddy." He says, sniffling.

"Scared of what? There's no one to be scared of here."

"Momma and me don't know no one. I heard yelling."

"That was just me and one of my brothers, buddy. Actually, his name is Cage and he's my cousin. We just do that sometimes. I promise everythin' will be good. Now, you want to go out and see what we can find to eat?"

Anthony slowly nods his head and doesn't unwind from me. I guess I'm carrying him. This is going to take some getting used to from him, and I'll help him in any way that I can. The rest of the guys will too, he just doesn't know that yet. Pops and Joker will definitely put him at ease. Plus, he hasn't met any of the other kids yet. So, once Jameson gets around him, it should help.

As I enter the common room, I see Melody talking and laughing with my brothers. Standing still, I watch them interact for a few minutes and I wonder why I didn't allow this to happen sooner. Is everything that my angel has been through my fault? If she had another way out, or knew about the club's move, would she have run here for safety? Or to just get away from her parents? Fuck!

"Daddy, what's wrong?" Anthony asks.

"Nothin' buddy. Just lookin' at your mama." I answer, ruffling his hair.

"She pretty." He states.

"Yeah, she is. The most beautiful woman I've ever seen."

Summer sees us standing there and asks if we want something to eat. I tell her to bring three plates out to us. There's no way that I'm letting Melody not eat this time. It's been a while since she ate anything really. When we were in the cabin, she was too sick to eat much more than broth for the most part. Since then, she's eaten really small portions of whatever she orders. I know it's going to take time for her to get used to having food in her stomach, but I can help her along with it.

"Mama!" Anthony yells out.

Everyone stops talking and looks in our direction. Pops is the first one to stand up and come over to us. Well, meet us half way. He doesn't say anything for the longest time, just stares at my son. Finally, clearing his throat, he speaks.

"Hey there little man. I'm Pops. What's your name?"

Anthony looks at me and I nod my head to him. "I'm Anthony."

"That's a strong name, a good name." Pops says. "Do you want to come meet more family?"

Nodding his head, I follow Pops back to the table. Grim and Joker are still sitting at the table, not saying anything. They're waiting to see what their next move should be. I'm sure they can see how nervous and unsure my boy is and want to make him feel at ease.

"Anthony this is Grim and Joker." I tell him. "They're my brothers."

For a few minutes, Anthony doesn't say anything. He just stares at Joker's hair. Today it's bright green with a little bit of black in it. This man changes his hair more than any female I know. It's fucking crazy!

"Daddy?" Anthony starts. "I want my hair like his."

I can't help the laughter that bursts from me. There's no way in hell Melody is going to let him have his hair done like Joker's. "I don't think mama will like that buddy."

"Well, since he won't be going to school right now, I don't see why not. I'm sure I could find some temporary hair stuff to do it." Melody responds, surprising the shit out of me.

"I got some stuff in the room. You bring him to me tomorrow and we'll get it done." Joker says, looking closer between the three of us.

"Yay!" Anthony shouts, and everyone laughs.

Looking at my family surrounding this table, I see the interaction going on between the guys sitting here, my angel, and my son. Anthony is watching the guys like a hawk to see them interact with one another and include the pieces of my heart into their conversation. Melody is eating a little of the food Summer brought out for us. And, I'm watching everyone. I wish that Cage were out here right now, but we'll get that shit worked out between us. Even if I have to bring Skylar into it so she can talk some sense into my stubborn ass cousin.

"Glock, we're havin' church in the mornin'." Grim tells me. "We'll keep it short since I don't know what you have goin' on. Melody, I know the girls are waitin' to meet you."

"Oh." Melody says, looking at me. "Well, um, I don't know any of them and what we'd talk about."

"They'll let you know." Joker says, laughing. "I'll tell you now that you aren't alone in a lot of things that you think you are. These girls have been through some shit and they have no problem sharin' their story with you. Especially Sky. They'll talk you through anythin'."

"Well, I think I'm going to try to get some sleep. Glock, I'll take Anthony in and put him to bed. Maybe give him a shower before taking one myself."

"Everythin' you need is in there. If we need to get our boy somethin' for the shower, let me know. Otherwise, I'm sure we can ask Joker for somethin' tonight."

"He can just use my stuff tonight." She tells me, taking my son's hand and leading him away from the table. I can't help but watch them walk away, knowing this time they won't ever be going very far from me.

"It's not your fault brother. You know that, right?" Grim asks me.

"I don't know that. If I had brought her around you guys in school, things would've been different. She would've had somewhere to go instead of bein' taken and havin' shit done to her that I don't wish on our worst enemy. That's the fuckin' mother of my son, the reason I breathe, and I let her the fuck down."

"Naw, she went through some shit, but you didn't let her down. You thought you were doin' what was best for her at the time. Now, she'll get to know us and we'll help her with whatever we can." Grim says to me.

"I'm goin' to head in and see if I can help her out with anythin'." I tell the guys, standing up and making my way to our room.

They all grunt their goodnights or whatever else as I make my way to our room. As I step through the door, I can hear Anthony and my angel talking. Well, my son is talking a million miles a minute about getting his hair done tomorrow. Melody is just listening to him chatter on while I'm assuming he gets washed up for bed. Stepping in the bathroom, I see Anthony sitting in a tub while his mother is sitting on the toilet watching him play with toys. His dark hair is already spiked up like Joker does to Jameson on a daily basis. The only difference is the color isn't there. Not until tomorrow anyway.

"How long you been standing there?" Melody asks me.

"Long enough to hear him talkin' about tomorrow like crazy. Does he ever stop once he gets started?" I ask, laughing at the thought of him talking like this all the time.

"When he's excited, you know it. Now, Anthony let's get cleaned up and get to bed." She says, standing and heading to sit on the edge of the tub.

"Can't daddy do it tonight mama?" Anthony asks, looking between the two of us.

"I'll do it, angel. You go find some clothes or whatever you need for your shower and I'll get our boy cleaned up."

As soon as Melody leaves the bathroom, I get down to the business of washing our boy up. I don't know how it happens, but by the time Anthony is done washing, I'm covered in more water than he is I think. There wasn't even that much water in the damn tub to get me as wet as I am. So, while grabbing him a towel, I grab one for myself, and drop two more on the floor to dry it up before Melody comes in and busts her ass.

Anthony is in his room getting dressed when I enter the bedroom and see my angel getting in her bag to dig some clothes out. Heading to the dresser, I pull a pair of sweats and nothing else. At this point, I'll sleep with sweats or shorts on. Sooner or later, we won't be sleeping with anything on. Melody just needs time to adjust since she just spent months upon months naked with no choice in the matter.

"What are you gonna do while I'm in the shower?" Melody asks me.

"I'm goin' to put Anthony to bed and then I'll wait in here for you." I tell her.

Melody heads into the other room to tell our son goodnight before heading into the bathroom. When I enter the other room, Anthony is lying in bed, with a book in his hands and waiting patiently for me to read him a story. This is going to be quite the experience since I've never read a child a bedtime story before. I hope he's ready for this.

Reading to Anthony is easier than I thought it would be. He actually only made it through about two pages before he was fast asleep. The move and excitement must have taken more out of him than we thought. So, I head back into the next room and lay down on the bed. Before I know it, I'm asleep.

Chapter Ten
Melody

WE'VE BEEN AT the clubhouse for about two weeks now. I've stayed in our room mostly, making sure that we can get more of our things in there and that Anthony has everything he needs. Kiera has been by my side when she's not glued to Blade's side. She keeps telling me that we can go out and relax with everyone else, but I don't want to right now. Kiera has been out getting to know everyone while keeping an eye on my son. Glock may be the one to take our son out to the other parts of the clubhouse, but Kiera still keeps an eye on him for me. She knows that it's hard to let him out of my sight right now. But, I'm not going to hold him back from anything his heart desires.

At night, I go out and clean up the common room and kitchen. Usually Skylar takes care of the kitchen, or so I've been told, but she's been busy with the kids and her men. So, I make sure that everything is cleaned up while Glock, Anthony, and everyone else are sleeping or otherwise engaged. I don't want to see that after everything that I witnessed while being held captive.

It's not that I stay up all night because I have nightmares or anything like that. Anthony had his days and nights mixed up when he was a baby and then I stayed awake as long as I could when I was in that damn cage so I would know of possible attacks coming against me. Now, I'm just used to being up at night. I usually end up in bed around three or four in the morning, get a few hours of sleep and then I get up with Anthony. It's exhausting, but there's nothing I can do about it right now.

Tonight is no different. I lay in bed next to Glock with his body wrapped around me until he falls asleep. Instead of laying here staring at nothing in the darkness, I slip out from under his arm and from between his legs. Tiptoeing to the door, I'm as quiet as possible until I make it through the door and softly close it behind me. Releasing my breath, I get the cleaning supplies out of the closet and make my way to the main room.

There's a smaller radio under the counter behind the bar and I quietly turn it on to hear *Come Over* by Sam Hunt playing. It's one of my favorite songs so I sing and dance to it while I clean the bar top, pile the dirty glasses to wash, and throw away empty bottles littering the top of the bar. Singing and dancing used to be one of my favorite things to do and I love having the freedom to do it again. It just doesn't happen where anyone else can see me. It never has and never will.

"Now we know who the bandit is sneaking in and cleaning the place from top to bottom." A female voice says, moving closer to me.

Startled, I jump and drop a glass. The only thing you can hear is the shattering of it hitting the floor and me standing completely still since I have bare feet. Looking up, I see five females standing before me. They are clearly not club girls, but more than likely the old ladies that I've heard talk about.

"Shit! I'm so sorry. I didn't mean to scare you." The dark-haired beauty says. "I'm Bailey and we had a feeling it was you cleaning everything up, but we wanted to see you."

"Um, hi. I'm Melody. Yeah, I have a hard time sleeping at night so I figure I can help out around here by cleaning and things like that."

"Oh, please don't think you're in trouble, you're not. Anyway, let me introduce you to the girls. This is Ma, Skylar, Summer, and Maddie."

"Hi everyone." I say, while the one introduced as Summer comes forward.

"Stay still honey. I'm going to clean up the glass so we can get you out from behind the bar." She says, grabbing the broom and dust pan from the end of the bar where I placed it earlier.

Making quick work of clearing away the glass, she stands back up and pats the bar top. The one introduced as Ma steps forward and tells me to hop up so she can look and make sure there aren't any cuts on my feet. Not wanting to get blood all over, I do as she says and turn so I'm facing her. Her gentle hands poke and prod my feet for a few minutes.

"You're fine honey. Now, what are you doing out here in the middle of the night cleaning up after these pigs instead of in bed with that sweet man Glock?" She asks.

"Oh. I was in bed, but I usually don't fall asleep until around three in the morning. So, I can clean while everyone sleeps and then get a few hours before our son gets up." I explain again.

"Nightmares?" The curvy blond asks me.

"No. It's always been like this. No story here guys, I promise."

"We'll get it out of you hun. It's what we do." The curvy blond responds again.

The girl that cleaned up the glass gets some shot glasses out and starts pouring shots of something before loading up a tray and heading over to the table I'm being steered to. After setting the tray down, she takes a seat and everyone sits there looking at me for a few minutes, not saying anything.

"Do I have something on my face?" I ask, rubbing my hand down one side of my face.

"No. I'm trying to figure out what the story is with you and Glock." The original girl says.

"Well, we met in high school when my family moved to the area. Glock and I were in a few classes together and got assigned to work on a few projects. From there I guess we kind of started hanging out without having projects due and then one thing led to another. Nine months later, Anthony was born and now here we are." I tell them, knowing I'm glossing over everything they're going to consider important.

"Okay. Well, we know more than that happ....You're her!" The one I'm assuming is Bailey practically shouts in excitement. "You're the one that fell asleep in the back of the truck with him shortly before you guys graduated!"

I can feel my face heating up and turning a bright red. In all the years that have passed, I can't believe someone still remembers the night we gave our virginity to one another. While I cherish that night, and remember every detail in crystal clear clarity, I would rather everyone forget one of Glock's friends finding us butt naked in the bed of the truck the next morning. Now, I need to steer the conversation away from me and onto them.

"So, I'm guessing that you're all old ladies?" I ask.

"Well, all of them are except for me." The girl that cleaned up the glass responds. "I'm a club girl that helps them out more than anyone else here. So, I get a few more privileges than the other club girls."

"Summer, you're more than a club girl sweetheart," The older woman begins. "You're one of us without the guy. And you know it!"

"Anyway, I'm with Cage and Joker. The VP and the Enforcer. Bailey is with the President. Ma is with Pops who is still a member. Maddie is with the Road Captain. And,

Caydence isn't here, but she's with Irish. You'll meet her at some point soon. The only other person we include in our circle is Darcy. She's a riot and you'll meet her soon too. She comes here from Dander Falls." The blond says. Thankfully she looks at everyone in turn.

"Why does she come all the way here?" I ask, confused.

"She does our hair for all major events and to get away from Crash and Trojan. You'll meet them too, if you haven't already done so." Bailey says.

"Okay. Well, I'm going to get back to cleaning and stuff before I go to bed." I tell them, standing up and feeling a little woozy. The shots we've been drinking must have gone straight to my head since I typically don't drink.

"Are you okay?" Bailey asks me.

"Yeah. I just really don't drink." I respond, falling ungracefully back into my chair.

"Well, then you can have a few more." One of them tells me, pouring another round of shots.

I don't know how long we've been out here, but things are starting to get rowdy. Summer is basically down to her bra and panties, Bailey is in her shorts and bra, Skylar isn't wearing any pants, and Ma is sitting back watching us all. Currently, I'm only wearing my panties and one of Glock's shirts that I've taken to sleeping in. We're all laughing, trying to sing, and dance around the room.

Out of nowhere, we hear someone clearing their throat and we all stop and turn. Standing at the opening of the common room are all the guys. A few have smirks on their faces, the older man I met earlier is trying to contain his laughter, and then there's Glock. He doesn't look thrilled, but he doesn't look pissed off either.

One by one, the men come in to gather their woman and take her back to their room for the remainder of the night. Well, with the exception of Skylar. Two hot as fuck men take her out of the room. Damn! Suddenly it's just Glock and me standing awkwardly in the room.

"I'm sorry. I didn't know they were going to come here and we'd end up drinking all night." I say.

"I know that, angel. You come out here every night when you think I've fallen asleep. I let you have this because I figure you're tryin' to escape from the demons in your nightmares. What's goin' on, angel?" He asks, taking a seat and pulling me in his lap after moving closer.

"I honestly haven't had a nightmare Glock. Since Anthony was born and got his days and nights mixed up, I typically don't go to bed until later. Then when I was with those fucking raping douche canoes, I figured it was best to see them coming. If I was awake, I'd be able to try to fight them off." I tell him, burying my face in his neck. Taking a deep breath, I smell the familiar scent of Glock. There's a faint smell of the soap he uses mixed with the faint, spicy smell of his cologne. It's a smell that I've known and has brought me comfort and memories.

"Are you sure?" He asks, lifting my chin so I'm looking in his eyes. "You know I would've been there from day one for you and our son. Don't you Melody?"

"I know. I tried looking for you when I finally managed to get away from my aunt's house. I didn't know where you had gone though."

"I know angel. We'll talk more when I know you're sober." He says lifting me up and carrying me to our room.

As soon as he closes the door, he sets me on the bed before starting to strip down to his boxers. Typically, he sleeps in sweats, but it gets pretty damn hot in this little room. I don't have the capri sleep pants I had on earlier, and I'm in no mood to look for something else to put on right now. So, I guess Glock's shirt and my panties will have to do tonight. Sleep finds me rather quickly.

The next morning, we're woken up by a pounding on the door to the room. Glock groans and tries to tuck me farther under his arm. I know with the pounding on the door that Anthony will be up and ready to go in a matter of seconds. My point is proven when I hear little feet pitter patter on the floor into the room and a little hand on my face.

"I'm up!" Glock calls out. "Give me a minute."

Before rolling over to get up, he kisses my temple and ruffles Anthony's hair. Shuffling to the door, he opens it and gets pushed to the side. Bailey comes storming in and tells me to get up, we're running late.

"Wh-where are we going?" I ask, pulling the blanket up farther around me.

"It's tattoo day. Don't you remember?" She asks, putting her hands on her hips and slightly tilting her head to me.

"No. I have no clue what you're talking about." I respond, trying to pull the memory of last night up so I know what I've gotten myself into.

"Maddie and us are getting our new tattoos today. You said you were getting one too." She answers. "Now up and at em so we can head out. You've got ten minutes to shower and dress."

Glock is standing in the doorway, watching the scene unfold and trying to hide his laughter. Bailey saunters out of the room after tapping him on the cheek. Poor Anthony is trying to figure out what's going on and what happened.

"So, I guess you're gettin' a tattoo today?" Glock asks, closing the door and walking towards the bed. "What are you gettin' angel?"

"I don't even know. I've got a few ideas floating around but I don't know yet."

"I always thought I'd be goin' with you for your first tattoo," Glock muses.

"How do you know that I don't have any already?" I ask him.

"I may not have seen everythin' yet, angel, but I haven't seen a tattoo anywhere on that deliciously creamy skin of yours."

There's no way I can respond to that. He always knows what to say to leave me speechless. I've thought about getting a tattoo for many years. Something to remind me every day of the feelings I had for Glock and what losing him meant to me. Nothing just seemed good enough or right though.

"Well, I don't have any yet. So, apparently today will be my first one ever. I guess I better go get in the shower. You good with keeping Anthony today?" I ask, starting to get out of bed.

"Of course I am. I'll take him to the garage to see my bike and he can help me work on it. That sound good little man?"

Anthony doesn't even bother answering him. He jumps up and down before running and wrapping himself around Glock's legs. I can already imagine how the questions are going to be firing out of his little mouth to Glock and anyone else that happens to come around them. It's going to be funny as hell and I wish I could watch it happen. Unfortunately, I'm on a time crunch.

The girls and I all load up in one of their SUV's and head to town. I'm told that the club owns a tattoo shop and that's where we're going. No one trusts anyone else to touch them as far as putting ink on their body. I guess I can't blame them considering this is going to be something that's forever. I try not to laugh at the excitement of I think it's Maddie. She's getting her first tattoo today too and is really excited. Apparently, she's covering up a scar from something that happened to her a little while ago.

"So, what are you getting done today?" Skylar asks me.

"I think I'm going to get some angel wings. There's a few reasons for this and I think it's fitting for my first one. It's going to be huge though."

"Why do you say that?" She asks.

"I want it to take up my entire back. With nothing but some shading in black or grey to give it a little color. I don't want any real color in it though since I've gone through some shit and I want it to be a darker color."

"That's kind of what I want." Maddie tells me. "I'm getting a phoenix to cover up a scar and represent the rebirth of me and who I truly am now."

"That sounds like an amazing idea." I tell her honestly.

The rest of the girls are talking about what they're going to be getting done and who they want to do the work. Their men all have their favorite artists, so of course, that's who the women want to use too. I don't know any of them, so I won't be picky about who does my tattoo. As long as it's done the way I want it done and it turns out amazing, I'll use the person again when I get another one. I still have to do something for Anthony too.

It doesn't take long before we're pulling up to a shop with a sign saying 'Wild Kings Ink'. Bailey leads us all in and tells the girl sitting at the counter that we're here for our appointments. Looking around I don't see anyone else in the shop. I'm surprised since I figured that there would be other people in here waiting to be tattooed.

"They closed the shop for a few hours to get us done honey." Ma says coming over to me. "This way they didn't have to send anyone with us and you can all get done at the same time."

"Oh. Well, that's nice." I tell her.

A girl that looks around my age walks over to me. She introduces herself as Tiffany and asks me to follow her to a room in the back. Thankfully I won't have to take my shirt off in the open. Not that it would matter since we're the only ones here, but I'll be more comfortable in a room alone. Well, that is until I see Ma following me.

"Just want to make sure you're okay." She tells me. "And we can get to know one another a little better while you're laying still on her chair."

I can't help the laughter that bubbles up. Ma definitely knows how to put the people around her at ease. There's no way I can even ask her to leave the room, I want her in here with me.

"So, what are we doing today?" Tiffany asks me.

"I want a pair of angel wings on my back. The only thing I want done to them is some shading in blacks and greys."

"Okay. No other color?" She asks.

"Nope."

"Sounds good. Let me draw it up and then I'll see what you think." She tells me.

Tiffany leaves the room while she draws the image that will go on my back. Ma uses this chance to grill me in what I'm guessing is her own special way. I don't really mind though. She wants to look out for Glock and for that I'm grateful. It's good to know he has people that care enough about him to make sure that I'm not going to hurt him. Someday I'll have that too.

"So, I don't know all the details about you and Glock, but I do know some." She tells me. "I know that when you left, he was a mess."

"What do you mean?" I ask, confused.

"Honey, he looked for you for days. He spent days and days sitting by the side of a road. Glock wouldn't talk to anyone and when someone did try to get him to talk, he blew up at them. There's more, but that's his story to tell you. Just know that he hit rock bottom when he didn't know what happened to you. Until I saw him after coming back, he wasn't the man that I've known and watched grow up."

"I didn't have a choice in the matter, Ma. If I could've stayed, I would have. No questions asked. I didn't even get to tell him about Anthony before I left."

"Your son is the reason you had to leave, isn't it?" She asks, looking straight through me.

"Yes. My parents found out and sent me away. I was able to get away before I gave birth to our son. That's when I met Kiera. She's been our savior ever since."

Before Ma can make any more comments, Tiffany comes back in the room. Holding up the paper, I see an impressive set of angel wings. She's already put the shading in and I love it. This is what's going to represent the loss of my innocence into the woman that I am today. I will mourn the girl that I didn't have a chance to be because I chose to love Glock. He and our son are the two most important things in my life and I will never regret the decisions that I made.

"This is perfect!" I tell Tiffany.

"Alright let's get started." She tells me, getting everything set up and ready to ink me.

I strip my shirt and bra off, noticing that Ma is holding her hand out for them, but allowing my modesty by turning her head away. Tiffany also has her back to me. She only tells me to lay down on my stomach and get comfortable. Doing as she says, I lay down and turn my head towards Ma so that we can still talk if she wants to. I'm not sure if I'll be able to handle the pain, but we're about to find out. Settling in, I wait for Tiffany to start so that I can get back to the clubhouse and see my son and Glock.

Chapter Eleven
Glock

AFTER WATCHING MELODY and the girls leave, I got Anthony his breakfast and ate a quick bite with him. Then it was time to get ready to spend the day in the garage with the bike. It's been awhile since I've ridden it while I was helping my girl through her recovery, so I'll give it a tune-up before I take it out. Melody will be on the back of it before too long.

"Daddy, are you ready to go now?" Anthony asks me, bouncing on his little feet.

"Almost buddy. We need to get you dressed and then I have to make sure that Grim doesn't need anythin'."

"Let's go daddy!" He says excitedly.

I chuckle to myself and lead him back to the room. He runs in his room and I hear drawers from his dresser opening and closing. Leaning against the door frame, I watch him pull out the clothes that he wants to wear today. I'm not sure if Melody lets him dress himself like this, but we'll go with it for today.

Anthony is busy pulling his shorts and shirt on while I make sure that I have everything I need when we go out back to the garage. As soon as he's done, he appears next to me and I see him wearing a pair of shorts and a button up shirt. There's a few buttons that have been missed, so I bend down and help him fix it. Taking his little hand we head out to the common room and I see the guys sitting at one of the tables in the corner. Since all the girls are gone, there's no one else really around the clubhouse. I'm sure the club girls are still resting after the night they had with different brothers.

"Guys, we're gonna be headin' for the garage to work on the bike if you don't need anythin'?" I ask looking at Grim.

"Nope. You go do your thing." Grim answers.

"I might head over there with you." Cage says, standing up. "Mind the company?"

"Not at all." I tell him. "You mind little man?"

Not saying anything, I look down to see Anthony staring at Cage as he stands from the table. I'm guessing that he's scared to see someone as big as Cage is. I can't wait to see his response when he sees Tank for the first time. His eyes will probably bug out of his head and I can see him wrapping himself around my legs.

"Do you care if Cage comes with us Anthony?" I ask him again.

He just nods his head and steps just a little bit closer to me. I know I've told him that we're family by blood, but he really hasn't had a chance to spend any time with Cage yet. Maybe that's what the problem is. We'll figure it out and he'll love him once they get to know one another better.

"Let's go to the bike," I tell him, trying to bring him back to the excited little boy he was minutes ago. "You gonna hand me tools bud?"

"Yes Daddy." His little voice responds, while he's peeking over his shoulder at Cage.

Making our way out to the garage, I open the door and flip the switch to turn on the lights. There's not really many bikes in here, so I won't have to roll mine out to work on it or move a ton of things around first. Anthony takes everything in with the few bikes that are in here. Mainly just beaters and ones that need to have a little work done to them before the owner wants to take them out for a long ride again.

"Which one is yours Daddy?" Anthony asks, a little of the excitement returning.

"This one over here bud." I tell him, leading him to my bike.

My bike has always been one of my first loves. Melody obviously has the first spot in my heart, but my bike was always a close second. Now, there's no question, Anthony has that spot. The parts of the bike that aren't chrome are painted a sky blue just like Melody's eyes. Some of my best memories are the times when Melody and I would lay in the back of my truck and watch the sky. There didn't have to be any talking or anything, we were content to just be together and do nothing. I've missed those days so much and I can't wait to get back to it.

Anthony runs a little bit ahead of us and starts inspecting my bike. It's like he knows exactly what he's looking at, but I'm pretty sure this is the first time he's seen a bike up close. So, Cage and I stand back and give him a few minutes to look his fill before I get to work on giving it a basic tune-up.

"Daddy?" Anthony asks, when he's gotten to my gas tank.

"Yeah bud."

"Why there wings on your bike?" He asks, hesitantly reaching out to touch the wings I have painted there.

Cage looks at me before walking over to look at what my son is talking about. No one has ever noticed the wings I have on both sides of the tank for Melody. She's always been my angel and always ridden by my side. Even when I didn't know where she was or what she was doing.

"Those are there for your mama. She's always been my angel." I answer looking at him and Cage.

"I'm sorry Glock. I didn't know." Cage says, coming back over next to me.

"There's a lot you don't know. Let me tell you."

Standing together I keep an eye on my boy as I tell Cage about Melody and what her leaving did to me. There's no judgment in his eyes, no questions until I'm done. I tell him about the time we spent together, the crazy things she got me to do, spending time not talking or anything else, losing my virginity to her, and every detail in between. Then I tell him about losing her and what it did to me. About the drugs, drinking, and random pussy. The time that I'm not proud of.

"That's why Pops and Ma took you in and wouldn't let anyone near the house?" He asks when I'm done. "They put you through detox with them and no outside help."

"They did. Ma and Pops saved my life and now I'm glad they did. At the time, I hated them for it." I answer honestly.

"I'm sorry for the blow up the other day. Didn't know it was like all that. Thought she was just some random you didn't want to share."

"How could you? No one did. Now, it's time for you all to know the truth. She's mine, they're mine. I'm claimin' her and no one is gonna stop me."

"Can't blame you."

"Uncle Cage?" Anthony asks, out of the blue.

"Yeah bud." Cage answers, getting down on his level.

"You gots a bike like my daddy?"

"I do. It's out front. We'll look at it later." Cage answers before turning to me. "He met Jameson yet?"

"I don't think so. Later, he can hang with him."

Cage keeps us company while I work on my bike with Anthony trying to help in any way he can. By the time we're done, he's got dirt smudges on his face and hands. Just like we used to when we helped our dads. I want to wash him up, but I know he'll see them as marks to be proud of just like we did. So, I'll wait until just before my girl gets back. I'm not sure how long they'll be or what else is planned for the day though.

Heading inside, I can hear the other kids in the common room and I'm guessing they're all here. Hopefully Tank is not standing or running his mouth at someone to scare Anthony. Looking around the corner I see him sitting with two of his boys while the third one is in his seat in front of Tank. Zoey isn't too far from him either. This might make it a little easier for him to meet Tank.

"Tank, want you to meet my boy." I say entering the room with Anthony and Cage following me. "Buddy, this is Tank. Tank, this is my son Anthony."

"Hey buddy. I see you've been workin'" Tank says, shifting one of his boys on his lap.

"I helpded my daddy and uncle Cage." He says, a smile lighting up his face like Melody used to look.

"You workin' on bikes now buddy?" Joker asks, joining us holding Reagan.

I watch Anthony take all the kids in and see his face lighting up again when Jameson starts heading in our direction. He probably thought the only other kids around were babies and girls. It doesn't stop him from scooting closer once again to me, placing himself between Cage and me.

"Dad, I was looking for you." Jameson says, looking at Cage.

"I was helpin' Glock and his son. Jameson this is Anthony. Anthony, this is my boy Jameson. He's just a little younger than you. Now, what did you need son?"

"I was just looking for you. No reason. Have you been out to the fenced in part yet Anthony?" Jameson asks.

"No. What's there?" My son asks, standing taller and trying not to hide.

"We got a playground and lots of toys out there." Jameson tells him. "Can we go dad? Please?"

"Yeah. Glock and I will go out with you."

"Where we goin'?" Grim asks, entering the common room with Alexa and Zander.

I just watch in amazement at the men that I'm proud to call family. A few years ago, none of us had kids and I'm pretty sure we didn't want any. We were content to party, drink, and fuck the club girls. Now, I can't imagine life without these kids around. The single guys are done bitching and whining about it and they spend time playing with the kids and helping out as much as they can.

"We're takin' Anthony out back Uncle Grim." Jameson responds.

"Well, let's go then. I think it will do good for all the kids to get some fresh air." Grim says, asking Summer to bring them lunch out back.

We all head out back and Joker opens the gate to the play area for the kids. Anthony and Jameson are the first two in and my boy stops dead in his tracks to take in the surrounding area. When it first started out, there was just a swing set basically and a covered area for Reagan. Now, we've had someone design and build a better swing set that has just about everything a kid could want to play with. There's one section just for the babies with swings. Then there's a fort for the girls and one for the boys in another area. A basketball court was just added to it since Jameson has decided that he likes certain sports. I honestly don't know what else we can add to it.

"Can I play Daddy?" My boy asks me.

"Go run around son." I respond.

The boys immediately take off and I make my way over to the tables under the canopy. Reagan is doing a lot better, but none of us still take any chances when it comes to her health. So, the canopy stays and we all watch her like a hawk when she's out playing. She's pretty good with knowing her limitations though. When she gets tired or hot, she sits under the canopy or finds a cool spot to lay down in.

Finally, Tank makes an appearance with Summer's help. He had to change the kids before bringing them out. A prospect is following them with two trays in his hands filled with sandwiches and whatever else Summer found them to eat. Slim Jim is following them all with drinks for everyone. At least that's what I'm guessing is in the huge cooler he's struggling to carry.

The boys are in the fort and I can just imagine what Jameson is telling my boy. Usually all the kids sit and eat at the tables, but I think today they'll just eat where they are. Well, the older kids can. The little ones will have to be helped and watched, so they can sit with us. Summer helps get all the plates ready and then takes the boys their plates. Reagan still hasn't really left our sides. I hope this isn't a sign that something is gonna happen with her.

Anthony

I can't believe all the cool stuff that's here. They've got more stuff than the big park my aunt Kiera used to take me to before the bad people showed up. She doesn't know that I listened to them from the stairs. They scared me.

"Anthony, there's something we gotta do." Jameson says, before there's a knock on the door.

A girl pokes her head in before holding out plates of lunch for us to take. We each take our food and a juice box before she leaves. Jameson starts talking again after taking a bite of his sandwich.

"The little kids need us. Both my daddies and our uncles look over us. It's up to us to protect the babies. Especially my sissy." He says.

"Okay. What's wrong with your sissy?" I ask him, taking a drink.

"She's sick. Not all the time, but sometimes. It's scary. So, we're the big men and look after them. You can help me, okay?"

"Okay." I answer, shrugging my shoulders. "Where's my mama?"

"They went for girl's day or something."

We continue to eat our lunch in silence. I take in everything that's been going on around me. I hope we don't have to leave here. Mama wasn't happy before and I hope my daddy can make her happy. I want to stay with both my parents.

Glock

It's been a little bit since Summer brought the food out and I want to check on my boy. Making my way over to the fort, I stop when I hear talking. Jameson is explaining how they have to watch over and protect the little kids like we do. Cage and Tank are behind me listening to their conversation. When it goes silent, we all head back to the tables and I shake my head. These two boys are going to be following in our footsteps. There's no doubt about it. I hope my angel is ready for it.

"So Glock, how are things with your girl?" Tank asks.

"I don't know. She wants her space since she gave a lot of her dreams up to have Anthony and make it as a single parent until she could find me. I want to let her have it, but she's mine regardless of what she wants to do." I tell him, looking at everyone around us.

"You're gonna be in for a fight then?" Joker asks.

"I am. I don't care what she does. She wants to go to school, she can. Work a full-time job, have at it. But, at the end of the day, she will be in my bed and under our roof. Rage is workin' on the house and I want to take her to see it. I have to check in with him and see the progress first though."

"Saw it on my way over and it's lookin' good." Tank says, lifting one of the boys onto his lap. "The outside is done already. He's had a bunch of guys workin' on it."

"Good. Maybe I'll run over there in a little bit and take a look around." I say, thinking about what I'll do with Anthony while I go.

"Go. He'll be fine. Joker is here and he's bonded with him the most. Plus, he's with Jameson and who knows what they'll be doin'." Cage says.

"I'll be right back." I say, standing up and looking at the fort. I'm torn. I want to check on him, but I don't want him to see the house yet. Not until I know Melody's plans.

Running out of the clubhouse, I make my way over behind Tank's house. The house Rage is building for us sits behind his house and off to the side. We're the closest ones to the trees that lead to Sky, Cage, and Joker's house. It's not like we need a lot of room for anything in the yard considering that we're all living in the same area and the pond is only a few feet away. The kids can go swimming and Melody can get what she wants for the yard by our home. I know she used to talk about things she wanted and I've tried to incorporate everything that I remember her talking about.

I stop a little before our house when I see that the outside is in fact complete. The siding is all up, windows and doors are in, and the path for the sidewalk is dug up. Avoiding the path, I make my way up to the door and open it before calling out for Rage. Inside, I can hear work being done from a few different areas. Guess Tank wasn't lying when he said Rage had guys working on it with him.

"Glock, that you?" I hear Rage call out from somewhere to my right.

"Yeah. Where you at?"

"Bathroom."

Walking in the general direction of where his voice came from, I find him in a bathroom almost as big as my room at the clubhouse. Well, the room that Anthony is sleeping in right now. I know I said I wanted two full baths at least, but this is crazy.

"How you doin' Glock?" He asks, wiping his hands on a rag.

"Good. This is huge Rage." I tell him my thoughts.

"Don't like it?"

"I didn't say that. Just wasn't expectin' a bathroom this big downstairs."

"Want a quick walk through?" He asks me.

"Sounds good."

He leads me from the room and into the living room. Like the rest of the guys, I went with an open floor plan. I can stand here and see the kitchen, dining room, and the downstairs bedroom for guests. It's huge, airy with a bunch of windows, and I hope that Mel will love it as much as I am right now imagining us as a family living here. Leading me upstairs, I see the four bedroom doors in the hallway. At the end is another bathroom.

Rage leads me into the smaller bedrooms first before we get to the master bedroom. It's exactly as I asked it to be. There's two walk-in closets, a bay window off to the side of where I imagine the bed going, plenty of room for whatever Melody wants to put in here, and a bathroom off the opposite side of the windows. Walking into the bathroom, I see the huge tub and then the shower on the opposite end of the room. From our talks in the past, I know that she loves to take baths but always wanted a shower where water would hit her body from every angle possible. Rage made this happen for her.

"You did a great job, Rage." I tell him honestly. "She'll love it."

"I'm glad you think so."

"How much longer before you're done?"

"I've got inspectors comin' in next week. So, we'll have to be done by then. The carpet is comin' in tomorrow. After that, it's just the small things. Paint will be done tonight too. I've got a second crew comin' in to do that when these guys leave."

"I appreciate you movin' so fast on this." I tell him, taking a step back.

"You said you wanted it done fast, so we're movin' as fast as we can."

"Alright. I might bring her over here later on. Gotta get back to my boy now."

"I'll be over to meet him when I can."

"Sounds good."

The girls have been gone for hours. I know they were getting tattoos today, but this is kind of crazy. Melody is probably scared shitless about how our son is and I don't have a way to contact her. We need to go out and get her a phone as soon as possible. This will not happen again after today.

"Daddy, where's Mama?" Anthony asks, rubbing his eyes.

"She'll be home soon bud." I tell him, pulling him up on the bed next to me.

I brought him to our rooms so that I could try to get him to take a nap after the excitement of playing with Jameson and the little kids today. Sure enough, they watched the little ones no matter where they were. It was kind of like a divide and conquer type of thing with Jameson on one side and

Anthony on the other. All of the kids that are big enough to toddle around were kept in the middle of them at all times.

Anthony cuddles into my side and throws his arm over me before laying his head on the pillow. Turning the volume on the t.v. down, I change the station to cartoons for him to watch until he falls asleep.

"Daddy, I like my uncles. Even Tank isn't so scary." He tells me, as his eyes droop again.

"No, he's not so scary bud." I agree, running my hand over his hair.

Within a few minutes, I see that his chest is rising and falling in an even pattern. He's finally out for the count. I lay there and think of everything that's happened since finding my angel and learning we had a son. She already has me wrapped around her finger and our son is quickly doing the same thing. Now, I can't imagine my life without either one of them in it.

Melody

After hours of laying in the chair while getting my tattoo done, we're finally making our way back to the clubhouse. The girls are all excited to see their men and show them the new artwork adorning their bodies. I'm torn between wanting to show mine off to Glock and keeping it to myself. One main thing is making my decision for me though, I need ointment rubbed onto it and since it's my back, I need some help with that.

As soon as we enter the clubhouse, the other women go in search of their men. I head down the hall to our room in search of the men in my life. I hear voices coming from one of the doorways halfway down the hall, peeking my head in I see the guys with the kids doing different things in the room. Bailey and the rest of the women are showing off their new tattoos. Searching the area, I don't see Glock or Anthony anywhere.

"Sweetheart, he took your boy to the room to lay down. Anthony had a bit of excitement today and was actin' tired." A huge man says to me after unwrapping Maddie from his body. This must be Tank.

"Thanks." I mumble, turning and heading to our rooms.

Trying the handle, I find the door unlocked and open the door as quietly as I can. My gaze immediately drifts to the bed where I see Glock sleeping with Anthony pulled into his side. They both look so peaceful that I don't want to disturb them. So, I quietly shut the door and head towards the door leading out back.

Almost there, I literally run into Kiera and she wraps her arms around me. I tell her that I'm heading outside while the boys are sleeping and she agrees to go with me. Honestly, I've missed my friend since we've been here. But, I'm not going to fault her for spending time with Blade. Apparently, there's something there between them, and I hope she's found her happy place with him. Who knows though?

"How have you been Mel?" She asks, as we find a bench to sit on.

"I'm okay. How are things with you and your new friend?" I ask, pasting a smile on my face to show her I'm not upset by the turn of events.

"Holy shit! Mel, he's everything I've ever wanted in a man. Polite, gentle, caring, but he can be rough when he needs to be too. He's shown me things I only read about in books. I am having a good time getting to know him."

"I'm glad. Do you think it's gonna lead to anything?"

"I don't know. He doesn't really seem the type to commit, but I don't know what's going on right now. Enough about me though, what's going on with you and Glock?" Kiera asks, settling in to get all the details.

"I don't know what's going on. I mean he's told me that I'm his and he's not letting either one of us go this time. But, there's so much I want to do still. I've always loved Glock, but I don't know if we are good together."

"Why not?" She asks, trying to figure out where I'm coming from.

"Before, he wouldn't let me around his friends. Now, he's back and I'm thrown into the mix with his friends. But, is it truly what he wants? I know he hasn't been a monk since I've been gone, but there's so many club girls here and they're all looking at me like I stole something away from them. I guess we need to just see what happens. The only thing I'm worried about right now is that he forms a lasting relationship with his son. Anthony is the priority here." I tell her, giving her just a small version of what I feel.

"Okay. We all know Anthony is number one in this situation. But, what do you want? Are you ready to write off anything that you and Glock could have?"

"No, I'm not. We're just not the same people we were before. I don't view everyone as good anymore. Now, I view everyone as a potential enemy. Besides, I want to go to school, find a job, a stable place to live with Anthony, and learn to live life. I've never gone out to a bar, never did anything that I wanted to do before. You know this."

"I do. But does Glock know all this?" She asks me, just as we hear the back door open.

Glock is disappearing in the door. This means he's heard at least part of our conversation, but I don't know what part he's heard. Shit! I guess this means it's time to talk things out with him. No more hiding behind the fact that he's getting to know Anthony and that's it. If it were up to me, I'd be with him again in a heartbeat. But, I need to know that we can still make it. We've both changed into new people, ones the other one may not like.

Knowing that I have to go talk to Glock, I tell Kiera good bye and we promise to hang out for more than a few minutes at a time, I leave her sitting outside on the bench. I think she just needs some time out of the clubhouse. Away from all the people we're still trying to get to know and all of the chaos. Granted, most of them go to their homes when they want to, but we're pretty much stuck here. I'm not even sure why Kiera wasn't asked to go with us today, but she didn't go and no one said anything about it to me. I'll have to find that out and soon because she's been in my life longer than any of the women here.

Going inside, I see Glock standing in the doorway to our room. It looks like he's on the phone so I hang back and let him finish up with whoever he's talking to. I can't hear anything since he's whispering to whoever is on the other end of the line. Maybe it's one of the club girls making arrangements to be with him. We sure as hell aren't fucking.

Finally, he hangs up and shoves the phone back in his pocket. Turning around, he sees me standing there and just looks at me for what feels like hours. Before I can move, he's moving towards me. Glock doesn't stop until he's got my back against the wall and he's leaving as little space as possible between us. One hand is braced next to my head while his other hand rests on my hip. This is really the first time that he's touched me since he found me in that warehouse.

"Stop thinkin' angel. It's always been you. I know that we need to talk, but there's somethin' you need to see first. Somethin' to show you how serious I am about keepin' you and our son. I don't give a fuck what you want to do, you do it. At the end of the day, you come home to our son and me. Not givin' a fuck about anythin' else though." He tells me before dipping his head and brushing his lips against mine. "Now, let's go before I decide to show you exactly how I feel about you."

"What about Anthony?" I ask, as my brain kicks back in.

"Bailey's sittin' with him. He's still passed out. Wasn't sure if you had him take naps anymore, but he's met a few new people, played with the kids, and helped me work on the bike. He was tired so he's sleepin'."

Grabbing my hand, Glock leads us out of the clubhouse through the back door. I see Kiera sitting on the bench with Blade next to her. They're talking and I can see that she's enjoying her time with him. Facing forward again, I see Glock leading us to the fence. It doesn't look like there's a way out, and I know I'm not scaling a fence after just getting a tattoo done. But, I put my trust in him and wait it out.

There ends up being a hidden door in the fence that he pushes open and lets me go before him. Shutting it behind us, Glock takes my hand again and leads me towards a few homes. As we walk, he tells me that one house is Bailey and Grim's while the other one belongs to Tank and Maddie. Pointing to the woods, he tells me that Skylar, Joker, and Cage live on the other side, and that we'll end up over there at some point in time for cookouts and parties.

I listen, but keep my gaze forward to see where Glock's taking us. There's a new house being built and I wonder to myself whose house it is. Instead of asking though, I just let Glock lead me where he's taking me. Probably somewhere in the woods so that we can have this out without anyone else overhearing. I'm shocked when he turns us to the house that looks the newest out of all of them. I mean there's not even a sidewalk there.

"Where are we Glock?" I ask, starting to hesitate my footsteps.

"You'll see angel. It's a surprise." He answers, leading us to the door. "Rage, where you at brother?"

"In here." Comes a muffled reply.

Glock leads us into the house and what I can only assume is a bathroom. A man that I haven't seen before stands up with a towel in his hands. He's looking around to make sure everything is the way he wants it. I'm looking between Glock and this man I can only assume is Rage while wondering what the hell is going on. If this is someone's home, I don't want to be in it before they've even been in it.

"I'll let you guys talk and I'll see you back at the clubhouse Glock." I tell him, turning to walk out of the house.

"Not so fast angel." He says, grabbing my arm to stop me. "You don't want to look around?"

"I'm not going through someone else's house. That's not right."

"Angel, this is our house. I told you I had already talked to Rage about gettin' started on buildin' it for us. He's almost done so we can move in." He answers, pulling me closer to him. "Now, let's do a walk through and see what the place looks like."

There's no response I can give him right now. I remember him telling me that a brother was building us a home back here, I just didn't believe it. When we were in school, we had a talk or two about our dream home. Mine was always open, big, and any place that I could call my own. Glock didn't really care one way or another as long as his family was all in one place.

We head out to the main area and I see that he's made sure that it's an open floor plan. You can stand in the kitchen and see everywhere around you. There's one door on the far side of the house and another just inside the door to come inside. I'm guessing one of them is a closet. Growing up, that was my one complaint, never enough closet space.

With his arm wrapped around my waist, Glock leads us upstairs and proceeds to show me the bedrooms. He leaves the master room for last and I'm amazed by it when he finally walks me through the door. The room itself is huge with two closets on the far wall. There's windows and a bench seat right between the two closets. On the other wall is a bathroom that I could probably live in. In the far corner is a garden tub with a ledge all the way around it. Across from it is the shower that's big enough for multiple people. There's his and her sinks with more than enough counter space and the toilet is kind of tucked away in the corner. Rage has also built a closet in where I can put all of our towels and things.

"I can't believe you did all this." I say, looking around in astonishment.

"Anythin' for you angel. Rage said it will be about a week before we can move in. So, the girls are gonna take you shoppin' for whatever you think we're gonna need in here. I don't have much furniture and we're gonna need to fill this house."

"You've already done so much Glock. I need to get a job to pay for it."

"You get a job if you want, but this is *our* home and for *our* family. I've got more than enough money to buy what we need and want."

Standing up on my toes, I press my lips against Glock's. My arms circle his waist and I let myself be pulled into the feelings he's always made me feel. Glock doesn't waste any time deepening the kiss and I can feel my heart race as I give in to what he's been telling me was gonna happen all along.

"As much as I want to continue this, angel, we need to get back to the clubhouse." He tells me, breaking the kiss. "Besides, we're gonna be leavin' in a little bit so we have to get ready."

"Where are we going?" I ask, wondering what he has up his sleeve.

"You need a phone and we're gonna look at cars. Can't have you stuck here with no way to get around."

There's nothing I can say to that. Glock has it in his mind that I need this stuff and I have to go along with it. There's no changing his mind once he gets an idea. I learned that in school and, apparently, that hasn't changed with time. It's only gotten worse.

"If you say so. I don't think I need any of it, but we'll go with what you say." I tell him.

"You want a job and I'm not guaranteed to be around to take you and pick you up all the time. Plus, I can check in when I'm not with you and you can check on our son when you're at work. It makes sense for you to have a car and a phone angel."

Glock took Anthony and I to the store to pick a phone up first. Now we're at the third dealership looking at cars. Well, Glock is looking at cars. Anthony and I are just trailing behind him. He knows what he's looking for and what I need to drive. The salesman here is trying to bend over backwards and kiss Glock's ass to get him to buy a vehicle from here today. I'm just laughing because he's treating him like he's royalty or something. Is this how everyone treats the guys of the club? I'll have to ask someone when we get back.

"Angel, what do you think about this one?" I hear asked.

Looking up I see Glock standing at a newer model SUV. The thing is huge and I should probably tell him I've never driven anything bigger than a small car. I'll probably kill someone in this damn thing. Or, I'll take out a few cars until I get used to the distance. Before I can open my mouth though, Anthony is already checking it out with his dad. He's excited and Glock is trying to tell him what he's looking at. Anthony is acting like he understands what he's being told, but I know he hasn't got a clue about the different parts of the car.

"Well, I don't know. I thought you said a car Glock?" I ask.

"You'll be safer in this than a small car."

"Yeah, but I'll probably take out small children and cars with this thing. It's huge!" I exclaim, trying to convey how nervous I am right now.

"You won't. It will be fine. You'll get used to it in no time. Let's take it for a test drive."

Glock was back in bossy mode so I knew there was no way I was going to get out of going for a test drive with him. I just wasn't prepared when he handed me the keys so that I could drive. Apparently, he'll be learning real quick just what I mean when I tell him that I can't drive anything this big. On trembling legs, I climb behind the wheel as Glock and Anthony climb in the passenger seat and back seat. As soon as I see everyone has their seatbelts on, I turn the key and prepare to drive away in this monstrous vehicle.

Just as I go to pull out on to the road, Glock braces himself and I slam on the brakes. Unfortunately, his seatbelt doesn't lock so he slams his head on the dash. I wasn't even going that fast.

"I'm so sorry Glock!" I exclaim. "I told you I couldn't drive something this big!"

"Yes, you can. Now, pull out and head towards the clubhouse. I want Cage and Joker to take a look at it before we do anythin' else."

"How's your head?" I ask, stifling my laughter.

"Cute angel. It's just fine. Now, let's get a move on."

Taking a second to regroup, I finally pull out and head towards the clubhouse. It really doesn't take all that long to get back there. Unfortunately, there's a whole group of guys out front to witness me pulling in. Looking nervously at Glock, he points in the direction that he wants me to go and I follow his gaze to see Cage and Joker sitting off to the side. I also notice that there's still a red mark on Glock's forehead that will tell anyone that sees him that he hit something.

"Park here angel. The guys are gonna do a quick once over before we make an offer."

"You sure you want me in this when your head is still red as hell from slamming it off the dash?"

Before he can answer, my door is pulled open by Anthony who is impatient to go over the SUV with the other two guys. So, I slide out and let the guys do their thing. Glock sits at the picnic table with me and he wraps an arm around my shoulders. We just sit back and watch our son try to learn what he can from the two men going through the gigantic SUV. I swear, this thing is huge and there's no way I'll get used to being behind the wheel.

"What you thinkin' angel?" Glock asks.

"I'm thinking that this is too big for me to handle. I mean, I've only driven a small car a few times and I don't know that I'll get used to driving something this big."

"You will angel. I have all the faith in the world in you that you'll not only get used to it, but that you'll excel at drivin' somethin' this big."

"We'll see. Let's just see what they have to say before we decide anything else."

Glock gets up and joins the guys checking out the SUV just as Kiera walks over to me and sits down. Must be Blade is busy or she needs a break from him.

"What's up hun?" I ask her.

"Nothing. What are they doing?" She asks, leaning back against the table.

"Glock decided that I need a new vehicle and that we should go with an SUV. So, they're going over everything before we make a final decision."

"Must be nice babe." She tells me.

"Where's Blade?"

"I don't know. I haven't seen him since I talked to you earlier. Oh well! I'll be leaving as soon as your man says it's clear anyway."

"I thought you guys were getting along good."

"We are. Neither one of us are looking for happily ever after. It's not in the cards for me."

"Kiera, you deserve the happy ending. How many people do you know that would step up and raise a child that wasn't theirs? I don't know anyone, other than you, that would do that. You could've taken Anthony to my parents and gone back to your normal life." I tell her, feeling the tears gather in my eyes at what she sacrificed for my son and me.

"No, I couldn't have done that hun. We both know what would've happened."

It's been a while and the guys have just gotten done looking the SUV over. Kiera went back in to find Blade and I've been watching the men argue, laugh, and play around while teaching Anthony a little about vehicles. My son is in heaven right now, surrounded by his new-found family members. I've done the best I can by him, but there's just certain things a mother can't teach her son. He now has Glock and the rest of the men of the Wild Kings to fulfill that empty space.

"Ready to head back, angel?" Glock asks, walking towards me.

"Yep. What's the verdict?" I ask, standing up and brushing my shorts off.

"It's all good. We're goin' back to finalize the sale and you'll drive it back here. Unless you want to go somewhere else first."

"Nope. Back here is fine by me."

"Mama, let's go!" Anthony hollers over.

"Coming baby boy."

"I'm not a baby anymore mama. I'm big and strong. Cage told me so." Anthony proclaims.

I try my hardest to hide my laughter, but I fail miserably. The guys don't even bother trying to hide their laughter. They stand there and laugh uncontrollably at my son's proclamation that he's not a baby anymore.

"Well, you'll always be my baby boy. No matter how old you get." I tell him, ruffling his hair and kissing the top of his head.

Glock

On the way back to the dealership, I can feel the nervousness radiating off of my angel. I lay my hand on her thigh to try to calm her down, but I can feel a different type of energy radiating off of her. Melody is definitely affected by me, all I have to do is be in the same room with her and I can feel the sexual tension bouncing between the two of us. Our chemistry is still there, now she just needs to see it.

If I can just keep her in this mood until we can get back to the clubhouse and get Anthony to bed, she will be mine tonight! The kiss we shared earlier today proved that we still have the chemistry. I just need to show her that we can make a go of this again. When I say that I'm claiming her and I'm not letting her go again, I'm dead serious.

Before I can continue on my line of thinking, I feel my phone vibrate in my pocket. Pulling it out, I see a message from Cage. Jameson wants to have Anthony stay the night with them tonight. Let's see if my angel is down with that idea.

"Angel, Jameson wants to know if Anthony can stay with them tonight." I tell her.

"Um, I guess it's okay. You said they live right by the clubhouse right?" She asks nervously.

"Yeah. I'll show you when we drop him off there. He'll be fine."

Now I just have to put a plan together so that Melody knows that I'm serious about us. And that I truly don't give a shit about what she does. If she wants to go out to a club with the girls, have at it. The girls want to go to a bar for a few drinks, go have fun. My intentions are not to be up her ass every minute of every day. I want to be there for her when she needs me, if she wants to talk I'm here to listen, and if she needs her body worked to the point of exhaustion then I'm the man for that too.

"We're goin' to go out to dinner tonight since little man won't be with us. Just the two of us to talk and start getting' to know one another again." I tell her, looking in the back to see Anthony passed out.

"I guess." Is the only reply I get back.

I know Mel is unsure about the two of us moving forward, but she needs to get it through her head that I'm not letting them go and that I'm going to be all the support she needs in her life. She'll have Kiera and the rest of the girls, the guys will even be there for her. We all know that Tank can get the girls to open up when they don't want to. But, at the end of the day, I'm the one that she needs to come to. I'm her man in every way.

Chapter Twelve
Glock

ANTHONY HAS BEEN DROPPED off, we've gotten changed to go out to dinner, and now we're on our way. Joker and Cage happened to tell me of a spot where there's some waterfalls. I know that they've taken Sky there on more than one occasion, so I'm sure it's a different spot than what they use. Honestly, it doesn't matter to me. As long as we find a spot we can spend some quality time together, I'll be happy. Melody doesn't have Anthony to hide behind this time. She will hear me and she will voice her feelings to me. I don't want her hiding anything from me. Not this time.

When we were in school, she never shared how cruel her parents truly were to her. I'm not sure what I could have done to help her, but I would have tried to do something. No one deserves to have someone else put their hands on them for any reason. Especially a woman! Between my dad, Pops, and the rest of the guys in the club, we could've found a solution. Then I'm sure I wouldn't have missed out on her pregnancy or the first almost nine years of my son's life. I can't dwell on that though. Today is the first day of the rest of our lives together.

"So, where are we going?" Melody asks as we head away from Skylar's house.

"We're goin' someplace I've never been before. First, we're gettin' take out and then tryin' to find this place Cage and Joker told me about."

"We're not eatin' at a restaurant?"

"Nope. I'm gettin' food from the diner and then we're eatin' outside. That okay?" I ask, suddenly hoping that she doesn't have a problem with it.

"I love the idea. Restaurants can be crowded and noisy. You said you wanted to talk, so we're going to talk." Melody responds, bringing some of her sass to the forefront.

"We do need to talk angel. There's a lot of things that need to be brought out in the open. Startin' with why you never told me about how your parents treated you. Then we'll move on to what's goin' to happen goin' forward."

Melody doesn't say anything this time. Instead she sits back and watches the scenery pass us by. It's warm with a slight breeze today. Sitting by the waterfalls should be great this time of the year. I've already got everything packed in the backseat of the truck and she truly has no clue. Today she will be mine again. At first I wanted our first time again to be in a bed, giving her the sweet that my angel deserves. But, we've never done anything the conventional way and I'm sure that being in a bed is just going to make things awkward. Our first time was in the bed of the very truck that we're in right now. Nothing could be more perfect than having my angel under me while hearing the sounds of the waterfalls in the background.

"I'll be right back out angel. You need anythin' else while I'm in here?" I ask, pulling to a stop outside of the diner.

"No. I'm sure you've got food and drinks. That's really all we need isn't it?"

"Yep.

After leaving the diner, it doesn't take long for me to find the park the guys told me about. They said they walked the path down to their waterfall, so we'll find a different path to take. I don't want to take my girl to the same spot they use. It won't be as special for her if I do. Parking the truck, I have

Melody get the bag and drinks from the diner out while I get everything else from the backseat.

"Let's go angel. I'm not sure exactly where we're goin', so it might take a little bit. You good to walk?"

"Yeah. You said dress comfortably so I did."

I look back over at her and see the nervousness and happiness radiating off of her. She chose to wear a pair of cut off shorts with a tight tank top displaying the club name. My girl has no makeup on and her hair is in a loose ponytail. Honestly, she has never looked as gorgeous as she does right now. Personally, I hate all of the makeup and other junk on a girl's face. To me it doesn't make them look better, it makes me think they're trying to hide something.

I stop walking once we get to the beginning of the path to determine which way we're going to head. Looking all around us, I see a path leading up. It's winding and I can see trees lining both sides of the path. This is the way I think we need to go. Even if there isn't a waterfall this way, I'm sure we'll be able to find the perfect spot to have our dinner and talk. As for anything else, that's all on her.

"Let's go this way angel." I tell her, taking her hand.

"Lead the way Romeo." Yep, the sass is coming back.

After walking for a few minutes, I can hear the sounds of running water getting louder. Maybe there's at least a stream up ahead that we can sit by. Melody loves anything that has to do with the outdoors and this will be something right up her alley. The only thing that would've made it better is if I had had the chance to get up here and find the perfect spot first. There just wasn't time for that though. Not this time.

All of a sudden I can see a clearing a few feet in front of us. Melody is partially blocked from seeing anything so I'll be able to get a quick glance and see what I have to work with. Continuing to make my way forward, I see there is indeed a stream winding parallel to the path. To the left I can see the spray from a waterfall and I'm waiting to see what my girl's response will be.

"You ready to see this angel?" I ask.

"Yeah."

Stepping to the side, I turn and watch her face. She can't hide anything if you know what to pay attention for. Melody takes a few steps around me and stops dead in her tracks. A serene calm covers her face and you can see the amazement in her eyes as she takes in the waterfalls, the stream, and just the rest of nature.

While she is taking in our surroundings, I spread out the blanket before grabbing the food and drinks from her. By the time she realizes that I've gotten everything set up, I am sitting waiting for her to come over to the blanket. Before I can blink she is sitting next to me. Not on the other side of the blanket, but right next to me. Something is changing in her and I'm not going to complain one bit.

"You ready to eat angel? Or do you want to talk first and get it out of the way?" I ask her.

"We can talk first I guess." She says, hesitating. "Where do you see this going Glock? I mean, we're both so different now. I've been through a ton of shit and I'm sure you've had your fair share too."

"I already told you that you're mine. I meant it. We will be a family and have more babies. Anthony needs brothers and sisters. You want to go out with the girls? Have at it. You want to go to school, work? Then tell me what I have to do to help you out with it. You need some time to yourself? Tell me to fuck off and get out of your face. But, rest assured that we will talk about whatever is bothering you when I get home. The house is almost done and we'll be moving in soon. Now, what else do you need me to clear up for you?" I tell her, looking in her eyes the entire time I'm talking so she knows I'm serious.

"So, you're basically saying that we'll be together and you'll let me do what I want to when I want to. Does this mean I'm your old lady? Or am I just the baby mama?" Melody asks, looking away from me and wringing her hands together. A sure sign she's nervous and isn't sure of what my answer is going to be.

"Angel, look at me." I tell her, waiting to continue until I have her eyes. "I've already told the guys I claimed you. So, as far as I'm concerned you are my old lady. I just have to get you the rag to make it official. You would never, and I mean ever, be just a 'baby mama' to me. You are home to me. I open up to you about things no one knows about and you don't even have to try to get me to do it. I want nothin' hidden between us. That bein' said, I can't and won't tell you club business. It's for your safety and I will only tell you things that you need to know for safety reasons."

"I can handle not knowing club business, Glock. It's not mine to know. I need you to understand that if we do this, you have to give me the room to find myself. My life so far has been as a daughter to parents that treated me like shit, a mother to Anthony while trying to find you, and then as a captive to those ass clowns. I need to learn what I like, what I want in life, and what I want to do with my life. Can you understand that?" She asks me.

"I can understand that, angel. And part of us bein' together is me supportin' you while you do that, watchin' our boy and teachin' him while you're learnin' what you want to do with your life, and makin' sure you have all the tools to accomplish what you want to. There's gonna be times I overstep my boundaries and you'll have to put me in check. I know you'll have no problem with that though. Now, I want to know why you never told me what was goin' on with your parents."

"I didn't want to be that girl. The one that runs to a boy she doesn't even know what to consider their relationship. I mean in school I didn't know if we were just friends or if we were more. There was no way I was going to tell you the extent of the shit I was dealing with at home. Now, you're going to tell me why you kept everyone away from me." She says, turning the tables on me.

"It was honestly nothin' to do with you angel. I didn't want them scarin' you off before I got the chance to know you and figure out where you saw us goin'. The guys can be loud, obnoxious, and over the top sometimes. They can take anythin' you say and turn it into somethin' perverted. I just didn't want you to feel uncomfortable because of somethin' they said or did." I tell her, trying to explain my decisions the best I can to her.

"Okay, but why keep me away even after we slept together?"

"I wanted you to myself. I didn't want to have to share you with them right away. But, I was already plannin' on takin' you to the clubhouse with me. My parents wanted to meet you, because the guys were talkin' about the girl I was hung up on. Everythin' else just happened before that could happen."

"Okay. Now, we know where we both stand, can we eat now? I'm starved!" Melody tells me, already leaning over to see what I ordered us.

Melody

I have to admit that I was surprised when Glock pulled up here and brought me to eat and talk by the waterfalls.

Before I never would've thought about doing something like this with him. It was almost enough when he'd lay in the bed of his truck with me doing nothing more than talking and looking at the stars. Now, I was sure it would be an impossible thing to do with him. He seems so different from the boy I knew. Glock is rougher and darker than when we were in school.

After our talk, and eating, I felt my back starting to bother me. It's a good thing I made sure to bring the ointment with me. Looking at Glock, I scooted closer and reached into my back pocket.

"Can you do me a favor?" I ask.

"Anythin' angel."

"I need this put on my tattoo. Can you do it for me please?"

"Where is it angel?" He asks, searching my body for the hundredth time looking for my tattoo.

"My back." Is the only thing I say before lifting the hem of my shirt until it's over my head.

For what feels like hours, I can feel nothing other than Glock's heated stare. I'm sure he's trying to figure out why I went with the darkened angel wings. And I'll explain it to him if he asks me. If anything has stayed the same about him, it's his curious nature.

"You gonna tell me why the dark angel wings?" He finally asks me.

"It's to symbolize the death of my innocence and the girl I used to be. Everything I've been through has shaped me into the woman I am starting to become now." I begin. "I guess I went with the dark colors because of the terrible things I went through. Not just with the kidnapping but with my parents and losing you too. Do you know what my main thought was when I found out we were having a son?"

"I can't even begin to think of what that was angel." He states, as I feel him moving behind me.

"The first thing I did was cry because I was sure that you would have been excited we were having a little boy that would hopefully look and act like you. Then I thought about all of the things he was going to miss out with having just me around to teach him things." I tell him as I feel his hands moving tenderly over my back.

"Angel, you would have found a way to teach him everythin' he needed to know. You are stronger than you give yourself credit for. And any child we have is goin' to be lucky as fuck to have you as their mother." He tells me, continuing to rub my back as he moves closer to me. "As far as bein' excited that our first child together was a son, to me it wouldn't have mattered. My only concern would've been whether or not you were both healthy and okay. The same way that I'll feel when we have more children."

Glock seems so sure that we're going to have more children, but I'm honestly not sure whether or not I want more. Don't get me wrong, I would love to give Anthony brothers or sisters. I'm just not sure that it's possible after everything that happened to me while I was held in a cage for six months of my life. Hell, I haven't even talked to any doctor about it. We'll just see what happens I guess.

Before I can get too deep in my own head, I feel Glock softly kissing my sweet spot. He knows that it's right where my neck and shoulder meet, behind my ear, or on the back of my neck. There's no stopping the shiver that runs from my head to my toes as he continues to kiss me with soft, gentle kisses.

"Glock," is the only thing I can get out.

"I got you angel. Let me have this. We need to have this." He tells me, and there's nothing I can say to disagree with him.

"Yes!" is my only response before I feel myself being pulled back and turned to lay on top of him.

"Angel, I want you so bad right now. You are the only one that's ever gotten under my skin and I can't wait to have you again. But, it's your show right now. You say no, then it's no."

Leaning down, I kiss him like the air I've needed to breath begins and ends with his kiss. Even though Glock deepens the kiss, he doesn't take complete control away from me. When he said it was my show, he truly meant it. Before I know it though, the kissing isn't enough. It's been nine, almost ten long years since I've had this man touch my soul. I need to feel his hands on me and be able to feel his skin along mine.

Sitting up, straddling his thighs, I start to pull the hem of the tee he's wearing up his body. The last time I saw Glock naked, he was muscular, but now, there's nothing that isn't rock hard on him. From his washboard stomach to his large arms, one of my favorite parts of a man, I can't take it in fast enough. Along with his harder body, I can't help but notice all of the ink adorning his body. The piece that captures my attention though is a set of angel wings tattooed right above his heart. In the center is my name in flowing script, and the surrounding area is free of any other ink. There's nothing I can do but draw my eyes up to his.

"Told you it was always gonna be you angel. One way or another I was goin' to have you with me every day no matter where I went. Ask our son about my bike too." He tells me, pulling me down and kissing away the lone tear rolling down my cheek.

Kissing me again, I let all that is Glock consume me. His hands are all over my exposed skin until they come to rest on my lower back. Angling my head, I deepen the kiss this time as I run my hands over his skin and down to the belt he's wearing. The entire time I can feel my hands shaking with nerves. I know Glock hasn't been a monk and that he's been with women while I was gone. It bothers me, but I can't change the past. However, I haven't willingly been with anyone other than Glock. He's the first and only person I've let in and I am scared that I'm not going to measure up.

"Angel, what's goin' on?" He asks, halting my progress by grabbing my hands in his. "You're shakin' like a leaf. If you aren't ready for this, tell me and we'll stop."

"I want this. I'm afraid that I'm not gonna measure up to the women that you've been with since I've been gone. Yes, before you ask, it bothers me but there's nothing I can do about it. You did what you did and there's no changing it."

"Okay. Why don't you think you'll measure up though?" Glock asks, pausing while I can see the wheels turning in his head. "Are you sayin' that I'm the only one you've been with? There's been no one else this entire time?"

"I honestly wish I could say yes to that. Willingly, you are the only person I've been with. I can't tell you how many men raped me over the six months I was kept there. It could've been one man repeatedly or several different ones." I answer, lowering my eyes knowing that there's a good chance he won't want anything to do with me now.

"Get out of your head angel." He tells me, lifting my face to meet his. "I don't give a fuck about them. They took somethin' that wasn't theirs to take from you. I am the only man that you have been with. There is one person that will know your taste, what you like and don't like, will teach you what they like, and will try anythin' that you want to. I am that man and I will be the only one that hears you scream out his name in pleasure and know what you sound like and look like completely sated."

I go back to undoing his belt while he moves his hands away and lets me do this at my pace. I'm still not sure of anything, but I can feel my confidence kick up a notch knowing that he's happy I've only ever been with him. I'm not going to say that I didn't go out on a date or two after meeting Kiera, but I never let it go anywhere. Glock was always right there in the forefront of my mind.

Once I have his jeans undone, I stand up to remove his jeans and take my shorts off. Glock makes himself comfortable and watches my every move. As I strip my shorts and panties off, I hear his sharp intake of breath and I want to cover myself. I know that I've changed since having our son. But I don't see that as a bad thing. My body changed giving nourishment and life to our boy. We'll see in time what he thinks of the changes.

"You are more stunnin' now then you were in school. I can see that you want to cover yourself and you are steelin' yourself against it. Come here angel."

Lowering myself back to straddling him, I move lower so that I can take him in my mouth. I've never done this before, so he's going to have to bear with me. This is something I want to give him. His eyes find me and I know he can see how unsure I am. He told me once before that my eyes were the window to my true feelings.

"You don't have to do this angel."

"I know I don't have to, I want to. It's just I'm not sure what I'm doing. So, you'll have to guide me."

"I can do that." He tells me, settling back down and letting me take my time.

Using my tongue, I lick down one side of his length before coming back up the other side. I don't take my eyes off of his face once while I open my mouth to take him inside. I already know there's no way I'm going to be able to take much of him in my mouth, but I'll do the best I can. So, I slowly take as much as I can in before I slide my mouth back up. While at the tip of his dick, I swirl my tongue around it, tasting the small drops of precum that are leaking out of him. Repeating the process, I hear him moan my name out as his hand snakes into my hair, releasing it from the ponytail I put it in earlier.

"I'm not goin' to push you to take more than what you can handle angel. Just want to see your face." He growls out.

I continue to increase my pace a little at a time and Glock stays true to his word and never forces me to take more of him. Changing to a more comfortable position, I find that I can actually take a little bit more of him in.

"Melody! Feels…so…good." Glock grunts out, pulling harder on my hair. "Not in your mouth, angel. Gotta stop."

I let Glock slide from my mouth as I sit up and make myself more comfortable straddling his legs still. I'm unprepared for him to pull my body up to his face as he settles my wet center over his mouth. Knowing that I'm going to protest, Glock swipes his tongue from my slit to my clit before sucking it into his mouth. All thought leaves me as I let him do what he wants to do.

There's no way that I can hold in the moans escaping my mouth as Glock continues his ministrations. I'm writhing and pressing myself as close as I can get to him. Until he pulls back a little bit. At first, I'm ready to yell at him since I was so close. Him inserting a finger in me stops me dead in my tracks though. While he continues sliding his finger in and out of me, Glock goes back to sucking and nibbling on my clit.

"So close, Glock." I murmur.

"Not Glock. Not while we're doin' this angel. It's Mason I want to hear comin' from your sweet lips." He says before going back to what he was doing.

While he continues to focus on my clit with his mouth, two fingers are inserted in me. He scissors them within me to make sure that I can handle his size after so long. The only reason I know this is because he did it the one and only other time we were together. Moving his other hand up to my breast, he starts to knead and pull on my nipple. Glock knows this is a sure way to ensure that I reach my release quicker than anything else.

"Mason!" I call out as my orgasm rushes through me.

As I stand over him, still quivering and shaking with my release, he begins to kiss his way up my body, not stopping until he reaches my tits. There he gives his full attention until I start squirming again. Instead of laying me down though, he holds me in place so that I'm kneeling before him. We're both on our knees right now as he pays attention to my chest.

"Since you just got your ink, you can't be on your back angel. You're gonna have to ride me."

I can feel myself beginning to shake again with nerves. I've never been on top and I don't know the first thing about what to do. Looking him in the eyes, I show him how nervous I am without opening my mouth at all.

"Don't worry angel. You can't get this wrong. There is no right or wrong way to do this. We'll find our rhythm and let one another know what we like and what we want."

"Okay." I tell him, pushing him backwards until he's lying flat on his back.

Taking a deep breath, I slowly lower myself onto his hard length. Glock closes his eyes and I can see his muscles straining as he holds himself back. He's letting me run the show today and I'm going to use this opportunity to find out exactly what he likes.

Pulling me from my thoughts, Glock releases a groan and moves his hands to my hips. He's not trying to take control, just guide me. After lowering myself on his length, I stay still for a minute to get used to him. Finally, I begin to raise myself back up before lowering down again. Every time I go up and down, I get a little bit faster and start swirling my hips. He keeps his hands in place and I can feel his grip tightening on me. He'll leave bruises and I couldn't care less. I relish the thought of having his mark on me.

"Angel, you feel so good." He grits out between clenched teeth.

I can't even respond, I can't. My body is already beginning to shudder with my impending orgasm. I've never been the one in control of anything sexual and I like the power I have. There's nothing like controlling the tempo, the amount I take in my body, and having the ability to make him lose his mind with what I'm doing. However, that doesn't last long. By the time my breathing is coming back under control, Glock is telling me to get on my hands and knees.

"I don't know." I murmur.

"Angel, I'm not gonna do anythin' to hurt you. Ever. Is there a reason you don't want to?" He asks.

"Never done it that way." Is my only response.

"You'll love it!"

Trusting Glock, I do as he asks and get settled on my hands and knees. I can feel him settling in behind me and reaching around to my clit. He's very careful and makes sure that he doesn't touch my back. At the same time, I can feel him getting as close as he can to me before plunging deep inside. This is definitely a position that I could get used to. I love feeling him so deep.

"Fuck!" He grunts out. "Get yours, angel."

Glock continues to pound away while pinching my clit at the same time. I can feel my release starting to grow as his movements become erratic and almost punishing. He would never hurt me, but I can feel him losing control because he's so close. Suddenly, my orgasm hits me and I can't even make a sound. I feel my entire body shaking and see stars behind my eyes. Glock growls out his release from behind me and I can barely hear it.

After a minute, Glock pulls out of me and lays us down so that I'm lying on his chest. He gently rubs my side as we get our breathing under control. I can feel myself starting to drift to sleep after being fully sated and then him rubbing my side is not helping me stay awake. At least until he starts talking.

"Angel, um, I wasn't thinkin' just now." He begins, tentatively. "I didn't wear anythin'."

"I'm not on anything. No birth control or anything else." I tell him, trying not to freak out.

"It's okay angel. We'll handle anythin' that happens."

"I don't know if I want more kids Glock. Hell, I don't even know if I can have any after everything that happened to me." I tell him, stressing out that this is going to be a deal breaker for him and what we're starting here.

"I've said multiple times I wanted more kids with you and you're just now sayin' this to me. What's goin' on in that head of yours angel?" He asks, changing positions so he can see my face better.

"I don't know. I guess a part of me didn't believe that you were serious. That you were only making sure that you could see Anthony and be a part of his life." I tell him honestly.

"You should know that I would never lie to you angel. If I didn't want to be with you, I wouldn't say that you're mine. Not even to make sure that I could be in Anthony's life." He tells me, pushing a piece of hair out of my face. "I said that you're mine because you are mine. We will be together and it's just you needin' to know that it's goin' to happen."

"We'll see, Glock. Like I said, we've both changed." I tell him, getting up and getting dressed again.

Glock follows suit and gets dressed. While he's finishing up, I start packing up everything. I know I need to apologize to him, but I'm not sure how to now. Even with him on the other side of the blanket, I can feel the pain, anger, and hurt radiating off of him. There's no way I can leave it like this.

"Glock, look, I'm sorry. I should've said something to you sooner. Maybe we'll go to the doctor and see what they have to say about me having kids. Then we can talk about it from there. Is that good with you?" I ask, walking closer to him.

"Angel, I'm good. But, you need to start talkin' to me. We should've already been to the doctor about this shit.

Tomorrow, I'm gettin' doc in to have a look at you and see what is goin' on. Anythin' else we need to talk about?"

"No. I just need time to get used to being an us again. I mean I thought that's where we were headed before and then everything changed."

"We were headed there before angel. I was already there with you but didn't know how to express that shit to you."

"Okay, well, give me some time and we'll get to that point again. I promise. Now let's get back to the clubhouse."

After the drive back to the clubhouse, we spend the rest of the time in our room. We just talk, laugh, plan, and explore each other's bodies. If our days consist of this and spending time with our son, I'll be happy to continue seeing where things go with Glock. However, nothing goes to plan in life and I wish we could've anticipated what was coming up.

Chapter Thirteen
Glock

THE PAST FEW DAYS have been interesting. I've spent more time with my son and angel than I have anyone else. My phone stayed quiet, Bailey and the rest of the girls stayed away, and my brothers have left us alone. This morning I woke up to find my family ready to start their day. Anthony is dressed in his usual outfit these days of shorts, a tank top, and his sneakers. Melody is dressed simply in a pair of cutoffs that show off her long legs, a tight tank top, sneakers, and one of my baseball hats on. She's not wearing any makeup and you can see that she's ready to let the day take her wherever it will.

"Where ya goin' angel?" I ask, my voice filled with sleep.

"Play ball at the park downtown. You getting up to join us or you staying in bed all day?" She asks, a playful smirk gracing her beautiful face.

"Yeah I'm goin'. Anyone else goin' with you?"

"Nope. Just us. Well, for right now it's just us."

"What's that mean?" I ask, sitting up and catching Anthony in my arms as he jumps on the bed.

"I haven't seen Kiera or the rest of the girls in a few days and who knows what they're going to want to do." She tells me like I should already know that.

While they go get breakfast, I get dressed and ready to start our day. Who knows what all we'll end up getting up to. One thing I've learned the last few days is that Melody can be unpredictable when she gets a wild hair up her ass. Yesterday, we ended up taking Anthony on a walk that was just supposed to be a short trek. Four hours later we returned home. They found a stream and decided to play in it. Then she decided that we were going to play hide and seek in the woods surrounding the clubhouse. She just goes with it. Which also means that we haven't talked to a doctor yet either.

Finally, completing my morning ritual, I find my family sitting at a table in the corner with Maddie, Kiera, and Tank. Anthony rushes over to me and lets me know that they're all going with us.

"Glock." Tank says in greeting. "Gettin' the boys ready and then we're takin' off I guess."

"Alright. That will give me time for coffee and a little breakfast."

As I sit down to eat the food Summer brought over, Anthony is telling me all about playing ball with my girl. Apparently before she was taken it was an event that took place almost daily. And she said that she wasn't a guy so she wouldn't know how to teach him what he needed to know. She knows more than she gives herself credit for. I'm sure if it came down to it, she'd do what she needed to do to learn everything she could to teach him everything he needed to know.

"Daddy, are you listenin' to me?" Anthony asks, bouncing in the chair next to me.

"Yeah, bud. I'm listenin'."

"Momma says that we're gonna get ice cream when we're done playing ball. You going for that too, daddy?"

"Yeah, bud. Ice cream sounds like a good thing to get after playin' ball."

"Can we go now? I've been waitin' forever!"

"Just waitin' on Tank and Maddie to get the boys ready."

A loud and long sigh escapes Anthony at the thought that he has to wait a little bit longer to get to the park. One he hasn't even been to yet. Melody and I both stifle our laughter at his dramatics. Tank and Maddie have getting the kids down to a science and shouldn't be more than a few minutes. Just as the thought leaves my head, I hear Zoey's little feet running back towards the common room.

"You can get ready to head out bud. I hear Zoey comin' down the hall." I tell him.

His excitement is contagious as he runs towards Zoey instead of outside. She stops beside him and he takes her little hand in his before walking towards the door. Looking up I see Tank standing there watching his daughter being led to the door by my son. We look at one another and give nod lifts. This is how Jameson and my boy are going to be with the little kids from now on. I can already see Anthony stepping into a protective role as the oldest kid here.

"Mommy, where's Aunt Kiera?" Anthony asks his mom without taking his eyes off of leading Zoey outside. "She said she's coming with us."

"I'm here big man. Don't think I'd let you get away with playing ball without me." Kiera says, entering the common room followed by Blade.

"You comin' too?" I ask him.

"Yep."

Blade always has been a man of few words. The most open I've ever seen him is since Kiera and my angel have been here. He spends more time in the common room, laughs and jokes with us, and keeps his eyes on Kiera. I don't know what's going on with them, nor do I care, but I like the way that he is these days. Blade has a past, like us all, and he needs to learn that it's not good to bottle that shit up. Hopefully spending time with us will help him with that.

"Daddy, you're still sitting there." Anthony calls out from the door. "Even Tank and Blade are outside."

Apparently, everyone went out while I was in my own head. Getting up, I make my way to Anthony so we can leave. Melody is at the SUV with the back passenger door open. Anthony sits in the middle so I'm sure she's waiting for him. Well, until I get closer and I can hear her talking to someone. Obviously, Anthony is next to me so it's not him.

"Who you talkin' to, angel?" I ask, stepping up behind her.

"Zoey. Anthony wanted her to ride with us. So, Tank and Maddie didn't care."

I peek in and wave to their little girl sitting in her car seat. She's waiting patiently for Anthony to climb in so I lift him up and carry him to the other side. As soon as we're all loaded up, I make the short drive to the park. Tank follows in his SUV while Blade and Kiera follow him on his bike. Kiera is the first and only woman I've ever seen on the back of that bike.

"You got everythin' we need angel?" I ask as I pull out of the clubhouse parking lot.

"Yeah. The bat, gloves, and balls are in the back. There's no point in bringing lunch when we can get something there. Unless you want to come back here for lunch."

"No. We can eat at the diner. It's not that far from the park."

"Okay."

Melody settles in for the short ride and watches the scenery pass by. She's pulling back into herself and I don't know why. We will be having a talk about it later on today though. I thought things were starting to change when we spent the weekend cocooned in our room not doing much other than being together. If someone said anything to her or she thinks someone is going to say something to her, I need to know so I can get it out of her head.

We've been at the park for a little over an hour and my girl and son are still going strong playing ball. Tank and I played for a little while before falling out. Blade has been keeping an eye on the rest of the kids. Right now, they're just playing catch and I can't take my eyes off of my angel. She's so graceful and can grab the wild throws out of nowhere. My girl should be a ball player or some shit like that.

"What's goin' on with you and her, brother?" Tank asks, sitting beside me.

"She's mine. Plain and simple."

"I know she's yours. What I want to know is whether or not she's on board with that."

"I honestly don't know. One minute things are good and now she seems like she's pullin' inside herself. We've talked and I know things are weighin' on her mind. Then she seems to not want to deal with it." I tell him honestly.

"Want me to talk to her?" Tank asks in all seriousness.

"I don't know if she'll open up to you like Skylar did."

"What's the harm in tryin'?"

"You want to give it a shot, go for it." I tell him, hoping that something can snap my girl out of whatever is going on in her head.

Melody

I am finally able to get Anthony to quit playing ball. Now, he's running around with Zoey for a little bit before we head out for lunch. Glock is talking to Blade and Kiera so I find a seat in some shade to cool down a little bit. Out of the corner of my eye I see Tank making his way toward me with two drinks in his hand. This is one huge guy and he kind of intimidates me. But, I see the way he is with his wife so I know he's more of the gentle giant type of guy. At least that's what I keep telling myself.

"Here, thought you could use a drink." He says, holding out a bottled water and taking a seat next to me.

"Thank you."

"So, I got to tell you somethin'. I haven't seen my boy Glock this happy since I've known him. And I met him a little while after you left. I know you didn't leave him of your choosin', but it killed somethin' inside my brother when you did."

I can feel the tears building up in my eyes. It's one thing for Glock to tell me what happened to him after I left, but it's a whole different story when I hear it from someone else. To know that I unintentionally caused him so much pain kills something inside of me.

"I'm not tellin' you this to make you upset sweetheart. I'm tellin' you this so you know when that man tells you he's all in, he is dead serious. Now, you have to make a decision as to whether or not you can go all in with him." Tank says, looking me dead in the eyes.

"I'm not clean. He deserves the girl he thinks I am. I'm not her anymore. And there's things I may not be able to give him. What happens then? What happens if I break him all over again?"

"You won't break that man. He's stronger than you know and you make him stronger. What do you think you can't give him? Because I'm not even touchin' you sayin' you're not the girl he fell in love with all those years ago. She's in there somewhere and you both can pull her back out."

"He wants kids. Lots of kids. I don't know if it's possible after everything they did to me." I say, a sob catching in my throat.

"Then you go to the doctor and find out. If he says you can't, the two of you will deal with it together and find a way to make it happen. If you can give him more babies, then you need to decide if that's what you want. Glock will never force you to make a decision you don't want to make."

"I know he won't. He's owned my heart for almost ten years. I'm never getting it back and I don't want it back." I tell Tank honestly.

"Then you need to talk to him and let him in. I'm here whenever you need to talk. Skylar and Bailey come to me more than their men some times. My girl can't have any more kids, so she'll know what you're goin' through if that's the answer you get. There are a ton of family behind the two of you. It's up to you to let us all in. Now, go get your man and tell him what you just told me sweetheart. He needs to hear it."

Getting up, I make my way to Glock. I know he had something to do with Tank coming over to talk to me and I'm happy about it. I'm not sure what it is about the big man, but he makes you feel at ease and that you can talk to him about anything. Before I can get to Glock, he turns and waits for me to be by his side.

"How did you know I was walking to you?" I ask, leaning against his shoulder.

"I always know where you are and when you're gettin' close to me angel." He tells me.

"Well, thank you for having Tank talk to me. There's some things we need to talk about." I tell him, fidgeting with the hem of my shirt.

"I know. We'll talk when we get back to the clubhouse and Anthony is sleepin'. No one is gonna interrupt us and no one is gonna know what's goin' on unless you tell them."

"Okay. Can we go eat now?" I ask, suddenly starving.

"Yeah angel."

After loading the kids up we all head to the diner to grab some lunch. I wasn't really planning on everyone coming to lunch with us, but I wouldn't trade it. These people are quickly becoming my family and some of my closest friends. And Kiera is going to be with us. I never turn down the opportunity to be with her.

Pulling up to the diner, we all pile out and I can't help but wonder what the employees of the diner are going to say at the number of people we're going in with. I shouldn't have even worried about it after seeing the guys and Maddie say 'hi' to everyone like they're frequent customers of the place. It should've occurred to me but it just didn't.

"You know the drill, sit anywhere big enough for you all." A waitress says as her gaze lingers on Glock.

"Thanks Ann." Tank responds, leading us towards the back of the place.

The guys push two tables together to accommodate us all and start talking without worrying about what they're going to eat. Going out on a limb, I'm going to guess they're regulars and know what they want to eat already though. Kiera, Anthony, and myself need to look at menus though, which brings a bout of laughter from the waitress.

"I don't see what's so funny." I speak up.

"Angel, it's okay. She's not laughin' at you, are ya Ann?"

"Oh, no. It's just we really don't have menus anymore. We don't get a lot of out of towners in here. So, how long are you staying?" She asks, looking directly at me.

"I'm not. We're here to stay." I say, my voice dripping with as much sweetness as I can put into it.

"Oh. Well, what can I get you all to drink? The usual guys?" She asks, standing closer to Glock.

He's not even paying attention, but I can feel the green-eyed monster wanting to come out and play. It's one thing for me to have to deal with the club girls, which I haven't had to yet, but it's another to have to deal with some waitress. I'm sure Glock fucked her since he said he wasn't all that picky and tons of different, willing woman go to the clubhouse to hook up with bikers.

"Since you don't know my usual," Kiera pipes in, sensing my anger, "I'll have a plain tea, little man here will have a chocolate milk, and my girl will have a sweet tea. Can you take your eyes off of her man long enough to write that down, or do you need some help with that?"

I should have known that she was going to run her mouth about something and stopped her, but she's right. Glock however, gives her the evil eye before turning to me. Without saying a word, I sit there and wait to see what his play is going to be. Unfortunately, he doesn't make the right one.

"Yeah, Ann, we'll have the normal drinks and the other three that mouth over there said. Thanks hun."

The last thing I'm going to do is cause a scene in a public place. Especially when I don't know if he's even done anything with her yet or not. However, that doesn't mean that I have to make it easy on him either. He's sitting across the table from me and Anthony is between Kiera and I. It will be really easy to ignore him and talk to them.

"Kiera, we're going to a nightclub tonight. I'm sure Glock won't have a problem keeping an eye on his son while we're out."

"Sounds good to me. Where we going?" She asks, knowing that I fully intend to stay away from Glock for the time being.

"I don't know. I'll find one and let you know when I do. We brought our going out clothes with us. Right?"

"Yep. I know that hot as hell little red dress you love is in with my stuff, but I'll get it for you when we get back."

"Where you guys goin'?" Blade asks, leaning in closer to Kiera.

"Out." Is my only response. "I need a break and I'm going to take one."

Glock is staring at me, letting me know with his eyes that we'll be talking about this later. And that I might not be going out. Well, he's got another thing coming. I haven't ever been out without worrying about my son and it's time that I do that. He said he'll support whatever I want to try and do. Guess this will be his first opportunity to prove that to me.

"I know this new club that's not far from my dad's clubhouse." Maddie pipes in. "Think we can bring all the girls out with you two tonight?"

"I don't see why not." I answer. "I wanted to spend time with Kiera and I'll still be able to do that. You got a problem with that, Kiera?"

"Nope. It's going to be awesome. In fact, why don't you guys stay here so we can go get ready?" Kiera answers.

"Well, it's a little bit of a drive to my dad's so maybe we can get ready there. Let me call and ask."

As Maddie walks away, Tank and Glock are staring a hole through me. I guess they're not on board with the idea of us going out tonight. Part of me is saying that this isn't a good idea, but the other part already said that I want to do things I never got the chance to do.

"A word Melody." Glock says, standing next to me.

Following him to the back of the restaurant, I stay quiet until I see where we're going to stop. He takes me through the kitchen and out the back door. Once we're away from the diner, he turns to face me. For several minutes, he doesn't say anything, Glock just looks at me trying to read me.

"What are you playin' at, Mel?" He finally asks.

"Nothing. I told you that I want to experience things that I never had the chance to. Going to a nightclub is one of those things. So, we're going out. You said you wouldn't have a problem with it at all. Or don't you remember that?" I ask.

"I don't have a problem with it. What I have a problem with is the reason you're doin' it."

"And what's that supposed to mean? You think that girl in there trying to stake a claim on you has anything to do with this? Get over yourself!" I yell.

"I know it has to do with that. And why would Kiera call her out like that?" He asks, the frustration and anger pouring through his voice.

"She called her out on it because you wouldn't say anything. You're the one pushing for this to work between us. I agree to give it a shot and within a few days I'm already seeing girls try to stake a claim on you. And it's not even a club girl!"

"Ann isn't staking anything. She's the waitress at the diner we go to. All she's doin' is bein' friendly."

"You keep telling yourself that big man. I'm going back in and I will be going out tonight. If you don't want Anthony with you then I'll find a sitter." I say before turning and walking away from him.

"Of course I want my son with me."

I hear Glock saying he wants his son with him, but I don't acknowledge him. You can say I'm being a bitch or whatever you need to tell yourself, but I simply don't know how to deal with Glock's past and women trying to act like they have a claim on him. In no way do I want to hurt him, but he needs to realize that instead of ignoring a woman that's blatantly trying to act like they're something more than what they are, he needs to say something. We'll talk about it later though, that I have no doubt about.

Walking back into the diner, I see everyone sitting around the table like nothing is going on. The kids are eating and Maddie tells me that her dad is happy to have us there to get ready to go out. He's even sending a prospect and some guys with us to the club. I'm sure that has more to do with the fact that he knows our men will want someone with us.

By the time Glock makes it back to the table, he's calmed down a little bit. Not enough for everyone at the table not to feel his rage simmering though. I should call off girl's night now, but we all need this. From what I've gathered, no one has really done anything in a long time. I want to blow off some steam and try something new. Who better to do that with than new friends and Kiera?

"When you guys get ready to head out, you know a prospect is tailin' you. Right?" Tank asks us.

"Yes, Tank, we do." Maddie answers him. "It's one night for us to go have some fun. You guys have your time and we need ours too. You know my dad isn't going to let anything happen to us. Hell, he and Playboy will probably be with us at the club."

"I know sweetness, but from what I'm gettin' Melody hasn't ever been to one and she'll need to be watched."

"I'm sitting right here. I may not have been out to a club before, but I do know how to get someone away from me when I don't want them near me. Just because I was able to be kidnapped doesn't mean anything. They had the unfair advantage of drugging me to kidnap me. I know not to take drinks from strangers and to make sure that I don't ever go back to a drink I've set down. We'll be fine."

Glock just sits there staring a hole through me. Guess he didn't realize that not only was I drugged when they found me in that cage, but that's how they got me too. I'm sure we'll be having a conversation about that one of these days too. However, my first order of business is getting to a doctor to find out what's going on and if it's going to be possible to give

Glock what he wants. I know he's not going to let me go either way, but I need to prepare myself in case I can't have any more kids.

"I can feel you thinkin' from over here angel. We will be talkin' about this more and we will be discussin' whatever else you got in that pretty little head of yours. You have your girl's night out and then we'll be sittin' down until everythin' is out in the open. Understand?"

"Yes. You know I'm sorry for acting like a bitch. Something I need to get used to and work on."

"Nope. We'll talk later. Now, let's eat so you guys can get on the road. Don't want you drivin' that far after dark. And you realize you'll be stayin' with Slim and his club tonight, right?" Glock asks, looking at the three of us. Tank sits there nodding his head in agreement.

"Dad already said the same thing guys. You know he's not gonna let us drive that far home after being out." Maddie says, putting a hand on her husband's arm. "We'll behave ourselves and be careful."

"The taken ones will behave themselves, but the single ones may not." Kiera pipes in.

I groan knowing this is not going to go over well with the three men sitting at our table. Figuring Tank or Glock would be the ones to voice their opinions about that statement, I'm surprised when I hear Blade growl out a response that I'm sure only Kiera hears. Glock and Tank sit back and watch their brother and my best friend. It's kind of funny considering, to my knowledge, neither one of them are saying they're together or that anything is going on between them. Interesting!

Before leaving the clubhouse, the guys all gave us a lecture about what they expected and reminding us to stay together and in sight of Slim's men. Not only did they have Slim Jim follow us, we also had Blade and another guy I'm not sure about. I haven't seen him yet, and he's pretty damn intimidating. He's about the size of Tank but scary looking. At least to me.

"Earth to Melody!" Maddie says, snapping her fingers close to my face.

"Yeah. Sorry, I zoned out there for a while."

"I got that babe. I was saying that Darcy is meeting us at my dad's clubhouse and then we'll all get ready. He's got two rooms for us to use, his and my brother's. Then a few of his guys will go with us. They'll let us have our fun but be there if we need them."

"Okay. Sounds good."

"You sure you're good Melody?" Bailey asks. "You've been quiet the entire ride and zoning out. I know something went down for you to call an impromptu girl's night out."

"I'm good. Just a lot on my mind. And things I need to get used to. It's a little overwhelming honestly." I answer.

"Let me guess, a woman acting like she was with your man?" Skylar asks.

"Yeah. A waitress was acting like I was just passing through and that she had some sort of claim on Glock."

"And he did nothing about it?" Bailey asks.

"Nope. He acted like nothing was wrong and told me he was just being friendly as usual."

"That girl was not being friendly." Kiera says. "She was trying to say, without words, that he's hers. And he ignored that shit."

Bailey and Skylar look at one another and have a silent communication. Finally, Bailey turns to me. "Listen, we've all been there and have had to deal with women thinking they have something more with our men. If Glock can't see it, or chooses to ignore it, then he needs a good ass kicking. Or just don't give him any for a day or two. Works wonders with Grim."

"Cage and Joker too. I don't even have to finish the sentence that I'm not giving it up and they're making sure I retract it." Skylar says, a faint blush creeping up her face.

"So, tell me what's it's like to be with two men at once." Kiera asks.

"Um…" Skylar starts.

"Can we please not have this conversation right now?" Bailey pleads. "One is my blood brother and the other one is close enough to be my brother. I'd rather not hear about their sex life."

"Oh. Well, in that case, put some ear phones in. I want to know since it's something I've always wanted to try."

"Without going into too much detail, let's just say that I never have to worry about being left unsatisfied. What one can't do, the other one does. I've been with both of them at once, one at a time, and with one while the other watched. I was nervous at first, but they both know how to relax me and make sure my mind stays on them and what they're doing."

"Okay. But what's it like when you're with them both at once?" Kiera asks, getting comfortable in her seat.

"Well, you just feel really full and it's amazing. Even if it were just something that happened a few times, I don't think I could go back to being with one man. Not after experiencing something like Cage and Joker."

"Okay. Enough!" Bailey interrupts. "I'm getting grossed out here."

"Alright. I might have to find some men to help me out with that." Kiera says thoughtfully.

"You find the right two at my dad's and you can experience it." Maddie says.

"Are you serious?" Kiera asks, sitting up.

"Yep. I'm not letting you know who it is, but I accidentally walked in on them. You figure it out and talk to them."

Tuning the conversation out, I think about Glock. I know he was still mad when we left, but he tried to hide it. Too bad he couldn't hide to storm clouds in his eyes from me. He told me when we were in school that I could read him like no one else and know what he was feeling before he did. And I could get him to open up about things no one else knew. Maybe I should call him when we get there. Or send him a quick message.

Me: I'm sorry for being a bitch. We will talk when I get back. I just need to get used to seeing women fall over themselves to get to you.

Setting my phone in my lap, I don't expect a response. Glock has other ideas though. He responds almost immediately.

Glock: Angel, Tank talked to me after you left. I'm sorry for not seein' what you did. You were right and she was tryin' to stake a claim. I've never been with her and I wouldn't. You are mine and I am yours. No one else.

A small smile appears on my face. I really needed to hear that. Even if I didn't know I did.

Me: You can make it up to me later.

I put my phone back in my lap and sit back for the rest of the ride. I'm guessing we should be there soon since we've been in the SUV for over an hour already. Tonight, I'm just going to relax and have a good time with the girls. Everything else will be waiting when I get back.

Chapter Fourteen
Glock

AFTER THE GIRLS LEFT, Tank sat me down and told me what made my girl so upset. Apparently, I was the only one that really didn't realize what Ann was doing. There will not be another chance for her to upset my angel. I'll be having a talk with her and if it continues, I'll be sure to let the owner know that we might have to take our business elsewhere. I'm not into playing games like that.

I'm sitting with my son eating our dinner when my phone goes off. Seeing a message from Melody immediately makes my heart race. The only thing I can think of is that something's wrong and she's reaching out. Once I read what she's written, I know I need to make this better. I was still pissed when she left and I know she knows it too.

If Melody thinks she's getting used to women throwing themselves at me or trying to stake a claim, she's dead wrong. That will not be something that she has to get used to. It's something that I won't tolerate. So, I respond telling her the truth. Melody is mine and I'm hers. There isn't anything anyone can do to change that fact. Not when my world is bright again and I can breathe without feeling like I'm gasping for air.

"Daddy, why are you upset?" Anthony finally asks me.

"I'm fine buddy. Mama and I just had a disagreement, but we're good."

"I know Mama was upset when she left."

"She was. But we're good now. I promise big man." I tell him, ruffling his hair.

Just as I go to pull him closer to me, my phone goes off again. Melody's telling me I can make it up to her later. You bet your ass I will! By the time I'm done ravishing her delectable body, she won't ever forget who owns her. She already owns my heart, body, and soul. And I wouldn't have it any other way.

"Slim sent a message that they're twenty minutes out. Boy Scout just picked them up and is following them with Blade, Dozer, and Slim Jim." Grim lets us know. He's been a moody bastard since we got back and the girls left. I'm guessing he's not happy they're going out for the night and staying at Slim's club.

"Thanks, brother." I tell him, looking around the common room.

The guys are all sitting with their kids while we eat dinner that Ma made. Not a single one of us is happy the girls went out so far away. It's been too quiet since we found my angel and released the rest of the girls. To say we're all expecting some blowback from that would be an understatement. We just don't know when it's going to happen, but it definitely will happen. Plus, there's the extra pressure with not knowing what Melody's parents are going to try to do next. I'm sure they know where they are by now. It's just a matter of time before they try something.

"Listen up boys!" Ma calls out. "You are moody assholes on a good day. I know that you worry about your girls while they're not in your sight. They need this girl's night out though. And you need to go make sure that they're okay. Now, go get cleaned up, dress nice for your girls, and get out of my sight. These kids are staying with Pops, me, and a few of the nomads. We're going to be turning your common room into a kid zone."

We all just stay where our asses are planted. At least until I hear Ma shout for us to get our asses in gear. Grim, Tank, Cage, Joker, and I all look at one another before we trip over ourselves to go get ready to head out. Ma and Pops are standing there, laughing their asses off at us.

Taking a ten-minute shower, I throw on a clean pair of jeans, my boots, a dark tank top under a black button up shirt that I leave half open, and my cut. I throw on a black ball cap backwards for now and head out to the hallway to see the rest of the guys ready to head out too.

"You know they're goin' to be pissed as fuck we're interruptin' their girl's night?" Joker asks us.

"Yep." Is our only response.

"Already called Slim and gave him a heads up. He's clearin' rooms for us and sendin' me the address of where to meet them. We'll hang back and watch them for a bit before we let them know we're there." Grim lets us all know. "Plus, Crash and Trojan will be meetin' us at the halfway point. Apparently, Darcy is with them."

Going into the common room, we see that Ma followed through on her statement about it being a kid zone. There's blankets, pillows, stuffed animals, games, and a ton of other stuff spread out. Couches have been moved so the kids can still watch t.v when they lay down for the night, and the tables are pushed so they can't get close to the bar. The men from Blaze's crew are standing guard while watching the kids with laughter in their eyes.

"Say bye to your daddy's." Ma says.

We all hug and kiss our kids before heading out to the bikes. Looks like Slim Jim will be driving the SUV back with his bike in a trailer. There's no way I'm not having my girl wrapped around me on the way back here tomorrow. Pulling out, we ride in formation and head to the women our worlds revolve around.

As Grim said, Crash and Trojan meet us at the halfway point. They get in behind us as we keep riding. I'm not saying we are, but there's a chance that we're pushing the speed limit a little. The only thing I can think about is seeing my girl in her red dress that looked skimpy as fuck. I didn't see much, but what I did see almost made me tie her to the bed after she put it on. I've been around the rest of the girls long enough to know that when they go out, they don't hold back. They all dress sexy as hell and the men wherever they are, want to push up on them. I know how my brothers feel about this, and I couldn't agree more. There is no way that any man is going to put his hands on what is mine.

We've been at the club, watching the girls, for about an hour now. They've danced in a group, had a few drinks, and now they're back on the dance floor. As soon as we walked in, I pulled my hat down low over my eyes and we all took up spots along one wall. The men in the club are leaving us alone and the women are trying to get something that doesn't belong to them. None of us have eyes for anyone but our own girl though.

I've watched Melody shake her ass and do things with her body that have me imagining all sorts of dirty things I want to do to her. My girl is sexy as fuck, flexible beyond belief, and watching her sway her hips has me adjusting my cock. Melody is currently dancing with Darcy and Crash, Trojan, and myself can't take our eyes off them. I swear to all that I love, if I were into sharing my angel, Darcy would be high on that list right now.

Unfortunately, some random douchebag decides now would be a good time to try to stake his claim on our girls. Melody and Darcy try to be polite and shut him out, but this guy just won't take a hint. Just as Crash and Trojan go to make a move, I see Wood coming out of nowhere. He's stalking through the crowd like it doesn't exist to get to them. Stopping the two men, I wait to see how this is going to play out. Wood better know what the fuck he's doing.

Melody

I've never had so much fun in my life. Dancing, having a few drinks, and dancing some more is something I've been missing in my life. I could do without the shots that we've had tonight, making me tipsy, but we're out to have fun and it's going to happen.

Since making our way back to the dance floor, I am dancing with Darcy. Kiera is off in a corner making out with some random guy. Guess it's a good thing that Blade chose to stay at the clubhouse with Maddie's brother. Her dad is around here somewhere though. As soon as I saw her dad, my jaw hit the floor. Glock is the only man I'll ever love and share my life with. But, Slim is hot as hell. And the power that radiates off him is something I've never seen before. With one look he can command an entire room.

Darcy and I are dancing like no one is there but us until a man I don't know tries to push his way in between us. I look at her and we try stepping away from him. This guy is either stupid, or too drunk to realize that we want nothing to do with him because he just doesn't get the hint. As I see him about to put his hands on Darcy, I speak up.

"Excuse me, I'm trying to dance with my friend." I say.

"Yeah, but there's always room for a man sweetheart. You can both dance with me." He says, trying again to put his hands on Darcy.

"Listen, I'm sure you're a great guy and all," Darcy begins, "But if you touch me with your grubby ass hands, I'll put your ass on the floor and walk all over it."

Before anyone can say anything else, I see Wood, who we met at Slim's club, on his way over to us. He grabs the guy's shirt and pulls him away from us.

"I've been standin' over there watchin' these two girls try to dance and have a good time. Then you come over and try to insert yourself where you're not wanted. I suggest you leave before I make you leave."

"You don't get a say in who they dance with." The guy blurts out.

"I might not, but their men certainly do."

Before we can question anything else, the guy goes to take a swing at Wood and misses wildly. Wood takes a step back and collides with Darcy. She has no way to stop her momentum so Wood grabs her around the waist as they both tumble towards the floor. Somehow, he spins midway down and she lands on top of him. The only thing I can hear is his 'oomph' as they hit the floor. Darcy lets her hands roam his upper body for a second before she's pulled off of him.

Two men, looking sexy as hell and pissed the fuck off, place her between them while they stare down the guy trying to dance with us and Wood. I can't move an inch, I want to see what's going to happen too bad to move, or look away. And then one of the men speak as I feel an arm wrap around my waist, startling me until I see that it's Glock.

"Wood, we'll deal with you in a minute." The guys grit out.

"Fuck my life." Is muttered from Wood as he gets up off the floor.

"Crash get the fuck out of here!" Darcy shrieks, trying to push away from the two men.

"Not happenin', spitfire. You're ours and you should know it by now." The other man says, snaking his arm around her waist possessively.

"Fuck off, Trojan. How many times do I have to tell you Neanderthals that?"

"Now, fuck face, you try to move in on somethin' that doesn't belong to you and then you try to make them dance with you when they don't want to. If they say no, they fuckin' mean no! Now, I'm goin' to give you one second to get your scrawny, nasty, desperate ass out of here, before we help you with that."

The guy takes off without a second's hesitation. Crash and Trojan now turn their attention to Wood. He stands there shaking his head and looks at Darcy. This must be the guy they were telling me about on our way here.

"Don't fuckin' look at her Wood." Trojan grits out. "Why is it every time you two are in the same place, you have your hands on him and he's got his cock near you?"

"I guess it's just my good luck!" Darcy says, staring between the two men. "You don't have a say in whose cock comes near me so back the fuck off!"

"We told you spitfire. You are ours and we're gonna make sure you know that." Crash says.

"Wood, I think I want to go back to the clubhouse now. These two ass clowns will be heading back where they came from." Darcy says before turning her back to them.

"Wrong spitfire. You wanna leave, you leave with us. Wood can find his own entertainment for the night."

"I'm not going anywhere with you! Mel, I'm leaving this area. There's too much testosterone for me right now. I'll be at the table."

I watch my new friend walk away and look between all the guys surrounding me. Glock looks amused, Wood looks defeated, Crash looks pissed off as he watches Darcy walk away, and Trojan looks ready to murder Wood. The only thing I can think is that these two have their work cut out for them if they think playing caveman is going to win her over. She's got something going on and we haven't been able to get it out of her yet.

"Well, that was fun." I murmur, losing my buzz a little bit. "What are you doing here?"

"We all came to be with our girls. The rest of the guys are here too." Glock tells me.

"Okay. Where are the kids?"

"Back at our clubhouse with Ma, Pops, and some nomads. We've been here a while watchin' you."

"I see. Let us have our girl's night out but make sure we don't cause trouble?"

"Nope. We were moody bastards and Ma kicked us out. Told us to come be with you."

"Oh. Well, then let's dance big man."

Glock doesn't say a word as he turns me so my back is against his front and we find our rhythm. I never once thought I would get him on a dance floor with me. Mainly because I never thought I'd be able to go out like this. Surprisingly, Glock does know how to dance and make me feel every inch of how much he wants me right now.

"When we get back, you're mine. All night." He murmurs in my ear before biting down on it.

"You think you're up for it?" I ask, rubbing my ass back against him.

"I'll take you right here angel. Don't tempt me unless you want to put a show on."

"Never tried that before. Why don't you find a place to take me then?"

Glock stands back and looks at me for a full minute before taking my hand and dragging me from the dance floor. He's looking all over for some place to take me. I know there's no way he's going to put a show on for anyone. He won't let anyone see me, I'm his and for his eyes only.

"Let's go outside." He tells me. "This is gonna be fast and hard angel. You good with that?"

"Mmmhmm." I mutter. Right now, I'll take him any way I can get him.

After opening the back door, I can already hear muffled moans and groans. Apparently, we're not the only one with this idea. Glock must change his mind about going outside because he quickly turns around.

"I'm not fuckin' you with someone else right next to us. We'll find somewhere else, angel."

"I'm following your lead big man."

For about ten minutes, Glock continues to look for somewhere to take me. At this point, I'm ready to say fuck it and give up looking. But, I know he won't change his mind and he'll get me back in the mood in no time. It looks like he found somewhere anyway as he's leading us towards the front of the club with his phone to his ear. Now really isn't the time to be on the phone, but what do I know.

Glock takes us to the corner farthest from the door and I see that it's almost completely dark. Every now and then one of the lights from the dance floor sheds a little light on the area, but for the most part it's dark. He pulls a chair over with us and I see a line of his brothers appear out of nowhere. They form a line in front of us with their backs facing us.

"Told you no one sees what's mine." Glock says, sitting down in the chair. "Can't have you against the wall with your tattoo so you're gonna ride me."

"Um…" I start to say.

"It's fine, angel. I'll let you know if you're doin' somethin' wrong, but I highly doubt it. Remember, hard and fast."

He sits down in the chair and opens his jeans so that just his cock is out. Before I straddle his thighs, I lean down and take him in my mouth. Immediately his hands thrust into my hair and control how much I take of him in my mouth. Just as I find my rhythm, Glock pulls me off of him and runs one of his hands up under my dress. Other than looking up at me, and finding out I'm not wearing any panties, he says nothing. I can feel my breathing pick up and come out in short pants as he inserts a finger in me to make sure I'm ready for him.

"You're so wet angel. I love it" He murmurs, pulling his finger from me and sucking it into his mouth. "Climb up."

Taking a peek behind me, I see the guys are still facing forward and that they haven't moved an inch. So, I face Glock again and straddle him while he lines his cock up with my entrance. I have never had sex this way, and I don't know how he expects me to do this without knowing what to do. Before I can think my way out of it though, he grips my hips and pulls me down on him as he thrusts his hips up. Instantly I'm filled with him and a moan escapes me.

"My noises angel. You need to make noise, bite me or kiss me. No one hears but me." He growls out while helping me move the way he needs me to.

Right from the start, the pace is fast and Glock meets me thrust for thrust. Soon, he lets go of my hips and pulls me to his mouth while moving one hand down to play with my clit. There's no way he's baring my chest so someone might see. With his torturous playing and pinching, I can feel my release starting to build and my movements start to become faster. Knowing I'm so close, I move my head in to take Glock's mouth with mine. Without hesitation, he opens up to me and I can feel a moan try to escape only to be swallowed by him.

"Give. It. To. Me." Glock growls out with every upward thrust.

That's all I need to push me over as he pinches my clit once more. I grind myself down on him as he continues to thrust into me. A few thrusts from him later and I can feel him tighten up and bite down on the spot just under my ear. A growl escapes him as he holds me in place and breathes heavily into my neck.

We continue to sit there for a few minutes while we get ourselves under control again. He rubs my back gently as I lean into him and wrap my arms around his neck. My face is buried in his neck as I struggle to get my breathing back to normal. I don't know if it's the alcohol or the fact that we could've been caught at any moment, but I've never been so turned on in my life.

"You like that, angel?" He asks finally.

"Mmhmm." Is the only answer I can murmur.

"Let's go get cleaned up. We're gonna be headin' back to Slim's in a few minutes and you're on my bike."

"In this dress?" I ask.

"Yep. You'll wear my coat and the clubhouse is only a few minutes away. No one will see anythin' with you wrapped around me."

Heading to the bathroom, I expect to hear comments from the guys or looks. They give no sign of what just happened and that they were a human shield. At the very least I expected some sort of comment made to Glock and there's just nothing. The girls on the other hand aren't so quiet about it. Following me into the bathroom, I hear all sorts of comments about fucking Glock in the club. Now all I want to do is leave and hide away for the rest of the night. It's a good thing we're leaving.

Chapter Fifteen
Glock

IT'S BEEN A FEW DAYS since the girls had their night out and things have been going good with Melody. The day after we got back, we went to the doctor and found out that it is possible for her to have more kids. My girl shed tears of happiness and we decided that it will happen when it happens. We also had a long talk about everything that was bothering her and we hashed it all out. Now, she knows where we stand and that if anything I'm the one that doesn't deserve her. Yeah, she's been through hell but that doesn't mean that she's no good for me. It means that I know she's a strong ass woman that has been through something horrible. Instead of letting it get her down, she's thrown herself into raising our boy and learning what it means to be my old lady.

Don't get me wrong, she hasn't dealt with everything that has happened to her. And I know that she's going to break down one of these days. We also talked about that. When she feels it's time, she's going to talk to Karen again. Right now, she's not ready to voice everything that happened to her. So, I'll be by her side and catch her when she falls.

"Glock, need ya brother." Grim calls walking out of his office.

"What's goin' on?" I ask, standing up and following him towards the main door.

"Got cops and a couple out here."

Immediately I know that shit's about to hit the fan. There's no doubt in my mind that it's my angel's parents here trying to stir shit up. Too bad for them that they're not going to find anything here and my girl and son aren't going anywhere near them. They can see for themselves that Melody and

Anthony are fine and then head back to the hole they crawled out of.

"Can I help you officer?" Grim asks, flinging the clubhouse door open before the cop can knock on it.

"I'm looking for a Melody Michaels and her son." The officer says. It's one that we've had run ins with before and he wasn't happy that he couldn't get shit on us then. I can only imagine what's running through his mind now.

"I'll get her." I say before turning and walking to our room.

Opening the door, I see Melody and Anthony sitting on our bed reading a book. Anthony loves to read to us these days. He takes every opportunity to read to us and only lets us read at bed time. After watching them for a minute, I walk in the door further and wait until Melody sees me.

"What's wrong?" She asks, seeing the anger on my face.

"Got a cop out here looking for you and our boy. Your parents are here." I tell her.

"You kidding me right now?"

"I wish I were angel. Need the two of you to come out so the officer can see you. It's up to you what you do from there." I tell her, silently letting her know that I will never keep her here.

"You know I'm not going anywhere. I'm home and no one is going to make us leave." She says defiantly.

Before I can say another word, Melody storms past me and heads out to the front. I grab Anthony and follow her knowing that the cop will want to see him too. Now, I need to get out there before Melody does something that can't be undone. Rounding the corner, I see Grim standing right next to my girl, almost as if he's holding her back from going on the attack. If Anthony didn't have to be here to see the cop, I would be turning around right now as my angel's words hit my ears.

"Officer, as you can see I'm fine." Melody starts, turning to look at us. "There's my son and you can see he's fine as well."

"Melody, oh my baby girl." Her mom says, wiping away fake tears. "We've been looking all over for you. We want you and your son to come home."

I don't miss the way that her mom says 'your son'. There's no way in hell that this bitch is going to get away with acting like Anthony is not my son. He is all me and everyone that spends one minute with him knows it.

"Mom, cut your bullshit. The only reason you want anything to do with us is to beat the sin out of us. Remember telling my friend that? Because you both did, on multiple occasions. Or is to beat the shit out of me some more? I mean, unless you've started smacking around Mom?" She says, looking at her dad.

"I don't know what you're talking about." Her dad finally pipes in.

"Yes, you do. You want me back so that you have someone to beat the shit out of and to take your anger out on. You're pissed that I didn't follow your orders and that I fell in love with someone that wouldn't treat me like a slave and beat the shit out of me. Glock is more of a man than any one of your followers. He treats our son with love and doesn't backhand him for making a mistake. When it comes to me, he shows me his love in multiple ways. Including letting me experience anything I want to for the first time. Officer, I'm sorry that they've wasted your time. But this is my home and I'm not being held here against my will." Melody says, flooring Grim and me.

"Thank you, ma'am. If you ever need anything, here's my card. Don't hesitate to call." The officer tells her.

As he's leaving, I see Melody's parents standing there, glaring at her. Now, it's my turn to talk. Melody played nice while the cop was here and now they're going to get a piece of my mind. We've all lost out on so much because of them. I'm not standing for it anymore. They are done playing games with my girl and son.

"This isn't over you little bitch!" Melody's mom speaks.

"Yes, it is." I say, striding up to the doorway after handing Anthony over to Summer. "You will *never* come around my girl again. *My* son will never know the kind of hypocritical assholes you truly are. You want to stand there on your high horse and try to control your daughter instead of lettin' her live her life by her own terms. I'm givin' you one warnin' to leave here and never come back. If I see you again, you'll be worm food before you can blink. Do I make myself clear?"

"You have no right to talk to us, you piece of trash. You're the reason our daughter is a sinner to begin with. We will have her back with us one way or another. Her and her bastard of a son."

Before anyone can say another word, the two turn and leave. Melody watches them leave. She's still standing in the doorway and her back is as straight as she can get it. It almost looks like she's holding her breath, waiting for them to leave. Like if she breathes, they'll turn around and start spouting more shit at her. Personally, I'm waiting for them to turn around and try to say something more. I'll pull my gun from my jeans so fast they won't know what hit them. They have no place in Melody and Anthony's lives. Not while I'm around.

"Angel, you okay?" I ask, as I see their car pulling out spitting gravel and dirt in their attempt to get out of here.

"I'm fine. I'm sorry you guys have to deal with this. If I thought they were going to find us here, I never would've come here." She tells us, and I can see the tears shimmering in her eyes.

"Is what you said true?" Grim asks, completely ignoring her comment about not coming here.

"Yes. I know Glock saw my dad backhand me the day I was forced to leave. That was pretty tame to what happened."

At Melody's statement, I see red. I knew he laid his hands on her, but I am betting it's even worse than what I thought. If I find out he did more to her, then I'm going to have fun doing every single thing they did to her to them. No one will stand in my way of getting to them. Even if I have to go alone, I will get my hands on them.

"Melody, I hate to say this, but we're gonna need to talk to you in church. If they're goin' to be a threat, we need to know as much as possible about what they did to you. If you know why they're pickin' now to come after you, we need to know that too. I'm callin' it for a half hour from now. That okay?" Grim says, stepping to her as if he were trying to protect her.

"Yeah. I figured this was coming. I'm sorry you have to hear this Glock. I never wanted you to know." My girl says, with tears in her eyes and one rolling a slow path down her cheek.

"Angel, there's nothin' you can say that's gonna make me think less of you. And no one outside those walls will know unless you tell them." I tell her, pulling her to my side and wrapping my arms around her.

"I know. I trust you all and I know that none of you will betray that unless it's absolutely necessary for others to know. It will be good for me to get this part out. I'm not saying that I'm going to go into detail about my kidnapping and what happened while I was there, but information about my parents I will."

Damn, my girl is strong. She's going to stand up in front of a group of men she's still getting to know to tell her story. And she's putting her faith in us to keep it to ourselves after the fact. Not many people would put that much faith in people after she's been through everything she has. I'm so fucking proud of her right now.

Melody

The last thing I expected when we got up this morning was for my parents to bring the cops to the front door of the clubhouse. They have some nerve to think that I would willingly leave with them. I meant every word when I said that I was home and that I wasn't going anywhere. Now, I don't know what's going to happen though. Not everyone might like what they hear today.

"Angel, you about ready?" Glock asks, breaking me out of my head.

"Yeah. Let's get this over with." I tell him, standing up and letting him lead me into the room they use for church.

Everyone is already there and seated around a massive table. At this point, Grim and Glock are the only two that really looked pissed. I know that will change when they all find out about the cops being here though.

"Alright," Grim starts, banging the gavel down. "We're here because we had a visit from the cops a little while ago. Melody's parents tried to get them involved sayin' we kidnapped her and their son. Melody let her parents have it and they did leave a warning that this wasn't over yet. So, she's here to give us all the information she can about them."

"In order for me to let you know everything about my parents, you need some back story. Please, don't interrupt me until the end and I need somewhere to be that's not right next to Glock. It's nothing against you babe, I just need to feel like I'm standing on my own and that you're not going to be there to protect me if you guys want me to get through everything."

No one says anything, but Grim motions for me to go stand next to him at the head of the table. Without looking back at Glock, I make my way over and look at no one. There's a spot on the wall that I focus on as I begin my story.

"Growing up, my dad was always a minister. The rules in the house were strict and punishment for me was always swift and painful. But always done in a way that there would be no visible bruising or anything like that. Not that any of my dad's followers would have said anything to anyone outside of the church. See, my dad isn't a minister for any type of church you have heard of. He's basically the leader of a cult." I pause as I let that sink in. "That's why we moved in the first place. My dad was running from charges being pressed against him. After that happened, my punishments got worse. It was almost like I was being punished for breathing most days. These ranged from having his belt on my ass, standing on a board with the tips of nails poking through for hours, being searched daily, kneeling on that same board, and finally the physical abuse started shortly after I started getting paired with Glock for projects. The last straw for them was finding out that I was pregnant before I had a chance to let Glock know. They shipped me off to an aunt's house that would keep me until the baby was given up for adoption. I knew there was no way I was going to give our baby up though. My plan was to run away and find Glock, one way or another. I just didn't have any idea about where to start."

I can hear Glock growling from his seat at the table. He knows that I'm not telling the whole story. Even if he doesn't know anything about the situation, he knows there's no way that I'm not leaving things out right now. It's just how it is with us.

"Yes, babe, I'm leaving things out. You guys don't need to hear everything they did to me. Or what my aunt tried to do to me while I was with her. If it weren't for my cousin, I don't know how I would've gotten out of there."

"You need to tell us everythin' angel. Why leave the shit out?" He asks, barely containing his rage at my parents.

"It's not important to the story. You all know they abused me and hid behind their fucked-up religion. That's enough of that part for now. Maybe, one day when I'm ready, I'll tell you the whole story Glock. Now, let me continue. Please." I silently plead with him, finally meeting his eyes so he knows I want to finish it and go decompress.

"Anyway, my parents know a ton of different people from all walks of life. We're talking politicians, cartel members, law enforcement, judges, and a ton more. When they were all in my father's presence, they didn't have job titles or anything like that. It was just a group of people. I heard more than one conversation between multiple men about owing favors and keeping secrets. I don't know more than that and I don't want to. But, you could pretty much tell which guys were in the cartel and which ones were not. My dad is 'owed' a lot of favors by them. Which is strange considering that the cartel is the one that wanted me and a few of the other girls. I'm surprised my parents didn't know where I was. Or maybe they have some sort of deal with the cartel to get me out of the way. I don't know and I really don't care. So, now you all know that my parents like to abuse children, they know people that scare the shit out of me, and that I'm sure there's a bigger plan in motion right now."

I am struggling to stay on my feet as I let them digest what I just laid on them. Grim must sense me swaying because in the blink of an eye, he's got his arm around me and leading me to Glock, who also made it out of his chair in a second. The guys are just looking at me as I'm led over to a couch sitting in the far corner. Glock cradles me in his lap as the guys talk amongst themselves. Faint murmurs are the only things I hear as they talk and try to use the information I gave them to come up with a plan of attack.

"Sweetheart, I have a question for you." Pops says, turning to face me in his chair.

"What is it?" I ask, interrupting Glock as he goes to speak.

"You said you could tell which guys were in the cartel. How is that?"

"They were among the few that followed my dad when we moved. So, not only did they have the money to follow him, but it was the way they dressed and acted. You could just tell they held themselves above the law and there was a hierarchy they followed."

"Okay sweetheart. Would you be able to pick them out if you saw them again?" Pops continues.

"Yeah. That was one of the reasons I was glad that I got sent away. They were in the process of setting up an arranged marriage to one of the sons. The entire family creeped me out and I knew that it wasn't going to be a good situation if I were to be married to him. Getting sent away was the best thing that could've happened to me." I answer honestly.

Glock sits up straighter at my admission and wraps his arms even tighter around me. His hands cradle my head and he keeps my face buried in his neck. I don't need protecting anymore though. They can't take away anything else from me.

"Angel, why didn't you tell me? I would've figured somethin' out. Even if it meant goin' to the courthouse to marry you myself."

I gasp and lift my head up, looking in his eyes and seeing the truth shining down at me. Tears are gathering in mine, knowing that he was willing to go that far in order to protect me when we were barely more than kids. While we were spending time together and getting to know one another, I had hoped one day we would make it that far, but I never got my hopes up.

"Do you think that they're tryin' to get you back to make you go with this guy?" Grim asks.

"I don't know. It's been so long and I don't know what their end game is here."

"Angel, I'm dead serious. If I thought it would help keep you out of their clutches, I would marry you today. Already told you, you weren't goin' anywhere. You're mine!" Glock tells me, leaning in real close.

I don't even know what to say right now. Never in my wildest dreams did I let myself believe I'd really marry Glock. Maybe be a part of his life as far as Anthony was concerned, but that's it. As far as I was concerned the most we would be was co-parents after he got over being angry that he didn't know about Anthony from the very beginning.

"You serious Glock?" Pop asks, with every other guy looking at us. "You gonna marry this girl?"

"I would marry her in an instant Pop. The only thing she has to say is yes." Glock says looking at me.

"I don't know about that Glock. We're just getting to know one another again." I say hesitantly.

I want to marry Glock, but it's really soon. I mean, our house isn't done yet and Anthony is just settling back into a routine. Unfortunately, I can feel everyone's eyes focused on the two of us. Glock is even staring down at me. My face is turning red if the heat I can feel is anything to go by. I guess I'm giving them an answer now and not waiting for another time.

"Well, if I have to give an answer now," I begin, "I say yes. It's always been you Glock. I don't want to do it tomorrow, or anything like that, but I will marry you."

"You have one month to plan it angel. That's what I'm givin' you. Now we have somethin' else to discuss too." Glock says, looking around the room.

"What's goin' on?" Grim asks.

"I had a talk with Kiera and she wants to know when she can leave here. I don't want her on her own yet though." Glock answers.

"What do you mean she wants to leave?" I ask, shocked and hurt that she went to Glock about this instead of me.

"Somethin' is goin' on with her and she wants to leave. She knew you'd pick it up in a heartbeat and didn't want to talk to you just yet about it. I'm sorry angel, I don't know what it is."

"Blade, if you hurt her, I swear I'll kick your nuts down your throat!" I scream out, knowing that this has something to do with him. Fuck!

"I didn't do anythin' to her. I have no clue why she wants to leave or that she did. Guess I should go talk to her." Blade says, starting to stand up.

"No." Glock says immediately. "She doesn't want to talk to you either. All she'll tell me is that it's time to move on."

Grim sits up and I can tell he's thinking about how to handle this situation so that no one gets hurt or pissed off. I'm not pissed off right now, I'm hurt beyond belief though. What is going on that she won't even talk to me about? We've been through a lot together during our friendship. Hell, she was with me when I had Anthony so I really have nothing to hide from her. It's upsetting to know that she can't say the same thing.

"Let me call Slim. I'll see if he can use the help somewhere so she can work and keep an eye on her." Grim says, looking at Blade.

"I don't like this prez. She needs to be here where we can keep an eye on her." Blade returns. "Let me talk to her and see what's goin' on. Then we can call Slim if she still wants to leave."

I just sit back against Glock and listen to everyone around me. Well, I try to. Really, I'm trying to figure out what's making my best friend want to up and run. Not a lot scares her and I know a little bit about the few things that do scare her. One thing is giving her heart away again. She was in a relationship just before I met her and the guy didn't know how to keep it in his pants. Kiera was the last to know and it devastated her. The one and only time she opens herself up, that happens. From that day forward it was one night, maybe two, and the guy was history. Blade is the first guy that captured her attention for longer than that which is how I know something happened.

Blade

Glock saying that Kiera wants to leave is a fucking shock to say the least. The last I knew, everything was good with us. Hell, I haven't touched anyone since I saw her when Slim Jim and I got to her house to help move them here. Something about all her red hair and vibrant green eyes pulled me in and hasn't let go since. She's everything that I've never liked in a woman and I can't get her out of my system.

Kiera is short and curvy. While I like my girls curvy, I don't necessarily like them short. Even in a pair of fuck me heels, Kiera doesn't come to my shoulder. Granted I'm over six-foot-tall, but heels should get her closer to my shoulders at least. Not my kitten though. Which is another thing that I don't usually like. She has no problem standing up to a man more than twice her size. With a mouth on her that puts most men I know to shame and the lack of being scared of a fight leads me to believe that I'll be fighting men more than not. Kitten is a good name for her. She's small and has no problem bringing her claws out to do some damage to you if you provoke her.

With Grim's permission, I leave church and head to my room. Right now, I'm hoping that's where she is so that we can talk. The closer I get to my door, the more noise I can hear. It's muffled with the door being closed, but I can hear packing and sobs. Why is she crying? Something is definitely wrong with this. Just this morning we were having a good time. After another round of the best sex I've ever had, we laid in bed talking.

Kiera got on the subject of kids. I don't know why, other than all the time she spent raising Anthony. She made a comment about how good I am with the kids and I let my feelings be quite known. I have no problem with kids. Hell, I love the kids around the clubhouse. When it comes to having my own kids, there's no way in hell that's ever going to happen. I have my reasons and I haven't shared them with a soul. I'm not about to start now. Even after that talk, my kitten was good.

Opening the door, I stop dead in my tracks. Kiera has almost everything she brought with her packed back up. In the middle of all the boxes and bags, she's sitting on the floor curled into herself. Her tears are just loud enough that she doesn't hear me enter the room and I make it right next to her before she realizes that she's not alone anymore.

"What's goin' on kitten?" I ask, crouching down next to her.

"Nothing."

"Then why you leavin'? I thought you were gonna move in with Glock and Melody for a while. Their house should be done in a few days and you can have your own space if that's what the problem is." I tell her, debating whether or not to reach out to her right now.

"I'm not getting in the way of them learning to love one another again. I would just be in the way." Kiera says, sitting up and trying to stop the tears from falling. "Besides, it's time that I move on. They have their life and I need to get on with mine."

"Okay. I thought we were havin' fun though. We good?"

"Yeah, we're good Blade. Neither one of us wanted more than fun. So, it was good while it lasted and now it's time to move on."

"If nothin' is wrong, why didn't you go to your girl? Why did you go to Glock instead to ask about this shit?" I ask, starting to get mad that she's calling quits on us.

"Nothing is wrong. Melody couldn't get me an answer even if she wanted to. So, why make her the middle man when I can go to Glock in the beginning? Now my stuff is all packed and ready to go. I'm just waiting to hear what the verdict is."

"You won't change your mind?" I ask, needing to make sure this is what she really wants.

"I'm not gonna change my mind Blade. I'm sure you're ready to get back to the easy pussy of the club girls and anyone else that wants a ride on a biker's cock." Kiera says before leaving my room.

I don't know how it happened, but I feel like my heart was just ripped out. Kiera got under my skin and I wanted to make something last with her. That's not something I take lightly because I've never wanted to commit to anyone. Easy pussy with no strings attached is the only thing I've ever wanted. It's not that I can't commit to someone, because I can. There's a reason for everything that I believe in and know is the way I want to live my life. Like the kid thing. My kitten is on birth control and we still used condoms. I don't take chances with this.

Falling on my ass, I look around my room at all of her things packed up. Part of me wants to rip the boxes to shreds and unpack every single item in here. Then maybe she'll get the hint that she's not going anywhere. I can't do that to her though. She's the one that put the limitations on us and I'm going to respect that. Even if it breaks my heart. So, I head back to church to let Grim know to call Slim and send her there.

Kiera

Telling Blade that I wanted to leave is one of the hardest things I've ever had to do. For my own reasons, it's time to go. Leaving everyone here is going to be hard, but I don't have a choice anymore. That choice left me this morning. Now, I have to find the courage to tell Melody a little bit without letting her know my true reasons. No one can know right now.

I find her walking towards her room and she pulls me along behind her. As soon as we get inside, she shuts the door and turns to look at me. Melody is trying to look in my face to see what's going on so I am making sure that I keep a blank mask firmly in place.

"Why?" Is the only word that leaves her mouth.

"I have to. It's time Mel. You and Glock are getting your life on track again and I'm not going to stand in the way of that. This is your time to grow, learn new things, and celebrate finding the man you love again." I tell her.

"Okay, but why do you have to leave here? Why can't we find you an apartment or something close by?"

"Mel, I'm still going to be close enough that we can visit. We'll talk all the time on the phone, and things will get back to normal. I just want to give the three of you a little time to get back to one another."

"I can't change your mind?"

"No, you can't babe. This is something I need to do."

"Okay. You better be back here in a month though. I'm not taking any excuses for you not showing up either."

"Why, what's going on?" I ask, intrigued.

"I'm getting married."

I stand there with my mouth opening and closing a few times. That is the last thing that I expected to hear coming from her mouth right now. This just makes me realize that I am making the right decision for everyone by moving on.

"What? How did this happen?" I ask, letting the excitement fill my voice.

"After I got done telling my story and Glock found out about the arranged marriage my parents were planning. He basically told me he would've married me then and he'd marry me today if I let him." She tells me, leaving out some things that I'll get out of her later.

"Okay. Well, I'll be back in a month then. We'll have to plan a bachelorette party and shit. Damn, I'm happy for you!"

Melody and I spend a little bit more time talking and laughing like we used to do before Glock comes in and tells me that Wood and Boy Scout will be here in an hour or so to get me. I still don't have a car, so they're driving a van down. Knowing that we still have things to talk about, he kisses Melody and leaves us alone again. He's going to make her so happy. She deserves it and I'll still be around for all the important things.

Before leaving, Anthony runs in to spend some time with me. Man, I'm going to miss this kid. He was my entire world for just over six months while his mom was gone. My days started and ended with making sure I was raising him the way that I knew Mel would want him raised and protecting him like he was my own flesh and blood. No one is more important in the world to me than Mel and her son. For now, anyways.

Tears are shed as I walk out the door. I'm crying more than Mel and Anthony combined I think. It's probably just the hormones though. Still, I don't turn around and see what I'm walking away from. I can't because I know I won't leave if I do. For a little while, I have to put some separation between us until I can spill everything to Melody without breaking down. I'm already leaving part of my heart behind, he just doesn't know it.

Chapter Sixteen
Melody

TODAY IS THE DAY we're going shopping for furniture and everything else that's needed at the house. The girls and I are going to Phantom Bastard territory and taking along a prospect or two. Darcy is meeting us there and I can't wait to see what kind of trouble we cause. Anthony is ready to hang out with his dad today. At least until Ma comes to get him so that Glock and a few guys can get some work done.

"Angel, you ready to go?" Glock asks, walking in the room.

"Yep." I respond, continuing to put my makeup on. I don't use a lot, mainly just some mascara and lip gloss.

"You guys have fun and don't worry about money. Bailey has the card and she knows there's no limit."

"Um….okay. I don't know what all you expect me to get besides the furniture." I start to tell him.

"It doesn't matter what you get. Just make sure it's what you would want in a home. It's not just about me or Anthony. Your wants and needs matter too." Glock tells me, leaning in for a kiss. To him, it doesn't matter if he ends up wearing my lip gloss or not. He wants a kiss, he takes one.

"Okay. You might be in trouble though." I say, trying to hide the smirk gracing my face.

"Why is that?" He asks, holding me to him.

"I might just end up having a spending problem, and you might end up with no money what so ever." I tell him, wrapping my arms around his neck and pulling him in close.

"You keep that up angel and you won't be goin' anywhere."

After planting a kiss on his open mouth, I wiggle out of his arms and go in search of the rest of the girls. They're all waiting in the common room for me, with smirks on their faces. I know immediately what they think was going on and why I took so long. Unfortunately, that is not the case since Anthony wanted to give me a list a mile long about what he wanted in his bedroom.

"Not what you're thinking guys. Let's get a move on before they decide we can't go." I say, knowing that I just left Glock hanging back there.

Just as we're heading out the door, I hear him tell me that I'll pay for it later. I'm hoping that I do. Glock told me once before that we'll try different things, anything that I want. I'm going to hold him to that.

We've made it to a furniture store where Slim and a prospect meet us. Slim Jim and one of the new prospects followed us so we could have our girl time. We laughed so hard we were crying at some points the entire ride. The only time they weren't directly behind us was when Darcy pulled in between us and the bikes so that the men could have eyes on all of us.

"Daddy," Maddie calls out as she runs towards the president of the Phantom Bastards. "Thanks for giving us Boy Scout again."

"You think I would do anythin' less knowin' my girl and her friends are in town?" He asks, wrapping her up in a hug.

"No. It's still nice that I get to see you."

"Yeah sweetheart it is. Now, you girls behave yourselves and I'll see you before you leave."

Walking into the furniture store, my eyes wander all over everything at once. Deciding to start with the living room, we make our way over as a salesman meets us. I tell him what I want and he leads us to the right section of the store. Bailey's already spoken up and told him that we'll be getting the same amount as her if not more.

"Start with the couches and work your way towards the back of the store for the living room." He tells us. "You'll find everything from couches, recliners, tables, lamps, and everything else in between."

After he walks away, I start looking at the furniture to pick out the pieces for our new home. Skylar is writing everything down so that it's easier when we're done. She'll just hand over the paper with the numbers on it and they'll pull everything to hold until the house is completed and ready for us to move in.

Within an hour, I've picked out everything that we'll need as far as the furniture is concerned. Maddie is hungry so we all decide to head to a diner they came to the last time they were here, Rosie's. Apparently, you don't get to order what you want to eat, they just bring you out food, drinks, everything. It seems crazy to me but I'll go with it.

"So," Darcy begins when we're all seated, "How long do you think it's going to be before the cavemen decide to follow us down here?"

"I give it about another hour or so. Hell, I'm sure they're already on their way." Bailey says matter of factly.

"They are. Ma already sent a text." Skylar announces. "And that includes Crash and Trojan."

"What the hell is up with those two asses?" Darcy asks, like she is truly in the dark.

"I'm new here and I can see that those two men are head over heels for you Darcy." I tell her.

"No, they just want someone that won't give it up when they snap their fingers. I'm not about to become the middle to whatever thing they have going on."

We all start laughing because we know that Darcy is well and truly fucked. Crash and Trojan won't give up until they have her right where they want her. She just doesn't realize what we already know. I can't wait to watch this unfold.

After filling up on burgers, fries, and the best dessert I've ever had in my life, we're on our way to the department store. Each one of us grabs a cart so that we can get everything we're going to need besides groceries. The girls follow me up and down every aisle as I pick and choose what to get. I ask for their opinions when I can't decide what I like more, and I get a million different responses making my decision harder.

Just as we're heading past the clothing section, Darcy gets the bright idea to try on some lingerie. Not just her though, she wants us all to. I cannot see anything good coming from this. Especially when she announces that she wants us all to show one another what we've tried on. Yeah, no good is definitely going to come from this trip.

Darcy goes from rack to rack pulling different pieces off until her arms are overloaded with clothes. The rest of us are looking at her like she's lost her damn mind. Until Bailey kind of shrugs and follows Darcy's little tornado of activity. One by one we all begin to follow suit and take arm loads in the fitting rooms.

I've never worn anything like this, so I've just picked a few pieces here and there, including a few bra and panty sets that I saw and fell in love with. One by one we all put our first choice on and open our doors. The rest of the girls look good in varying degrees of nighties. Some are almost see through, Darcy's is almost completely see through and she's parading around like she's in her own home. I'm the most covered by far in a bra and panty set covered by a thin silk robe in the same deep, dark red.

"Damn Darcy!" Bailey says, looking at her. "You got a hot body. Can't wait to see Crash and Trojan drooling over that."

"Stop with them! They will never see all this." Darcy says, spinning around and smacking her own ass.

I'm the first one back in my dressing room and changing my set. This time I'm choosing a short nightie that's little more than a see-through scrap of silk. There's a matching robe that is just a little bit longer, but only reaches the middle of my thigh. Before I can tie the robe, I hear a commotion right outside the doors. It sounds like there's yelling and someone possibly hitting something in the aisles surrounding the fitting room.

Opening the door, I see that the rest of the girls have also opened theirs. Crash and Trojan are standing between Darcy and Wood. Oh no, not again! Wood is leaning against the fitting room counter holding his nose and I can see blood dripping down his hand. Just as I go to look back towards Darcy, movement catches my eye and I look up to see all of our men standing there with their mouths open. Fuck! This is *definitely* not going to end well!

My eyes search out Glock and I can see the anger, lust, heat, and frustration all swirling for dominance. All of those emotions I can deal with. If I see disappointment in his eyes, for any reason, I won't be able to handle that. Disappointment is an emotion that I've become familiar with throughout my life. My parents were constantly disappointed in me, as were the members of their "church." So, I never want to see it shining from Glock's eyes. Ever.

"What the fuck are you doin'?" Grim asks. We know he's mainly talking to Bailey, but he's looking at all of us.

"It was my idea, Grim." Darcy says. "Lingerie is my one guilty pleasure and I couldn't resist."

"Okay." Cage says. "That doesn't mean you all have to parade around out of the fittin' rooms for everyone in the fuckin' place to see what belongs to us."

"No one else saw." Skylar pipes in.

"Wood, how much did you see?" Glock asks.

"Um, well, I saw Darcy. No one else, I swear it." He says, hesitantly.

I can hear growls coming from two men and I can only assume it's Crash and Trojan. Glock is steadily moving closer to me and I'm almost afraid of what he's going to do when he gets to me. The only thing I can see flaring in his eyes right now is hunger. A hunger that I haven't seen in years. This could get interesting in a hurry.

"Is there a problem here?" One of two security guards asks, coming up behind the men.

"No sir. No problem here." Darcy says, trying to cover herself.

"There's been several reports of a disturbance over here in the last few minutes. Now, I'm going to have to ask you ladies to get dressed and the men to come with us."

"Yes sir." I say, before turning to head back into the dressing room. "We'll get dressed and complete our purchases."

After shutting the door behind me, I hear the men grumbling and grow distant as they follow the security guards somewhere else. I'm glad I wasn't expecting this to be a normal day and that there was going to be some trouble caused. Now hopefully we can get the rest of what we need and be on our merry way.

Glock

I never expected to walk around the corner and see Melody, and the rest of the girls, standing there virtually naked in the middle of a department store. Before, Melody would have never done something like that. I'm honestly not mad about it at all, though Melody will be getting punished for allowing others to see what is mine. Though, I'm sure she'll like it before I'm done with her.

Melody is about to get taught the way that I truly like to fuck sometimes. I'm not hardcore into the punishment thing, but she will be getting a red ass. I haven't pushed her sexually up until this point in time, but I think things are about to get more interesting.

We all follow the wanna be cops to their office so they make it look like they know what they're doing. Hell, they think they're going to get something out of us and that's the last thing that's going to happen. Not a single one of us is going to tell them anything for their little 'report.' As we all follow them into their cramped little shoe box, we take up more room then is available. When I say their office is a shoe box, that's giving it more credit than what it deserves. Honestly, I don't know how they managed to fit two desks and a mini fridge in here.

"You," the security guard starts, "What happened to you?"

Wood stands up straighter and crosses his arms over his chest. "I don't know what you're talkin' about. Nothin' happened to me."

"That why you got a bloody nose and blood down the front of your shirt?" The second guard asks.

"Got hurt before I got in the store. Was workin' on my bike and the wrench slipped." Wood deadpans.

"That's your story, huh?"

"Yep. Now, you got what you need. I'm leavin'."

With that, we all file out of the little shoe box and make our way to the front of the store. The girls will have to get a few more things I'm sure, so we'll wait for them here. Grim looks at all of us and we make sure that Crash and Trojan are on one end while Wood is on the opposite end of all of us. They don't need to have any more communication right now. Not when the image of Darcy almost naked is still fresh in all their minds. Hell, all of our minds.

"You guys headin' back today or goin' to Slim's?" I ask no one in particular.

"We're goin' to Slim's." Grim answers. "What about you?"

"I think we'll probably head back today. I want to let Mel in on some things. Time to christen the new house I think." I answer seeing all the men smirk.

Yeah, they know what's about to happen when we get home. We don't need furniture in the house or anything else for what I have in mind. I'm perfectly happy to bend her ass over the kitchen counter, the bathroom counter, the seat in the shower, or anything else I can find. As long as there's carpet laid down, I'm content to lay down a blanket and take her there. Actually, that doesn't sound like a bad idea.

After waiting for almost another two hours for the girls to get done, we have loaded up two trucks, a van, and the bed of my truck. Everything will be fine while the guys are at Slim's clubhouse overnight. We're taking the stuff home with us that goes outside. She decided we need a swing, a table and chairs, a place for her to read, a bonfire pit, and a few other things. I'm surprised we fit it all in the truck, but we did.

"What are we doing when we get back?" Melody asks me.

"Headin' over to the house for a bit. Why?"

"Just asking. Are we taking Anthony over with us?"

"Not now. We need to have a talk and stuff. You're goin' to learn some things tonight that I like. If at any point in time it's too much, let me know and we'll stop. Immediately."

"I'm getting nervous." She tells me. "Are you sure I'm ready."

"We'll take it as slow as you need. But, we're goin' to start this now."

I can feel the nervousness radiating off of my angel. There's nothing for her to be nervous or scared about though. We are going to take this slow, as slow as she needs us to. Tonight, she'll just get a little taste of things to come. As time goes, I'll do more and more to her in order to get her ready.

While we were still waiting, I called Pops and Ma to get me what I need at the house. Rage was still working to finish everything up today, so he'll let Pops in before we get back. Now, I just hope my girl enjoys herself and lets herself open up enough to relax and just enjoy what happens tonight. I know I'm going to enjoy teaching her and teaching her new things.

"You won't tell me anything about what you're going to do?" She asks me, looking away from the passing scenery.

"No."

"If I guess?"

"No."

Melody huffs and crosses her arms over her chest. The only thing she's accomplishing is pushing up her tits so that I can see even more in the deep v neck of her shirt. If I weren't driving right now, I'd be diving head first into her chest. There's time for that later though, they will receive more than enough attention when I'm not concentrating on getting us back to Clifton Falls.

Pulling into the section where our house is being built, I park the truck and turn to face my angel. She's sleeping with her head against the window, her face full of peace. I know that it's one of the few times that she's been able to sleep without having a nightmare, but she won't talk about what they are.

I'm guessing that it's about the kidnapping and torture she went through, but I can't say for sure. The only thing I can tell her in those times is that I'm here when she wants to talk and I'll help her fight her demons off.

"Angel, we're here. Let's go inside." I tell her, putting my hand on her shoulder so she doesn't jump up and get hurt.

"Wh-what?" She asks.

"We're at the house angel. Let's go inside." I tell her again.

Melody gets up and out of the truck as she's rubbing the sleep from her eyes. I can still sense the fear of what I'm about to do to her radiating from her, but it's not quite as bad as before. She did say that she wanted to try new things, and this is just going to be a taste of that.

I lead her inside and see that there's a picnic basket sitting on the kitchen table along with a blanket folded up next to it. Rage isn't here any longer so there won't be any interruptions. The only other thing I need to check is the bathroom in our room. So, I grab everything from the counter and lead my girl upstairs. She's holding onto my hand with both of hers, but she's putting her trust in me by letting me lead.

Instead of keeping her in the bedroom, I tell her to head into the bathroom and strip while I set things up in the bedroom. Once the door is closed, I spread the blanket out and then the food. Ma made sandwiches, cut up fruit and vegetables, and put a piece of cake in there too. Instead of beer or whiskey, she put in a bottle of wine. There's nowhere to keep it cold, so for now, I'll leave it in the basket.

Opening the door, I see Melody, naked, and bending over the tub to light the candles Pop set up around the edge. I stop dead in my tracks as I see her delicious ass up in the air and wiggling to music that only she can hear. My girl always has a song in her head that she hums or sings softly. Not being able to stay away any longer, I walk up behind her and run my hands up her thighs before grabbing her ass.

I can hear the intake of her breath from feeling my hands on her. Before she can say anything, I land a smack to one ass cheek before moving my hand up to the middle of her back. Landing a smack to her other ass cheek, I her the sharp gasp come from her mouth. I can tell it's not from pain, but from excitement. Especially when she looks back over her shoulder and I can see the flush on her face and the hunger in her eyes.

I use my hand and rub it over both ass cheeks to take the sting out a bit as I look down and see the nice red marks from my hand on her smooth, pale skin. It's a good look on her. Wrapping my arm around her waist, I pull her up flush to my front. Kissing her soundly on her mouth, I move around her and turn the water on, adjusting the temperature so it won't burn her. At the same time, Melody starts undressing me.

Releasing my belt, she undoes my pants and slides them down my legs. The thud of them hitting the floor is loud since neither one of us are talking. Melody's staring up into my eyes as I look into hers. Next, she runs her hands up my body, ignoring my cock, moving her body up until she's standing in front of me. Her hands slide over my shoulders as she pushes my cut down my shoulders. She doesn't let it hit the floor though, my girl folds it in half and lays it on the counter between the two sinks. Turning back around, my shirt is the next thing to come off. I raise my hands up so there's nothing to stop her from finishing removing it. My boots are the last thing to come off as I simply toe them off.

"Get in the tub angel." I tell her, my voice a growl with want and need for my girl.

Melody doesn't hesitate to do as I say. The only other thing she does is pile her long hair on the top of her head. I slide in behind her pull her back so that she's resting comfortably against me. My girl is impatient though and I can feel her rubbing her ass against me. I'm already hard as fuck and she's not helping matters right now. Yeah, this isn't going to go as planned.

"Angel, you don't stop that, I'll smack my ass again." I tell her, nipping the side of her neck before soothing the sting with my tongue.

"Maybe that's what I want."

"You're askin' for it right now. As soon as we get out, I'll smack your ass all you want. Right now, let's relax a little bit." I say as she relaxes back into me. "Now, there's only a little over three weeks until the wedding. What all do we need to do?"

"There's so much we need to do that I don't know how it's going to get done in so little time."

"We have the whole club to help and the girls will have everythin' as far as decorations taken care of. All we need to worry about are the guests and what we're wearin'." I tell her, running my hands up and down her arms.

"Do I get any say in the wedding?" She asks.

"Yeah angel, you do. They just want to help make it a special day. And if they can take some of the pressure off you by handlin' the decorations and things, they will. Otherwise, talk to them when they get back tomorrow and you guys can get everythin' set up."

"Okay." She tells me, relaxing once again.

For a while we just sit in the tub and watch the flickering of the candles in the mirror and I watch Melody. She's running her hands up and down my legs and starting to rub her ass against me again. I think bath time is going to be cut short now, even though I love having her in my arms this way.

"Up angel." I tell her. "Blow the candles out while I get the towels."

Before drying myself off, I use a towel to dry her off. Instead of letting me dry myself off, Melody returns the favor and makes sure that I'm as dry as I'm going to get. Well, as dry as I'll let her get me with her teasing.

This time, Melody leads me into the bedroom, stopping when she sees the blanket and food. Looking up at me, I see the tears shimmering in her eyes. I keep forgetting that no one has ever done anything like this for her. Well, that's going to change. Cupping her face with my hands, I use my thumbs to wipe the tears away before they can fall.

"Don't cry angel." I tell her. "This is only a taste of how it's goin' to be. And you're the only one that gets this side of me. You and our kids."

"It's just I've never had this. I've missed out on so much."

"You did. And you had to grow up way too fast. Now, you get to experience things we've missed out on together."

Melody pushes me down on the blanket, following me down. She puts one of my legs on each side of her and leans down over my aching cock. Using one of her hands, she lifts it up so that she can take me in her mouth while using her hand on me. In this position, I can't touch any part of her other than her hair. So, I shove a hand in it to pull her hair tie out and watch her hair float down around her upper body. This doesn't last long though since I can't see anything. My hand goes back in her hair to hold it back. Yes, her hair tie was doing an excellent job of this, but I want my hands in her hair instead.

My girl swirls her tongue all around me while taking as much of me in as she can. Her inexperience still shows, but that doesn't matter to me. Knowing that I'm the only one that Melody has ever done this to is hotter than words can describe. We may not get every single first thing together, but to me, anything she gives me is better.

I can feel myself getting close and I'm not blowing my load in her mouth. Not this time. Gripping her hair a little bit harder in my hand, I let her know that I want her to stop. She looks up at me with questioning eyes.

"Not in your mouth angel." I tell her. "One day, but not today. There's too much I want to do to you."

"Okay. I'm nervous, but I'll trust you and what you do to me."

She's giving me her trust and that's one of the most precious gifts that she has ever given to me. Melody doesn't trust easily, she never has, and this is huge for her to give it to me so freely. Especially with an unknown experience. We've already started a little bit of spanking, which I will continue. Now, she's going to try something else new.

"Lay down on your back angel. Eyes closed and hands at your side for right now. You also need to lift your head just a little bit."

Without fail, my angel does as I ask. I take out a blindfold and tie it a little loose at the back of her head. Checking to make sure she's okay, I make sure her head is on the blanket. Next, I run my hands over her velvety smooth skin and watch as the goose bumps rise following my path. Pop grabbed my bag from my room at the clubhouse before coming over here, so I grab it and pull out the new feather tickler I got. Running it up and down her body, I change the path and pace continuously so Melody never knows what is going to happen to her. I can see her trying to anticipate where my next touch is going to be while her breathing level picks up in excitement.

"You okay angel?" I ask her.

"Y-yes." She stammers.

Dropping the feather tickler, I continue using my hands and mouth to keep her aroused. Moving between her legs, I slowly lower myself so that I don't startle her. I can see her arousal and it fills my senses. Tonight is going to be mainly about my girl and making it a night she'll never forget. Well, until our wedding night that is.

Melody

I am still blindfolded as Glock consumes me. The sensations he's creating within me ensure that I'm not going to last long. Especially when he puts his mouth on me. He licks, sucks, nips, and teases me until I'm pushing closer to him. Trying to get him where I want him to be. Too bad for me he has other plans though.

"So....close." I murmur.

Glock just growls as he inserts a finger into me as he continues to suck and nip my clit. My body arches up into him so that I can get him to do more without having to say words I don't know how to voice. It's a good thing he knows how to read me because he adds another finger to me, sliding them in and out while scissoring them to prepare me for taking him.

Unexpectedly, Glock removes the blindfold from me. I can see his handsome face looming over me, watching to make sure that I'm okay. Honestly, it was an intense experience not being able to see what he was doing to me. One that I want to happen again, multiple times. Glock gets up on his knees and takes himself in hand, sliding his hard cock through my wetness before slowly sliding inside me.

"Damn angel, you're still tight as fuck!" He growls out, inching his way in me.

After working himself in and out, Glock sinks all the way in and I arch up into him at the fullness. He stays still for a minute while pulling my legs up over his so that I'm closer to him as he pulls my upper body up to him. Now, I'm sitting on him and he's wrapping my legs around his waist. It's my turn to take the lead apparently. And I do.

I use my hands on his shoulders to lift myself up before sinking back down on him. His hands dig into my ass as he helps me lift up before making sure I don't sink back onto him too fast. Swirling my hips, I continue to increase my pace slightly. I can feel myself getting to my first release. If it's like any other time, there will be multiple.

"Fuck angel, keep going." He growls out.

My pace is becoming almost erratic as I feel the build-up threatening to overwhelm me. Sensing what I need, Glock starts meeting me thrust for thrust instead of concentrating on making sure I don't fall back down too fast. Digging my nails into his shoulders, I know I'm going to leave marks. So, I wrap one arm around his neck to continue to have leverage while I run my nails up and down his back.

"Mason!" I yell, feeling the explosion.

He holds me through my release and as I start to come back down, never losing the pace that we've set. At least until he tells me to get on my hands and knees, which I do without hesitation. Once I'm in position, I feel the sting on my ass as he once again spanks me. I never thought I would like being spanked, but if Glock's doing it, it's more than fine. Landing four more smacks in different areas on my ass, I can feel Glock getting closer to my body. There's no way he's going to hold off much longer from being back inside me. I saw the raw hunger on his face after he spanked me earlier.

"Please!" I almost beg. "I need you Mason."

That's all it takes for him to enter me in one thrust. Since I've already had one release, he's not as worried about hurting me. So, he sinks all the way in me. In this position, I really feel full. And he knows just how to move so that I can find my release quickly. I have to say it's one of my favorite positions so far.

"Give. It. To. Me." Glock growls out on every thrust.

Reaching down, Glock pinches my clit before beginning to rub tight circles around it. He knows just what I need to make sure that I'm going to reach mine before he reaches his. Out of nowhere, I can feel my body begin to coil and tighten with my impending release.

"Mason!" I scream out.

After a few more thrusts, I can feel him go still and know that he's reached his release too. I'm still coming down from my release and I can feel him settle on me before rolling us to the side. He continues to rub my back and plant kisses on my temple and forehead while our breathing goes back to normal.

"Love you angel. Always." He says, before getting up to get us cleaned up.

"Love you too."

Glock returns with a warm washcloth from somewhere and takes the time to clean me up before settling back in next to me. For the rest of the night, we eat, talk, laugh, and share what we want to happen with us. It reminds me of days when we were younger. Now, in just a few weeks, I'll be his wife and we'll be starting a new chapter in our lives. I hope we're ready for this.

Chapter Seventeen
Melody

A few weeks later

TODAY IS THE DAY that I've been dreading and waiting for. I'm getting married today. We decided that Anthony was going to be a part of our celebration so he'll be walking me down the aisle to his dad. My bridesmaids are the other old ladies while Kiera is my maid of honor. Glock chose to have a few of his brothers as his groomsmen while Cage is his best man. Thankfully Blade will not be walking with Kiera back down the aisle because it was all I could do to talk her into coming back here for my wedding. I'm not sure what is going on with her, or them, but I will find out. Just not on my wedding day.

"Mom, Aunt Kiera is here!" Anthony yells, running into the room we're all getting ready in.

"Thank you honey." I tell him before turning to see Kiera, with tears in her eyes, enter the room. "Oh babe, what's wrong?"

"Nothing. I'm fine sweetie. This is your day and we need to get you ready." She tells me, wiping the tears from her lashes and plastering on a fake smile.

"I know you well enough to know you're lying. But, I'll leave it alone for right now. I'm almost ready, I just need to get my dress on so I can get my makeup done."

All of us are in varying forms of dress and finishing up when there's a knock on the door. Pops is standing on the other side telling us that if we're not ready to go soon, Glock will be up here tearing the door down. Knowing that he's not lying, we all hurry up and finish getting ready in about ten minutes. It's not like we weren't almost ready to go as it was.

"You ready for this girl?" Kiera asks me.

"I am."

The ceremony is taking place out back, so we'll exit through the back door. Pop makes sure that I'm standing off to the side so that Glock can't see me as everyone else makes their way down the aisle. Finally, it's time for our son to walk me down the aisle to the man that has always tempted me to be who I truly want to be, the man that I love.

"Mama, you're real pretty today." Anthony tells me, grabbing my hand to begin our way to his dad.

"Thank you, baby. I love you."

"I love you too. Daddy too." He says, making sure that I don't trip going out of the doorway.

As we make our way down to my man, I can feel the tears starting to pool in my eyes and I don't want to cry. I'm not sad, but I see Glock waiting for us to meet him and I can see the love shining from his eyes. This is not something he's doing to make sure that Anthony is with him all the time, us getting married is what he truly wants to happen. All of my doubts and fears melt away knowing that he's going to make sure that we have everything we want out of life. Including let me learn new things, growing as a person and not just a wife and mother, and that Anthony gets every opportunity he can to do what he wants to accomplish in life. Glock doesn't care if Anthony follows in his footsteps and becomes a Wild King, he wants him to do whatever will truly make our son happy.

Glock doesn't wait for us to get to him, instead he meets us a few steps from the altar. We chose to go with an arbor one of the guys made covered in flowers. He tells Anthony thank you for walking me down to him safely and gives our boy a kiss on the top of his head before Anthony goes to sit with Ma and Pops. Taking my hand in his, he kisses me sweetly on the cheek before leading us the rest of the way to the justice of the peace that has married everyone else in the club.

Before I know it, we're ready to say our vows. Glock goes first.

"My angel, from the very first day I saw you, I knew you would be mine. There was such a light shinin' from you that I knew I had to have it light up my darkness and make me whole. Even though we are just findin' our way back to one another, you are the one that's always been in my heart. My tattoo and the design on my bike will show you that. You have given me the greatest gift by having my son and agreeing to be my wife. For the rest of my days, I will love you, protect you, and let you spread your wings to fly. I love you!"

There's no stopping the tears after his vows. So, I take a moment to compose myself before I begin mine. "The first day I met you, you stole my heart and I never got it back. Even through the separation, you were always the only one I wanted and needed. You rescuing me was the greatest day of my life because it brought you back to me. While you let us grow and spread our wings, we'll support every move you make and decision that is made to protect the family. I will honor you, love you, and protect you all the days of my life. I love you with all of my heart!"

I'm so wrapped up in Glock's eyes, seeing the love he has for us, that I don't hear the justice of the peace announce us as married and that Glock can kiss me. He places a hand on each side of my face and gently leans in to kiss me. The kiss is soft and tender, nothing like the heated ones we've shared before. This is Glock's soft and sweet side coming out while everyone watches on. He doesn't stop kissing me until the whistles and cheers break through and bring us back out of our own little world.

Glock turns us to look at our family surrounding us and we begin our descent back towards the clubhouse. The party will be outside, but I know we're going to want a minute or two to ourselves. Once inside, the rest of the wedding party gets a drink, and the girls shorten their dresses with the hidden connectors. We make our way up to our room at the clubhouse.

Once inside, Glock pushes me against the wall before devouring my mouth. I quickly lose my breath and wrap my arms around him to pull him in closer to me. There's no way I'm letting him consume me to the point that we end up having sex right now. Too many people are waiting for us downstairs. And, I know that he won't care, but I do. I want us to be able to celebrate and share our day with them.

"Slow down, husband." I stammer, pulling my lips away from his. "I want to wait until later for that. Help me pin this dress up and then we'll go back downstairs."

"You're killin' me wife. I'll never get tired of sayin' that." He tells me, giving me one last kiss before helping me pin my dress up in the back.

Glock

Today has been the best day of my life! Melody is now my wife and no one can take her away from me. The second she stepped through the back door of the clubhouse, my eyes about popped out of my head. Her dress is short in the front and fans out behind her. It's strapless and I can see the swell of her tits from the end of the aisle. My angel is barefoot, which is something she always used to do in school. Her hair is swept up with curls framing her face and laying down her bare back. As she gets closer to me, I can't help myself, I need to be touching her in some way.

The ceremony takes too long for me, but I stand there and get through it because I know this is what she wants. To me, it seems to take hours to get to the part where I get to kiss my girl and hear that we're husband and wife though.

We've been celebrating with our family for a few hours now. There's been drinking, laughing, dancing, and now it's time to take my girl in my arms for our dance. She let me pick the song and has no clue what it's going to be. I just nod to the DJ to get ready to play the song I chose while I grab my angel and lead her to the make-shift dance floor.

As soon as we come to a stop, *Die a Happy Man* by Thomas Rhett comes on. Melody looks up at me and I can see the tears shimmering in her eyes. I remembered and she's shocked as hell that I did. This is the song that was playing when we were together for the first time. I've remembered every single thing about that night every day since.

"Yeah, angel, I remember." Is the only thing I say before we start dancing.

Melody lays her head on my shoulder with her arms wrapped around me as we get lost in our own little world while dancing. I can see a few people dancing on the outer edges of the dance floor, but they're giving us our moment. Kiera had been sitting by herself though and I know it's ripping my girl apart. Well, she was until I saw her disappear with our boy a few minutes ago. Blade is a dumbass for letting some club girl hang all over him knowing he wants Kiera and that she's miserable right now. But, he'll learn.

Once our song is done, I soundly kiss my girl before we hear screaming coming from the front of the clubhouse. Whipping my head around, I get a horrible feeling in the pit of my stomach that something just happened to our boy and I'm going to kill someone.

"Glock! Melody!" Kiera screams, running around the corner.

"What's the matter Kiera?" My girl asks, and I can feel her body shaking. "Where's Anthony?"

"They took him. I tried to stop them, I swear I did!" Kiera responds.

"Who took my boy?" I growl out, wrapping my arms around Melody before she falls to the ground.

"Her parents. They grabbed him as we were coming back outside and I just couldn't stand up to both of them. I'm so, so sorry!" Kiera cries, sinking to the ground.

I can see Blade wanting to go to her, but he has no clue how to now. It's my fucking problem and I can't worry about his love life when my boy was just taken off our property.

"What were they drivin'?" I ask, frantic and knowing that we need to get moving soon.

"Black sedan." Kiera says, dropping her head back down.

"Someone get Irish out here and tell him to get on the fuckin' computers. Tank head in there now and get started, see what you can find. The rest of you mount up and head out. Look for any black sedan." Grim calls out.

About thirty of my brothers head out. Since other chapters of the Wild Kings are here along with the Phantom Bastards, I won't have to worry about only a few guys being spread too thin.

"Angel, I'm goin' with them. You go with Kiera and I'll call you as soon as I know anythin'."

"You better." She says with tears streaming down her face. "We need to bring him home Glock."

"I will angel." I tell her, wrapping her in my arms to lead her inside.

"No. I'm meeting you where they are. I'll be behind you in a few minutes." She says.

"I'm not arguin' with you about this. I know you want to be involved. The only thing I'm gonna say is if it's not your parents, you're not involved." I tell her, looking her straight in the eyes so she knows I'm serious.

"Fine. But I'm gonna be there when our boy is brought out. And if it's my parents that did this, I'm gonna kill them after telling them what I think of them. I *need* this babe." My angel pleads with me.

I give her a quick kiss before turning to follow the rest of the guys out to our bikes. We're going to be following the ones that already left while Tank talks us through what he sees on the security footage. He and Irish will follow my girl when she leaves since Tank won't need long to see what he has to see.

For this ride, there's no formation followed or anything else. At least for me there isn't. I'm ready to meet up with the rest of the guys so that we can find these fuckers and get my son back. I'm riding like a bat out of hell and hoping that I don't come across any cops because I'm not stopping for anyone or anything.

It's only taken about an hour to catch up with the black sedan that we're thinking has my son. We've all communicated with the Bluetooth devices in our helmets and decided to hang back so that we can follow them wherever they're going. I'm not risking my son in an accident because they got nervous or scared. His life is more important than catching them this second.

I can see that they're slowing down as we get to a wooded area outside of town. I'm not sure what's out here, but if it's something secluded, I'm not going to complain one bit. That just means that I can handle business without the chance of an innocent bystander getting hurt or hearing something they don't need to.

We've followed them for another ten miles before they pull onto some dirt road. It's twisting and turning from the little bit I can see and there's no way we're following them down it on our bikes. After passing the road, as if we're just out for a drive, we all pull over and hide as many of our bikes as we can. Then a bunch of us jump in the SUV Melody is driving to follow them up the road they turned on. Hopefully there's not a lot of different roads off of this one.

Melody doesn't say a word as we pile in or start driving down the path. The only thing she's done is move over so that one of us could drive. She knows the importance of getting back behind them and wasn't going to mess something up. My girl wants our boy back as bad as I do and isn't going to take any chances with his safe return.

Tank is driving because he knows my nerves are on edge and I'm going to be too worried about getting to my boy and making sure Melody is safe. We're all ready to go out guns blazing when we reach wherever my boy is. We won't though because no one is going to let anything happen to my boy. Anthony is the most important person in this situation. Once we get him to safety, we'll be ready to do our thing and make sure my family is safe for good.

Up ahead I point out the black sedan that's parked in front of what looks like an abandoned warehouse. I point it out and we pull in behind it. There's no way they're getting out of here. After parking, we wait a few minutes for the rest of the guys to catch up to us. Meanwhile, the rest of us try to get a look inside to know what we're dealing with.

Looking up in a window, I see a whole group of people sitting in what looks like pews and mismatched chairs. They're all looking forward, so I let my gaze follow up to where they're looking. There in the front of the building is my son and his grandparents. One on each side of him with their hands clamped on his shoulders, preventing him from going anywhere. Fuck!

Hearing a gasp come from behind me, I see Melody is looking in the window with me and can see everything I am right now. Her face has gone pale and there's genuine fear in her eyes. This must be what she was talking about when she was telling us how she grew up. She's reliving every detail right now.

"They're all here." She stammers out. "They've got our son in there with everyone from their cult. We have to get him out of there. Now!"

Tank and Grim have come up behind us and can hear the desperation in her voice. Making the ultimate decision, we look at one another and know that we're going in without waiting for the rest. Grim goes over and tells the rest of the guys with us that we're heading in now.

"Angel, we're goin' in now. We're not waitin' for the rest of the guys." I tell her, pulling her into me.

"I love you Glock! Know that I love you with everything I am." Melody tells me, looking me in the eyes and

I know. I know that she's going to do something I won't want her to.

"Angel, you stay with me. You're not goin' in there alone."

"I have to. Don't you see, I'm the one they want. The one they need to complete this, whatever it is they're doing."

"I can't lose either one of you. Can't you see that?" I plead with her.

"You won't lose either one of us babe. I'll be fine. Honestly, whatever is meant to happen will and in the end, we won't have to worry about them anymore. Let me do this without being pissed at me."

Grim returns and takes my attention from my girl for a split second and that's all she needs to make her move. Before any of us can stop her, she's around the corner and inside the building. I'm going to make her ass bright red when I get my hands on her again. Damn her!

Melody

I know that Glock is going to be pissed at me for not waiting for them, but Anthony is in here and I'm not waiting anymore to get our boy back. If I have to sacrifice myself in the process that's what I'll do. I'm the one my parents truly want anyway. Too bad they can't do what they want and have me marry someone of their choosing since we're already married.

As soon as I enter the building, I can hear my father preaching to his followers. His booming voice sends chills down my spine as I remember all too clearly the things he's said to me growing up, things he's done and allowed to be done to me. I want to freeze and stay hidden in the shadows, but my boy needs my help and I'm not going to let my fear overrule his safety.

"Ladies and gentleman, as you can see, this is a child created in sin. He's been allowed to roam free and not have any guidance under His word. Yes, he is my grandson, and now that he's in my control he will know right from wrong." My father pauses, and I hold my breath.

"You're a fucking crazy man!" Anthony shouts. "My Daddy and uncles are going to get me back and you'll pay."

Gasping, I know that now is when I must make my move. Anthony can't suffer because he knows that we've been hiding from these people for longer than we should have. Stepping out of the shadows, I put myself right in my father's line of vision.

"Your right son, Daddy is here to get you. They're all right outside and waiting to come in for you." I pause, letting all the murmurs and voices die down. "I'm who you want Dad. I'm the one who sinned, right?"

"You're no daughter of mine!" He yells, his face turning bright red. "My daughter wouldn't be living in sin and wouldn't have raised a bastard instead of doing what was laid out for her. Men, get her and bring her up here. She needs to relearn the ways of His word!"

Two of my dad's followers roughly grab my arms and lead me to the front where they're holding my son. As I get closer, I can see that their holding him so tight that they're hands are turning white. Glock sees that they're going to leave marks on him and they're already dead.

The first thing my dad does as soon as I'm close enough is reach out and back hand me. He hits me so hard, my head whips to the side and my vision turns a little blurry. It's nothing new, it's just been a while since I've been hit by this man.

"Is that all you got? I remember it hurting a lot more when you used to hit me. And not a single one of these brain washed assholes did anything to stop you." I grind out through the pain.

"You've got quite the mouth on you these days young lady." My mother speaks for the first time.

"Yeah, and you're still the brain washed bitch I remember. Now, my son will be walking out of here and going to his father. I will be taking his place and you can do what you think you have to."

"You'll be getting married today my dear." My dad says.

"No, I really won't. I'm already married douche canoe! Think on that for a minute and know that any plans you had regarding marrying me off to some abusive bitch is not going to work."

"And who are you married to?" He asks.

"She's married to me you dumb mother fucker!" I hear Glock call out from somewhere.

"Obviously, you're not man enough to face me, so why should I believe that you're really married to my daughter?"

"Oh, we're married alright. And you're touchin' what belongs to me." Glock says, stepping into view from the side. His face turns to a look of murderous rage as he takes in the fact that I've been hit.

Before anyone else can say anything, my dad pulls me in front of him and my mom pulls Anthony in front of her.

They're going to try to use us to make their escape. Honestly, as long as Anthony makes it out of here, there's nothing else they can do to me that hasn't already been done.

Plus, I know where my dad keeps his gun. It's not in his hand so I'm betting it's in the same place. I just have to get Anthony out of here and to safety before I can grab it. So, I'm going to make sure he gets there right now. Once Glock has him, the rest of the guys will shield him and make sure he's protected.

"Anthony, I want you to go over there to Daddy." I tell him. "If my mother values her life, she'll let you go right now so you can make your way over there."

"He's not going anywhere." My dad growls out. "He's where he belongs right now. Not with that miscreant pretending to be a father to some child that's probably not his."

"You better watch what the fuck you're sayin'!" Glock growls out.

"Anthony, go on. Go to Daddy now." I tell him again.

Anthony twists and turns until he can get out of my mother's grasp. Running as fast as his little legs can carry him, he maneuvers around everyone until he's safely in Glock's arms. Now is the time for me to make my move and get this shit taken care of once and for all.

I twist and turn like I'm trying to get away. I'm not, but it's the only way I'm going to be able to get my arms behind him enough to grab the gun. It's always there and always loaded. There's no way he'd go anywhere without it. Especially knowing that he had taken my son and knew I would be there behind him soon.

Finally, I can feel the gun in my hand and it's not strapped in the holster. So, I know it will pull free quickly and easily. In less than two seconds it's in my hand and I'm pointing it directly at my dad's head. The shock is evident on his face as well as my mom's. They never thought I'd have the balls to do this.

"Now, here's how this is going to work. Everyone in here is going to get up and leave. Right now!" I yell out.

"You heard the lady!" Grim calls out. "If you don't want to be included in whatever is about to happen, I suggest you leave here and forget anythin' that you happened to see."

It doesn't take that long for everyone to file out and peel out of the make-shift parking lot. In that time, I'm still pointing the gun at my dad's head and Glock now has his trained on my mother. I spare him a glance but not long enough to let my dad try anything.

"This is how it's going to play out." I begin. "You are going to sit in that first row and listen to every single thing I have to say to your condescending assess."

As my dad goes to say something, Glock reaches out and backhands him. He's seen him do it to me and now he's repaying the favor. Just as my mom goes to bitch at Glock, I backhand her. She may have never put a hand to me, but she sure as fuck never stopped it either.

"My entire life, you tried to make sure I was following His word. It was never about Him, it was everything that you wanted everyone to see and hear. It didn't matter if you abused me, never let me do anything, made me stand in front of everyone in nothing more than my bra and panties so everyone could see what you were offering to the highest bidder. As long as you got what you wanted and had someone in the wings, waiting to marry me as soon as they could, you were happy." I begin. "The only time I was allowed out of your sight was if it was for a school project or some other sort of homework. No dances, parties, or hanging out with friends. Hell, I couldn't have any friends unless they were part of your supposed church. Now, I'm living for me and loving someone that isn't afraid to let me spread my wings and fly. He lets me learn new things and loves me while I grow. Glock doesn't hold me back or keep me from experiencing new things. What is it you were truly afraid of me doing?"

"Obviously, you're doing what we were afraid of you doing." My mother spits out. "You're living in sin and have a bastard son."

"Our son is not a bastard!" I scream out at him. "We're married and he has always had his father's last name. My son is loved and cared for, allowed to live and grow, do things he wants to do."

"Exactly! You allow your son to live in sin, following your footsteps!" My dad bellows.

There is no point in continuing with saying anything to him. No matter what I have to say, they're not going to listen anyway. It's what they want to hear that's important and matters. If anyone else that's not in their church tries to tell them anything, they don't listen. The only ones that matter are the ones that choose to follow them.

Before anyone can say anything more or stop me from doing anything, I pull the trigger on my dad's gun. I hit him square between the eyes. Yeah, I may have had someone teach me to shoot. There were days I'd spend at the gun range before we moved learning everything I could because I knew eventually, it would come down to them or me.

My mother is screaming and covered in blood. I'm standing there, feeling no remorse when I think about everything they've ever done or said to me. How they took our son away from us. Even if they didn't get a chance to do anything to him. Once my mother's screeching pierces through the fog in my brain, I turn my gun towards her. Almost immediately, she stops screeching and starts pleading her case to try to live. It's not going to happen though.

"Angel, don't you do it. One murder is more than enough. Put the gun down." Glock tells me, trying to get me to hand it to him.

"I can't do that babe. I need to be the one to end this shit once and for all. I was the one they tortured and treated like nothing more than a piece of meat. It was my life that they tried to sell off to the highest bidder. And it was our son that they tried to take and use to get to me. This is on me Glock, no one else." I tell them, staring at my mom the entire time.

"Sweetheart, let us take this burden from you. You got your dad, now let us deal with your mom." Tank says.

"Thank you Tank, but this is on me." I tell them all again.

Without a hesitation, I pull the trigger again and nail my mom in the shoulder. "Maybe I will let them handle you mom. I'm sure they know multiple ways to torture you and make you pay for everything you didn't stop him from doing to me."

I hand the gun over to Glock and turn away from the people that gave me life. They are not my parents and haven't been for a very long time. Honestly, I don't know which part of my life was worse. The time growing up with my parents, or being kidnapped, tortured, and raped almost daily for six months. It's over now though, and I helped end that shit. At least when it comes to my dad. Now, we can get on with the rest of our lives, watch our son grow, and grow together with one another.

"Angel, why don't you go check on our boy while we handle this in here." Glock tells me. "I'll be out once it's done and we'll get him home."

I nod my head to my man and turn to leave the building. Outside, I see Maddie's dad sitting with Anthony in the back of the SUV. They're talking and I can tell that Anthony is excited about what they're talking about. His hands are all over the place and his little face is lit up with excitement. This is what means the most to me, what I live for. Anthony and Glock are my entire world, they make me want to be a better person and help them learn things that they need and want to learn.

It doesn't take Glock and the rest of the guys long to make their way out of the old warehouse. When they do, I can see my man searching for me and our son. So, I stand up and start to run to him. I'll always run to him.

"Babe," I start, "Please tell me it's all over."

"It is angel. You won't ever have to worry about either one of them ever again. Now, let's get our boy home. And I do mean to our home. The girls got everythin' all set up."

I shouldn't be surprised, but I am. A few days before the wedding, the girls wouldn't take my calls or anything until later in the day. Part of me thought that I had pissed them off for some reason, but the other part thought it was something like putting our home together. When the wedding planning began, I told them I didn't want a bachelorette party, and they respected my wishes and didn't throw me one. Now, I can't wait to get home and see what they did.

"Let's go home Glock. I want to relax with my two favorite men in the world and shut everyone else out for a while." I tell him, wrapping my arms around him.

"Some weddin' day huh?" He asks. "One we'll definitely never forget any time soon angel."

"Definitely won't forget it any time soon. Not only will we not have to worry about my crazy ass parents anymore, but I got to marry the man that has tempted me in living for my family and myself. You give me the strength and courage to fulfill everything I want to accomplish and more. I love you!"

"I love you too angel. Let's go home." He says before turning to Grim. "You make sure my bike gets home? Not lettin' my family out of my sight any time soon."

"Got it covered." Grim says.

We make our way over to Anthony who is now telling Cage and Joker all about his adventure. He's trying to sound so grown up and tough for his uncles. The two men are standing with him like I've seen them do countless times with the rest of the men in the club, listening to every word spilling from our boy's lips. Anthony is definitely stepping into his legacy at a young age, but I couldn't be happier for him to follow in the footsteps of these men.

"Let's go home son." Glock says, pulling Anthony into our embrace. "Know you're dyin' to see your new room bud."

"I am! Let's go Daddy!" Anthony says, forgetting all about the other two men.

As Anthony climbs into the backseat, we can't stop the laughing. He goes from full on macho little man to little boy in an instant. Glock does his man hug thing with the men left standing around us before opening my door. Once he's in, we

don't wait for anyone else. He takes off towards home.
Towards our future.

Chapter Eighteen
Glock

IT'S BEEN A LITTLE over a month since I married the best woman I know. Every day she grows more and I love watching her spread her wings. Now, she's enrolled in school for her degree in accounting. Melody is also working at the diner in town. It's more to get out of the house a few times a week than anything else. With me working and Anthony in school, she wanted to do something.

Anthony continues to grow and learn every day. He and Jameson have become best friends and they both watch over the younger kids. It's amazing to watch the two of them take on their roles as protectors. My son is so smart and the conversations we have amaze me just a little bit more each day. Our last one was regarding a brother or sister for him.

"Daddy," Anthony called out to me. "Can I ask you something?"

"Sure bud. What's on your mind?"

"Well, Jameson and the rest of the kids all have brothers and sisters. Why don't I?" He asks, sitting right next to me and looking at me. "I really want a brother or sister Daddy. I'll protect them, I promise I will."

"I know you will buddy. But, it's not just up to me when you get a brother or sister. Momma wants to do some things before we talk about havin' another baby."

"If I help her though, she can still do the things that she wants to do Daddy. I mean, I don't know about the diapers, but I can help with the other things."

My boy is trying so hard to convince me to give him a brother or sister and I wish it were that easy. Melody just isn't sure about the timing right now though. She wants to wait just a little bit longer and make sure that we're stable and going to make it before any more kids are brought into the picture. I can't blame her, but I know she's it for me. My family is here to stay and we'll get through anything life throws at us.

"Well, bud, I'll talk to momma again and see what she says. That sound good?"

"I guess so." Is the only thing he says before heading back outside.

I can see movement out of the corner of my eye and I know that my girl overheard our conversation. She was up laying down because she wasn't feeling good this morning. So, I'm guessing she needed something to eat or drink and came downstairs.

"You hear that angel?" I ask her, waiting for her to come sit with me.

"I did babe. Apparently, he's ready for a brother or sister." She responds with laughter dancing in her eyes.

"Yep. So, now I'm keepin' my word to our little man and talkin' to you about it." I tell her, pulling her down in my lap.

"And what do we need to talk about? Is it the practicing of making the baby? Because I'm pretty sure we've got that down pat. Or is it actually having said baby brother or sister?" She asks, snuggling into my neck.

"Well, I definitely don't mind practicin' with you angel. But, I think it's time we seriously talk about havin' another baby. I missed out on everythin' with Anthony and I want to experience that with you. I want to watch you grow round with my baby and know that you're doin' everythin' in your power to keep him or her safe and healthy until their time to be born. I'm ready to make trips in the middle of the night for crazy pregnancy food and rubbing your back and feet when they hurt."

"I know, babe. But…" She starts to say.

"I know, you're not ready." I say in defeat.

"Not what I was gonna say. I was going to say that we don't have to worry about trying any more. I have an appointment tomorrow afternoon to confirm, but I took a home test this morning."

"Are you serious? You're givin' me another baby?" I ask, shock and excitement coursing through me.

"I am serious babe. Just don't tell Anthony yet. I want to make sure everything is okay before we get his hopes up."

"Okay, angel. I can keep quiet for now." I tell her laying her down beneath me on the couch.

Scooting down, I spread my hands over her stomach, under her tee. Her stomach is still flat and there's no way you can tell that there is a baby in there. But, I'm going to do everything in my power to make sure that they are protected from today until I take my last breath.

Melody

Coming home with Anthony the day of our wedding was like walking into a dream. The girls had our house decorated and the furniture exactly where I wanted it to go. It probably helps that we talked about it a million and one times until they did it.

We had a house warming party and I met even more of the guys in the Wild Kings. Some nomad members were in town and came along with a few more chapters that aren't too far from here. The Phantom Bastards were obviously here too.

And Darcy caused yet another scene. I don't know how that woman survives a day with the way trouble finds her.

The only good thing is that Wood wasn't involved in Darcy's little mishap. Unfortunately, Boy Scout was. Crash and Trojan weren't too far behind and saw the whole thing. Wood had to pull Boy Scout away before the other two men killed him. We didn't see Boy Scout too much the rest of the night.

This morning, taking the pregnancy test, I have mixed emotions. On one hand, I'm excited to be carrying Glock's baby again. But, there's still things I want to do and I'm worried that I'll never get to do them with two kids in the mix. Glock won't let that happen though, so I should just focus on being happy. Right?

After telling Glock about the baby, he went all macho caveman on me. He didn't want me getting up off the couch for the rest of the day or doing anything until after I go to the doctor tomorrow to confirm it. I can see already how this next seven or eight months is going to go. We'll be fighting for sure about me working, doing too much around the house, too much he thinks I shouldn't be, and a million other things. Help me now!

It's times like this that make me miss Kiera even more. We've talked on the phone and made plans to visit, me going there. But every time it gets close to me leaving, she cancels. I feel like on one hand I've gained the world with my husband, my son, and our new little peanut. On the other hand, I feel like I've lost my sister from another mister. Kiera doesn't seem to want anything to do with me these days and I truly don't know what is going on to make me feel like that.

One of these days, if I can get away from Glock, I'm going to be heading down to her with no warning. This shit is going to end with her ignoring me and breaking our plans. If it's something to do with Blade, there's no reason to be ignoring me and breaking plans for me to go to her.

Now, I'm ready to just relax with my family and see what this day has in store for us. Thoughts of Kiera and what's going on have to go to the back of my brain so that I can be in the moment with my guys. I'm thinking of going to the park again to play catch and then a picnic lunch. Glock is going to just have to suck it up and deal with the fact that I'm not glass and I won't break just because I'm pregnant. This is going to be an amazing journey that he'll be able to experience with me this time around.

Epilogue
Kiera

I FEEL LIKE THE worst friend ever. Melody has never been anything but kind and there for me. Now, I've been ignoring her and cancelling our plans. Mainly at the last second so that she can't refuse or try to get me to explain what's going on. I just don't want her to try to 'fix' it for me. There's nothing to fix. I've learned everything I need to know from watching her raise Anthony as a single parent.

Yes, I found out I am pregnant with Blade's baby. It was never supposed to be a forever thing between us. We were just supposed to be having fun and spending time with one another until I could move on. I'm not one for relationships when every guy I've ever been with has cheated on me or abused me in one form or another. I don't know what Blade's issue with relationships is, but I know this is the last thing he's going to want in his life.

Eventually I will tell him that he's going to be a dad. But, right now, I'm trying to wrap my head around the fact that in about six or seven months, I'm going to be a mommy. I'd love to have a little boy that looks just like his daddy, but really I don't care what gender the baby is.

Blade wormed his way into my heart without even trying and now I can't forget him. He's everything I never wanted in a man. He's quiet, reserved, demanding in bed, and is the complete opposite of the guys I usually go for. However, I am completely in love with him. And, I'm so fucked right now.

Slim and the Phantom Bastards have been amazing though. They helped me find a place to live, a little two-bedroom house with a yard. It's close to their clubhouse and my job. Slim hired me on as a bar tender at their strip club, Vixen. I don't strip and I don't wear any less than I absolutely have to. My tips are great and I'm making quite the nest egg for myself.

The only one bad spot in the whole thing is that Slim knows what's going on with me and he isn't happy with the decision that I'm making to hold off on telling Blade about the baby. Hell, he's not happy with the guy I've been seeing either. His name is Jason and I didn't really want to start dating him in the first place. Jason just wouldn't take no for an answer.

Now, I wish I would have talked to the guys in the club. He's turning abusive and it doesn't matter to him whether I'm pregnant or not. The only thing I'm thankful for is that he's not hitting me anywhere near my stomach to hurt the baby.

One of these days I'll learn. Until then, I'm just going to live my life and continue to grow as a person. A baby is only going to add to it for me and enhance my life.

Blade

Since Anthony was kidnapped, things have quieted down around the clubhouse. I've mainly stayed in my room, not socializing or anything else, including fucking the club girls. Kiera left a while ago and took my heart with her.

This wasn't supposed to be anything more than a fun time. When I was with her, there was no one else and I was the only one she was with. Something spooked her though and I can't figure it out. When I do, I'll be using it to get her back. No matter what happens, my kitten will be coming back to me. Kiera can bare her claws all she wants, and I will gladly take the scratches.

From my way of thinking, there's only two reasons that would send her running. Either she fell in love with me and ran before she talked to me. Or, she's pregnant and thinks I'm going to accuse her of trapping me. While I never wanted any kids of my own, I would never turn my back on a child I fathered either. After the up-bringing I had, there's no way that I feel I would be a good father to an innocent child.

I do have eyes on her though, knowing that she's in Phantom Bastard territory takes a little bit of the edge away from the fear of something happening to her. Wood and Boy Scout are on Kiera duty for now. And I will be making trips down there to see her myself. Especially being told that she's working at Vixen. No woman of mine is working at a fucking strip club. If it's the last thing I do, Kiera will be mine again. And I will find out what made her run!

The End

Melody's Temptation Playlist

I Won't Give Up – Jason Mraz

Broken Strings – James Morrison

You Make It Real – James Morrison

Just Like A Child – James Morrison

Day Is Gone – Noah Gundersen

Break In – Halestorm

Come Over – Sam Hunt

Goodbye – Sam Hunt

Forever Girl – Jon Langston

I Don't Care Anymore – HellYeah

Falling Apart – Papa Roach

Stronger – Through Fire

Die A Happy Man – Thomas Rhett

The Day You Stop Looking Back – Thomas Rhett

That Don't Sound Like You – Lee Brice

Withdrawals – Tyler Farr

Acknowledgements

First, and foremost, I'd like to give a huge thank you to the ladies of the street team I share with Darlene, The Clubhouse. They have shown us so much support by getting our names out there, helping us figure things out, and countless other ways. Without you, none of us would be living our dream.

My beta readers are some amazing women. They not only read Melody's Temptation once, they read it twice. And, they provided me with some amazing feedback and talks while working things out in the story.

Vicky, my amazing PA deserves a huge shout out. She listens to me complain when the characters won't talk, lets me bounce ideas off of her when I get stuck, and helps get our names out there as much as possible. And, the daily inspiration helps too!! Thanks for cracking the whip when I've needed it!!

Darlene, as busy as she is, helps me out in numerous ways. From being there to help bounce ideas back and forth to listening when I need someone in my personal life. We have laughed, bounced ideas back and forth, and listened when the other one needed an ear. Can't wait for Dallas!!

Finally, to my amazing family. Without their support, love, and understanding, I wouldn't be where I am today. My children are completely amazing and try to help me out as much as they possibly can. Now, I have the ability to write during the day while they are at school and spend more time with them at night.

And, I can't forget all of the amazing readers. Without your support, I wouldn't be able to do what I love to do. Thank you for everything!!

About The Author

I am a single mom to three amazing kids. They inspire me every single day, and make me want to be better. When it comes to my writing, they encourage me more than anyone else in my life.

I have been an avid reader since the time I was old enough to read. My grandmother was the one that got me into reading and I love all types of books. My kids are following in my footsteps, and I love it.

When I'm not spending time with my kids, family, and friends, writing, or working around the house, I spend my time watching NASCAR and relaxing as much as I can. Not that relaxing really works out that much.

I am the shyest person I know and it's crazy how hard it is to talk to people. However, I love meeting new people and hearing their story. You can learn a lot from people if you take the time to listen. If I can say one thing to you, please, don't ever hesitate to follow your dreams.